I0762077

# Silas LaMontaie

Lawrence Weill

Black Rose Writing | Texas

The author grants the final approval for this literary material.

First printing, Hardcover edition



ISBN: 978-1-68433-380-6
PUBLISHED BY BLACK ROSE WRITING
www.blackrosewriting.com

Printed in the United States of America
Suggested Retail Price (SRP) $22.95

*Silas LaMontaie* is printed in Chaparral Pro
Music by Travis Tench, lyrics by the author:
http://lawrenceweill.com/?page_id=577

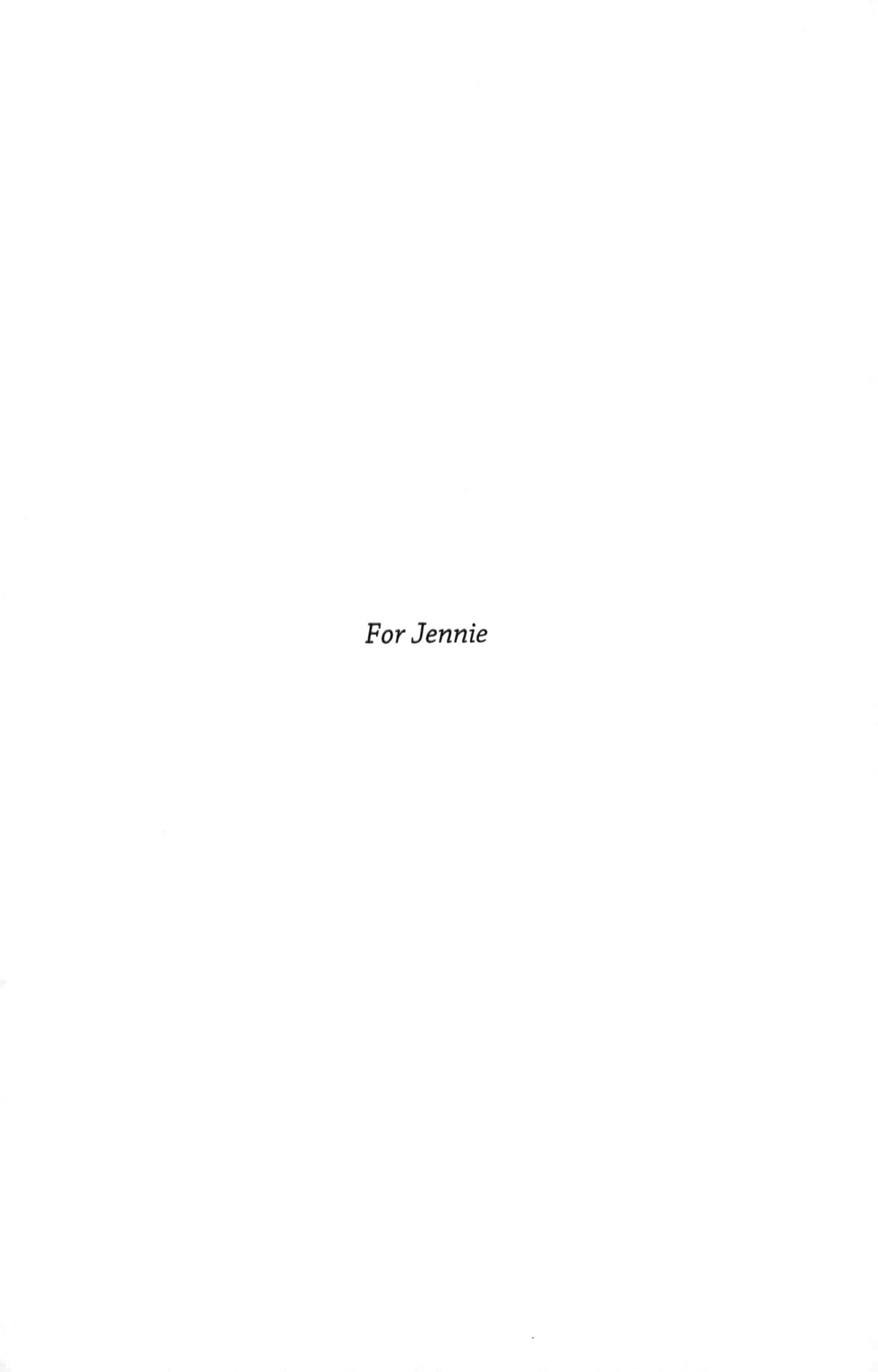

*For Jennie*

Silas LaMontaie

# Foreword

We are all but tiny droplets of water flowing along the vast river of time, waiting to arrive at the ocean to be set free in some beautiful tide. As we flow down this river, we are surrounded by millions of other drops, sometimes sharing a bit of our make up with these other drops, sometimes taking from them. One drop pushed and pulled by the multitude of other drops. We are all pulled downstream just the same, headlong and heedless, dreaming of briny bliss, inexorably powered by the invisible forces of gravity and current. But sometimes, there's a drop of water that comes along, and it's different. Sometimes there's a drop of water that bounces through the eddies, and it takes a notion all its own, and it decides to go another direction, its own direction. That's when that little water globule decides go to the side of the river bed, or maybe the bottom, and to beat its soft head against the river bank, just to do it, to see what will happen, and by doing that, it makes a dent in that shoreline. To be sure, it may be a tiny dent. But you see, that drop of water is followed by a host of fellow water beads who all see the wondrousness of that decision, an option they never knew was possible. So those beads of water follow and they are chased by yet more drops, and after a while, all those dewdrops change the flow of the water. The next thing you know, they have changed the currents in the river. And that eventually changes the route of the river itself. Then, nothing is the same. It seems to me, that is how our world changes when one little drop decides it's time to beat its head against the shoreline. Sometimes that brave drop is a hero, sometimes it's an artist, sometimes it's a lunatic, and sometimes it's a lover. But one thing is certain: if you're ever around them, you will remember it. In my life, I have met only a handful of people who are such determined droplets. If you meet one, you will know it.

# Chapter 1

Mr. Kohler was a man of his word, and for some reason, people admired him for that despite the fact that he had the moral compass of a scorpion. But he swore to ruin my Daddy, and that's just what he did, although Daddy never gave in and, just maybe, got the last blow in. Daddy could fix anything, and he loved getting his hands dirty. He fixed motors for folks who had boats on the Bayou Teche and over on Lake Dauterive. Sometimes he worked on cars for folks taking a back way from Lafayette to New Orleans. And occasionally, if people asked him nicely, he even worked on things like radios and fans. He had his shop out behind our house off Bourgeois Avenue. There was a sign he had painted next to the driveway that said Motor Repairs on the top and Réparation Moteur below it and at the bottom, his name, Benoit LaMontaie, but everyone knew he was there and everyone counted on him. He had more work than he could handle, and he had trouble saying no to people. He knew all of them, of course, and he knew they needed the motor fixed on their boat to get back out and get to work, or that they needed their car fixed so they could get to their job in Lafayette, maybe. Consequently, he always had lots of stuff in the back yard. I used to love to go out there and see what he was working on and climb around on the tractors and cars. He kept a lot of what other folks might call junk, but he called them parts. But what he really liked working on was the big things – big trucks and bulldozers and earth movers and industrial stuff. He had a reputation for being good and being exact, and he was the man companies called when they needed someone to fix a big piece of equipment. They would call sometimes in the middle of the night, and he would be up and gone before breakfast. He was gone often for a week or so, fixing some piece of equipment out of town. But he was good. He could just look at a roller and tell it was off by a sixteenth of an inch. It was amazing. That's why he liked to work on the big contraptions at the sugar mills around our area. They had wonderful, terrifying devices my Daddy told me, from this one that had these rotating knives that could take a man's arm off in seconds to the crusher that weighed a ton and consisted of two giant drums with meshing teeth. Then there were the rollers. They weighed twelve tons, he told me, and they had to be aligned just right, or the cane wouldn't be squeezed right, and it wasn't like he could pick up one end and adjust it: it was all very exact and mechanical. Daddy loved it.

Mr. Kohler owned the mill outside our little village of Loreauville, but he lived over in New Iberia. He owned a lot of stuff, and he liked to splash around in the pond a lot as if to prove what a big fish he thought he was. Daddy rarely said anything mean about people, but I could tell he didn't like the way old man Kohler strutted his wealth in front of folks who struggled to get by despite working hard. When the sugar production went down because the rollers were off, they'd call Daddy to fix it, and he and the crew at the mill would make the adjustments and go on their way, but I'd see Daddy give Momma a look when the subject came up on whether Kohler was timely in paying or not. Kohler was a good one for looking rich, but a bad one for paying his bills, it seems. Momma would just shake her head. That last time, it finally got to her. I remember it because I was just getting ready to start school the next day, the first grade, and I was upstairs in my room organizing and reorganizing my cigar box of crayons and pencils and rulers. Momma and Daddy were just below me on the front porch, just swinging slowly, but more, trying not to move, because even in September, it is hot and muggy in south Louisiana.

"Bennie, did Kohler pay you yet?" Momma asked quietly.

"Not yet, Cher." The porch swing squeaked lazily.

"It's always like this. He needs it fixed, and you fix it, but then he doesn't want to pay you. And when you're gone fixing his stuff, the other stuff here doesn't get done. You were off fixing his big sugar mill and not fixing Robert's Evinrude, and Robert would've paid you cash. And Robert needs that motor right now. It's not right."

"I'll fix that old inboard tomorrow, Hon. Don't worry."

"I know, Bennie. But it makes me mad. It feels like he's taking advantage of you. And us too, for that matter."

"He's just an old snapping turtle, Abella. He's waiting for some thunder before he lets go of his money. But I'll get paid."

Momma laughed, but it wasn't a happy laugh. "Maybe you need to bring the thunder, Bennie."

"Well..."

"And how much is he going to pay?"

"We won't go hungry. Trust me, darlin'."

"I don't see why you even go over there and work on his old mill if he's so bad about paying you. You don't deserve to be treated like this."

"He'll pay me eventually, Cher, and meanwhile, half the folks we know work at the mill. They're counting on that mill for their jobs. If I don't fix it, they don't work, and that doesn't help anything, does it? He keeps threatening to close it down anyway. We don't want to see people out of work."

"No, no, we don't. But you know he's taking advantage of you. And it's not fair. You work hard, and you do the best job of anyone, but he tries to cheat you and whittle you down so you can barely pay for your gas over there and back. I don't understand why it doesn't make you mad."

"What good does it do for me to get mad?"

"Well, I don't know. Maybe if you got mad, you'd get him to pay you."

"Cher, you are the one who told me I had to control my temper. You remember. Now, as I recall, you used to tell me I was going to hurt somebody or get myself killed trying, as I remember it."

"Oh, Bennie. That was then and that man by the..." They grew suddenly quiet, almost like they knew I was listening.

"Darlin', it's not that bad. He'll pay. He'll pay."

"You think you'll get what's fair from that Kohler?"

"Darlin', let's just relax, okay? Can we just drop it for now? I promise you I will work on it." The swing creaked again.

"Okay, Bennie. Fine. I need to get some stuff ready for tomorrow anyway." I heard the swing creak again as Momma stood, then the raspy complaint of the screen door as she came inside. Momma was an English teacher over at the high school. She had gone to college up at Louisiana State Normal School in Natchitoches, and she loved teaching. In fact, she named me after one of her favorite characters, Silas Marner, and she would remind me often that the message of the book was that love conquers all and that she expected I would learn that lesson well. And I did.

It was kind of funny in some ways, Momma and Daddy being together. Momma was as pretty a woman as you wanted to see, all auburn hair and blue eyes, tall and elegant. She looked to me like a graceful willow blowing in the breeze when she walked. She came from a fairly well-to-do family up in Winn Parish, and she went to college and even studied classical music. Daddy was just about the opposite of Momma with his olive skin and hair black as a peppercorn. He wasn't big, but he was very strong. Daddy's family wasn't exactly poor, but they weren't rich either. Whenever we visited them at Grandma Boudreaux's house, they would have a dinner outside, with fried chicken and ham and fish and crawfish and shrimp and a dozen different vegetables. There would be twenty or twenty-five cousins and aunts and uncles who all looked like Daddy and me, although I got Momma's eyes. At the end of the meal, they would all get out instruments and make music. Sometimes, Grandma Boudreaux would read the tarot cards for people. And this was all because it was Saturday. Or Sunday. They were bayou people, through and through, and as generous and kind as they were tough and rambunctious. And Daddy knew his music too, just a different kind of music than Momma had learned. Whenever someone would ask how Momma and Daddy met up, they would just shoot a look across the room at each other and share a wonderfully mysterious smile and mumble at the same time, "New Orleans." And if it was a short reply, no one ever asked for details, as if simply saying that answered every question they had asked or thought to ask. Later, when everyone else had left, Momma would nuzzle up to Daddy and say, "The tiger of Vieux Carré." And then I would go to my room and leave them be. It was from Momma and Daddy I learned that you can fall so deeply in love, you can never climb out of love, not that you'd ever want to. I applied that lesson well in just a few short years.

The next day, I walked to school with my best friend Charlie Blanchard and his mom. Charlie was nervous about going to school and cried the whole way there, but I wasn't scared. I was excited, because Momma had already taught me to read and I couldn't wait to read more books. Momma left early for the high school, and Daddy fed me kush kush and milk and sent me on my way as if I had been doing this forever. Then he went out to his garage, and I went to school over behind Our Lady of Victory Church. I carried a brown paper bag Momma had filled with a peanut butter sandwich and potato chips, and I had my cigar box, which I had reorganized that morning, although nothing stayed in place once I picked it up, of course. I loved school.

That night, after dinner, we sat on the porch, Daddy with a beer and Momma with a glass of wine and me holding a big glass of lemonade. It had rained during the day, which had cooled things off some but added a whole new layer of moisture to the air. When you sit outside near the bayou after a rain, the hair on your arm forms little drops of water that are cool to your touch. Frogs and crickets took up a chorus and Daddy played his guitar softly and hummed a faint melody and then Momma hummed with him but in harmony. It was as if they were serenading the frogs and the frogs were answering them. I could have sat there forever listening to that music, but then Momma shoo-ed me off to bed, and they sat together on the swing, sometimes going for long stretches never saying a word, with only the creaking chain of the porch swing reminding me they were still there. It was an intoxicating lullaby.

By the end of the week, though, the mood around the house had changed. No one said anything for long stretches of time, and Momma sometimes left the room when my Daddy came in, and she wouldn't even look at him. I knew she was mad. Daddy knew too. He would look after her after she had left the room, his arms dangling at his sides, and he'd look so sorrowful. When Saturday morning came, Daddy came in from messing around in his shop early in the morning. Momma was drinking a cup of coffee, sitting at the kitchen table. I was coloring a picture I had brought home from school, sitting in my usual spot at the table.

"What are you coloring, Little Man?" Daddy sat at his place. Momma didn't look up.

"It's a fish." I colored away.

"What kind of fish?" Daddy peered over at my paper.

I held it up. "See? It's a red fish. It's not the right shape, though, but he's red anyway."

"So it is. So it is." Daddy took the picture from me and held it for Momma to see. "Cher, you think you can cook this up for us for supper?" Momma looked at the paper, looked at me, then looked at Daddy.

"Bennie, I don't want to be mad at you."

"Lord knows, Abella, I don't want you mad at me." Daddy paused and shook his head. "Little Man, why don't you go out in the yard and see if you can find me an alternator that's still got good brushes on it for Mr. Raymond's Chevy, okay?"

"Okay, Daddy. It's a Bel-Air, right?

"That's right, Sy." He tousled my hair, and I headed out the back door.

"Don't let the screen door . . ." But the door slammed before Momma could finish her sentence.

"Sorry." I turned and sent a wave, but I knew just where Daddy kept the electrical things in the shop. I loved it when he let me help him, although I never really had the knack he did. But before I made it to the shop, I heard my Momma's voice rise, something I very rarely heard.

"You can't let him get away with it, Bennie. You just can't! We need that money." Daddy said something much softer, in his calming tone that I knew, but it didn't calm Momma down. In fact, it seemed to make her madder. "No! No! I won't let it go! You said he was going to pay, and you said it would keep the mill going, and you said not to worry. But now he's cheating you on the money, he's laying off folks at the mill even before the harvest is all done, and guess what? I'm worried. I'm worried about our friends, and I'm worried about the bills. And I am worried about you letting him get away with it." Then I heard my Momma cry, which was something I had never heard before. It made me scared and sad, and I wanted to go inside and hug her, but I had never known them to fight, so I didn't know what to do. And then Daddy got loud too, which scared me.

"Abella, what is it you want me to do with that fils-putain? If I don't take what he says he'll pay, I might not get anything. What am I supposed to do?"

Momma sniffled. Now she spoke more quietly. "Benoit LaMontaie, I want you to make it right. I know I've spent a lot of years getting you to be calm, but this is different. He's making you look like a couillon, and that's not right. You need to stand up for yourself and for our friends." There was a pause.

"A couillon? You think I'm a fool?"

"No, Bennie. But he does." It grew quieter again. I went back to looking for the alternator.

"You're right, Bele. You're right. I can't let him do this."

"Thank you."

"I got to make sure he knows . . ."

"You need to get paid."

"Maybe he won't pay, at least in money."

"But he . . ."

"No, Cher, you are right. I have to make it right."

"Wait, Bennie, . . ." And I heard the front door screen screech and slam. I had found the car part, but now Daddy was gone somewhere, and Momma didn't like dirty parts on her kitchen table. I put the alternator on Daddy's workbench and went back inside. Momma was staring out the window, biting her lower lip.

"Momma?"

Momma looked down at me and squatted down, so her eyes were almost the same level as mine. "What is it, honey child?" She caressed my check with her thumb.

"Where's Daddy going?" I looked through the archway that led towards the front door.

"Daddy's got some business with a man. That's all. Don't you worry." Momma stood now and spoke to the archway. "Ne laissez pas le tigre de sa cage."

# Chapter 2

Then Momma turned back around, smiled, and picked up my red fish picture. "My little artist! Let's put this on the icebox, okay?" Momma put the picture on the round-fronted refrigerator and affixed it with a magnet Daddy had brought in from some motor he had taken apart. Suddenly, Momma was all happy, but it didn't feel quite right, like she was hiding something. "Where's Charlie today, Silas?"

"I don't know." I had not thought about my friend yet that day. There had been so much going on, I hadn't really thought of anything but Momma and Daddy and their argument.

"Why don't you see if he wants to play, hmm?"

"Okay." I ran through the back screen door. Such was my age, I was immediately distracted by play.

The screen slammed shut just as Momma said, "Don't let the screen door slam."

Charlie and I spent the cool of the morning exploring the cemetery behind the church. We hid behind the mausoleums and played army with sticks-become-rifles. I read some of the names to Charlie, and we knew some of the families, or at least the children of those families. I wanted to go on over to the bayou, but neither of us was really allowed to go there without our parents, presumably because we would fall in, and it was true, Charlie couldn't swim, but I could. And there were the alligators to be concerned with, of course. So instead we walked over to the road that led to the drawbridge and sat on the flat ground with its closely mowed grass and watched the farmers bring in sugar cane loaded on wagons pulled by tractors. We waited for the bridge to rise, but there weren't any big boats, so it stayed down. It grew warmer by that afternoon, so we retreated to my house for lemonade and bologna sandwiches and the cooler shade of our front porch. Whatever play was next would be generated by our imaginations.

When we got to my house, Momma was working on cutting out some letters for her bulletin board in her classroom. Ordinarily, I would have just sat at the table, watching her hands as she manipulated the scissors like magical tools, it seemed to me, and maybe hear some stories about my grandparents up in Winn Parish. There was some talk we were related to Huey Long, but Momma always said that was just kinfolks putting on airs. But she wasn't very chatty, which was unusual. She didn't talk a lot to other people necessarily, but she always talked to me. But this day, she was off someplace else. When I asked her if we could have some lemonade, she only waved towards the cabinet where we kept the glasses. "Can you pour it, Sy? Momma's working on something." She didn't even look at me. Even at six years old, I knew it wasn't the letters she was working on. There was only one thing that could distract my Momma like that, and it was Daddy.

"Momma?" I retrieved two metal glasses from the cabinet, one green, for me, the other one blue.

"Yes, Sy?"

"Where's Daddy?" I went to the refrigerator and pulled the lever that unlatched the door.

"Oh, he went fishing with his cousins. You know, Beau and Johnny? The funny ones. They always like to joke with you." I did know Beau and Johnny, and my memory was that they liked to make fun of me, and every other kid who showed up at the old home place when we went. I would've taken a permanent disliking to them, but they were equally mean to all the kids there. When they picked on me, all my cousins laughed and took part, and when they picked on one of them, I did the same. Somehow, knowing I wasn't the only one being bullied made me feel less picked on in the long run. I guess a bird really doesn't care who puts out the seed as long as they get fed.

"Sometimes, I think Beau and Johnny are mean." I pulled the lemonade out with both hands. It wasn't a huge pitcher, but it was the one Momma always liked to use. I knew it was her favorite. I left the door of the refrigerator open.

"Yeah, well, they can be, they can be. But sometimes, it's meanness that gets people through the day. Sometimes, if someone didn't have some meanness to hold them together, they might just blow away like a dandelion head. Then, there's no telling where they might end up." I considered her comment. Were the Boudreaux brothers deep down as fragile as a dandelion in the wind? The concept was hard for me to grasp. "Close the icebox, Sy." Momma didn't look up; she just knew.

"Daddy bringing home redfish for dinner?" I poured the drinks carefully and put the pitcher back into the refrigerator and closed it.

"I don't know, honey child. You boys go on outside and play." Momma kept looking at the electric clock on the kitchen wall.

"But Momma, we're hungry."

"Go play." She said it sharply, and it surprised me because she almost never got mad at me. True, up to that point, I had been a pretty good boy, but I think it surprised her too. She softened her tone now. "Charlie, is your mother home?" I gulped my lemonade down.

Charlie stepped forward out of the archway that led to the living room. He had been nearly invisible, but that was normal for Charlie. "Yes, Ma'am." I handed him his drink.

"Charlie, would you ask your Mother if you boys can play at your house this afternoon?"

"Yes, Ma'am." Charlie chugged down his lemonade, and we put the glasses on the countertop. We both left through the back door. I remembered to not let the screen door slam this time. We knew Charlie's mom wouldn't care if we played there. It was only two doors down, and in Loreauville, every mother was watching out the windows and checking on every kid. If we had been inclined to get into mischief, we would have been found out immediately, and our parents would have known before we got home. We went the two doors down to Charlie's house and sat beneath a crepe myrtle that still had deep pink blooms on it. The blossoms accentuated the dark greens and deep blues of Loreauville. I came home when the streetlights came on.

Just after dark, Daddy got home, and he looked like first one thing and then another. He did have a mess of redfish, already cleaned and smoked, but he looked like he had had to fight an alligator maybe to get them. His face was dirty and sweaty, and he had mud all over his khaki work pants. There was a black smudge on his tee shirt that had once been white but was now grey. I wondered how he got his shirt so dirty from fishing. But he came in while Momma was upstairs and he put the redfish filets on a plate on the counter next to the sink, and he started washing. He scrubbed his face and arms and even took off his shirt to wash his neck. I was sitting at the table watching him, drinking water from my green metal cup. It was funny seeing my Daddy without a shirt. Unless we were at the beach, I rarely saw him shirtless. I was fascinated watching his arms move as he washed. He was cat-like. When Momma came into the room, Daddy was just rinsing off. He dried his face and neck, and arms, and the dishtowel was splotched with grey-black smudge.

Momma picked up the plate of smoked fish. "Well, Benoit LaMontaie, I do believe you've had a successful day fishing." She spoke to him while she moved the fish to the table and then went over to the refrigerator and pulled back on the latch, retrieving a plastic bowl of slaw.

"Yes, I did, Cher. Me and Beau and Johnny got into a mess of them over on Vermillion Bay. Then we went on over to Aunt Ouida's and fixed them all up so you wouldn't even have to cook them."

Momma pulled out another bowl, this one a rice salad. "Thank you, Darling. I do appreciate that." It wasn't really like Momma to have things ready like this. It was almost as if the entire scene had been written out and they were reciting lines for a play. She turned and looked at Daddy, and they stood looking at each other a moment, something passing between them I did not understand. "Bennie, why don't you go get a clean shirt for dinner? I've got one on the bed for you." Daddy gave her a quick smile and left the room. Before he came back, we heard sirens – lots of sirens. I went over to the window to see what the commotion was about but Momma shoo-ed me away. "Sy, go wash up. It's time for supper." I could not believe she didn't want to see what was going on. Sirens? Red lights? Excitement of this sort was rare for Loreauville. Who would want to miss it? I went down the hallway and washed my hands in the sink. The three of us sat at the dinette table and ate dinner. I always loved redfish. The mood was quiet at first, then Daddy started asking me questions about my day, about Charlie, about goings on around town. I did my best to fill him in. He told me I had inspired him to get some redfish with my coloring project. I looked over, and my picture still hung on the front of the refrigerator. Momma was unusually quiet through supper. After we had eaten, we went out to sit on the front porch. The air was thick with an acrid smoke.

"It smells funny out here, Daddy." Daddy shot a look at Momma.

"Yeah, it smells like a fire or something, doesn't it?"

"It smells like when Grandma Boudreaux burned the pralines that time we went there for a cookout. Remember?" I looked up at my Daddy, and he gave me a smirk.

"It does indeed, little man. It does indeed."

Other folks were walking around tonight, pointing and murmuring amongst themselves. I saw Charlie walking with his Mom and Dad. I rarely saw Charlie at night.

"Hey, Charlie!" I waved, and he waved back and ran over towards the porch. His parents called for him to wait but then followed him to the front steps.

"Charlie, we need to let Silas and his parents...," his mother started.

"Good evening, Frank, Claudine." My Dad stood from the swing and walked over to the steps where they stood now. Charlie's dad stuck his hand out, and the two of them shook hands. There was a brief pause as their eyes met. "Frank, can I get you a beer? Claudine?"

"Oh, No. Thanks." Charlie's mom shook her head.

"Yeah, thank you, Ben. Don't mind if I do," Charlie's dad said at the same time. Claudine looked over at Frank as if he were doing something wrong.

"Claudine?" Daddy turned to go inside and get the beer.

"Oh, well, ..."

"How about a glass of wine?" Momma offered.

"Well, okay . . ."

"I'll get it, Cher." Daddy said to Momma, then went inside. Charlie and I went to the other end of the porch and watched the people milling around. It was a busy night. Usually, in Loreauville, after eight o'clock, everyone was inside or no farther out than their front porches. But tonight, everyone was out. Daddy had brought out two stiff ladder-back chairs, and he and Charlie's Dad were sitting in them. Charlie's Mom sat on the swing with Momma. They were talking, so Charlie and I dangled our feet over the end of the porch.

Charlie kicked his legs back and forth. "My daddy says the mill burned."

"The sugar mill?"

"Yeah."

"Wow. Wonder why?"

"Daddy says it happens all the time. Says they use the used-up cane to run the boiler and that sugar burns pretty easy, so it's sometimes just a matter of time."

"Huh." I thought about my grandmother's pralines, and then I thought about Daddy coming home from fishing so dirty. "Huh," I said again.

"What?"

"Nothing." I looked over at my Momma and Daddy, and as if she knew I was looking, my Momma gave me a look too. She smiled at me, but it was an odd smile like she was thinking of something else maybe.

"Daddy said they were closing it anyway."

"They were? We just saw all those wagons . . ."

"Daddy said they were taking everything over to Morgan City 'cause the mill was newer and didn't need fixing as much." I knew Charlie's father worked at the mill as some sort of manager, so I figured he was right.

I processed the past few days in my head, and I tried to make sense of what my thoughts were leading to, but I couldn't quite nail down a conclusion for some reason. Then the sheriff pulled his car up alongside the street, and Sheriff Landry climbed out. A big Buick pulled up behind him, and Old Man Kohler got out of the passenger side. Sheriff Landry was someone who came by Daddy's shop often, getting the patrol car fixed or the motor on his skiff running, but he looked very serious when he strolled up the sidewalk. Kohler was a short, fat, bald man and he swayed back and forth as he fell in behind Sheriff Landry. The sheriff turned around and faced Kohler.

"Let me handle this, Mr. Kohler." The sheriff was making stop motions with both of his hands, but Kohler kept walking until he was right behind the sheriff. I heard Daddy's chair scoot, and I looked over. Daddy stood and leaned against the post by the steps that led to the sidewalk.

"Evening, Remy," Daddy called to the sheriff.

"Look here, Sheriff," Kohler's voice was nasal, whiney. "I know you Cajuns all stick together. . ."

"Let me handle this." This time Sheriff Landry's voice was sterner and Kohler stopped and looked up at the sheriff, who was a head and a half taller than he was. The sheriff turned around and walked slowly but familiarly up to the porch. He took off his wide-brimmed hat and held it in front of him and nodded towards Momma. "Abella." Momma nodded back. "Claudine."

Charlie's mom nodded and said, "Evening."

"Frank." The sheriff took his time.

Mr. Kohler piped up. "Why aren't you over at the mill, Blanchard?"

I nudged Charlie. "He sounds like Mrs. Underwood's rat terrier." Charlie giggled, but my Momma shot me a look, and I stopped talking.

Charlie's dad stood now too. He and Daddy were both wiry men, but the picture of the two of them standing side-by-side on the top step was formidable. "Good evening, Mr. Kohler." Charlie's dad said slowly. "Last I heard, there was no mill to be at." The sheriff turned and looked at Kohler, who immediately stepped back.

"What can I do for you, Remy?" Daddy didn't move.

Sheriff Landy turned back around. "Ben, you see the big fire at the mill?"

"No, I saw the commotion and figured I best keep clear of it, so I didn't get in the way. Was it bad?"

"Yeah. Total loss." The sheriff looked at the sidewalk then back at my Daddy. "You know anything about it, Ben? Folks say you had a beef with Mr. Kohler here."

"Well, he's a man of low moral character, so I do have that beef with him. But, no, I don't know anything about it. And I'm very sorry you felt the need to ask me."

"See here . . ."

"Shut up, Kohler." Sheriff Landry turned and barked at Kohler. "I said I would handle this and I will. Go on, get back in your car." Kohler backed up a few steps but then stopped. I noticed the driver of his big Buick was standing beside the car now, his hands folded before him, waiting. The sheriff turned back around. "Ben, I have to ask. Where were you today?"

"I was over on Vermillion Bay with Beau and Johnny Boudreaux all day, except when we went over to Ouida Jean's place to clean and smoke the big mess of redfish we caught." I thought I saw the sheriff lick his lips and swallow just then. "Remy, you think I had something to do with the fire at the mill?"

"Well, Kohler said you two had a row . . ."

"He owes me four hundred dollars, so yeah we had a discussion about that." It sounded like all the money in the world to me. Four hundred dollars? "But he said it wasn't worth paying me for my time and effort, so he wants to pay me seventy-five. Sound fair, Remy?"

"No, but . . ."

"I'm not paying you a cent now. That place is gone, and so is your money. How you like that?" Kohler shook his finger towards my Daddy. If my Daddy was put off by this, he didn't show it. He remained calm, leaning up against the post. All this time, Charlie's Dad had watched the sheriff quietly, intently.

"Maybe it was an accident, Sheriff." Daddy scratched his cheek absently.

"That fire was started, Ben, and by someone who knew what they were doing."

Daddy shifted his weight and stood up straight. "Sheriff, if you want to find out what happened, I suggest you look at who had something to gain from burning it down. And that wasn't me, and I didn't burn anything except a few fish scales today." Daddy turned around and returned to his chair but remained standing. Then he turned to face the sidewalk again and called out to Kohler. "How much insurance did you have on it, Kohler?"

Kohler stiffened and fairly hopped up and down with anger. Sheriff Landry held up his hand behind him to tell Kohler not to speak, but Kohler couldn't help himself. "I wasn't about to pay those ridiculous rates the insurance companies want. I didn't have anything on it, damn you!"

Charlie's mom made a slight gasp, but Momma only raised her eyebrows. We heard far stronger language any time we went to see Daddy's folks. But

Sheriff Landry was not happy. "Kohler, that's enough. We got ladies present, and you won't talk that way around them." He put his hat back on and marched towards Kohler, and I thought he was going to beat him up or something he looked so angry.

I guess Kohler did too because he turned and ran back to his car so fast his driver barely had time to open the door. He jumped in and rolled down the window and yelled as they drove off. "You're done in this town, LaMontaie, you hear me? Done!" They sped off down the street in a cloud of gas fumes and gravel dust.

The sheriff came back up the sidewalk and walked right up to the bottom step that led to our porch. "Ben, I'm going to have to go talk to Johnny and Beau and all. Just to cover my bases, you know. I'm just doing my job here. But I believe you. I do." He put his hat back on and tipped his head towards Momma and Charlie's mom. "Ladies, I apologize for the unpleasantries tonight. I hope you will have a good evening." He turned now and looked at Charlie's dad and didn't say anything for a moment, then simply pressed his lips together and said, "Frank."

"Sheriff."

Sheriff Landry left, and nobody said anything for a few minutes. Daddy looked at Charlie's dad without saying anything several times. A mosquito landed on my arm, and I swatted it, and just the slap on my arm seemed to break things up. Charlie and his parents went home, and Momma and Daddy and I went inside, but it was very quiet all evening as if someone had died and no one wanted to talk about it.

# Chapter 3

We become accustomed to thinking that our everyday lives should operate somewhere in the middle, between utter disaster and overwhelming good fortune. It can even frustrate us when we find that isn't always so, that at times we may have too little or even too much and we aren't sure how to deal with those extremes. We think somewhere in the middle is what is normal, and anything else is strange, an aberration. We aim the car down the middle of the road to avoid the edges. But life seldom cooperates. We often find ourselves pressed by the excesses of fortune. It's a bit like the weather. We look for the daily weather to be not so hot or not that cold, with a bit of rain now and then to make things grow, but not too much. And we make sure to comment on how hot is or how wet it is as if those things were abnormal. But any weatherman will tell you that a fact of our weather year in and year out is that droughts are often followed by floods and floods are followed by droughts. Extreme in one direction followed by extreme in the other. Our lives are very much the same way. So much of everything or too little. But it isn't the want or the plenty that defines us any more than the sunshine or the cold on any given day explains the weather. It's all in how we respond to those excesses.

Three things happened after that night of the big fire that changed my life dramatically. Everyone in town talked about the mill burning down. They gathered around storefronts and stopped in parking lots, car windows down. They paused in their routines to share any latest news, or, more likely, rumor. Even the kids at school talked about it before Miss Cosler called them to pay attention to the lesson. But whenever I came into the room, people stopped talking about it and just looked at me. It was like I was an animal in a zoo. I still played with Charlie, and we did all the usual things, but I noticed people on the street nudging each other and whispering when they saw me. I knew what they thought, and I didn't like it. It made me mad. Finally, after school one day, Bobby Lee Daltry said it to my face.

"Your Daddy is going to prison because he burned down the mill." He stuck his face forward down into mine. There was a gaggle of other boys behind him. He was one of the bigger boys and in the second grade, but I had tussled with so many cousins at family get-togethers, I was not one bit afraid. One thing I had learned from fighting with cousins is whoever lands the first blow often wins the fight, so instead of giving him some denial that might have led to yelling and pushing and shoving and then maybe a fight, I simply turned around to Charlie, who was at my side as usual, handed him my books and came around swinging, catching Bobby Lee, who was still leading with his chin, flush in the check with a right hand. He stepped back and blinked hard, and I came at him as fast and furious as I could, raining lefts and rights until he finally fell to the ground and curled up in a ball like a newborn kitten, crying. He lay on the dusty ground of the school playground, sniffling. I stood over him and looked down, my heart filled with scorn.

"My Daddy did not burn the mill down, and you are a liar, Bobby Lee. And my Momma says a liar is the worst thing there ever was." I turned around to get my books, and Charlie was staring at me with his eyes bugged out and his mouth open. I looked around, and all the other boys looked the same way, gawking at me like I was some sort of oddity. They reminded me of a dock full of sac-a-laits on Lake Dauterive when I went out fishing with Daddy in springtime. "Let's go home, Charlie." I turned and walked down Victory Drive towards home.

"'Kay." Charlie fell in beside me, but he was quiet. I figured he was thinking Bobby Lee might have had it coming, but he was only saying what everyone else thought. But if he was thinking that, he had the good sense to keep it to himself. My blood was pumping from the fight, and it wouldn't have taken much to set me afire a second time. I went into my room and fumed for a long time. I finally fell asleep until Momma woke me for supper. The phone rang during supper, and Momma excused herself to answer it. There was some murmuring and Momma said, "Uh huh" and "I see" a couple of times. Then her voice grew quieter, and she said something in a low hiss into the receiver, her hand covering her mouth so we couldn't hear what she said. She put the phone back in its cradle hard then came back to the table. She gave me a look I had not seen before. I couldn't tell if she was angry at me or happy with me. It was a look that somehow made me feel older. She also looked up at Daddy and just pressed her lips together. Daddy only blinked. They did that frequently, having whole conversations in a couple of nods and blinks. We finished supper in silence.

It was going on Thanksgiving and was cool enough in the mornings for jackets on the way to school. The next day, I saw Charlie walking to school without me, and I yelled for him to wait and started to run to the door to catch up with him. Momma made me stop and put on a jacket, and by the time I got outside, Charlie had turned the corner, almost as quickly as if he had run the last half a block. That is when my friendship with Charlie started ebbing away. That was the first big thing that happened after that night of the fire.

We didn't play after school anymore. It was true, the weather had an impact, with days of cool afternoons followed by heavy dewfalls that made the morning feel extra chilly. But even on the warmer Saturdays, Charlie seemed to disappear somewhere. At first, I couldn't believe he had stopped being my best friend. We had been constant companions for most of our short lives. He knew about all my secrets, like how I had eaten all the cream candy that Momma had brought back that time from visiting her folks up in Calvin and even that I had a crush on a girl in my class named Lynn. And I knew his secrets as well, including the time he had pilfered a set of paraffin vampire teeth from the dry goods store. But all of that seemed lost now. I decided that it was just a mistake, that he was not avoiding me, but it was just a lull, a time when he was somehow pulled away by other people. I tried to be sure I was where he would be going, either on the way to school or hiding out in the cemetery in case he came by to explore, but he walked on the other side of the street on the way to school with Roy, who was a goofy third grader in my estimation, and somebody that nobody would want to be around. But there they walked, and when I called to Charlie, he acted like he didn't hear me. He didn't come by the cemetery at all.

Then my frustration got the best of me. If Charlie didn't want to be my friend, I didn't want to be his. Besides, I told myself, he was boring. So instead of playing with Charlie, I hung out in my Daddy's workshop with him in the afternoons. I walked alone to school, and that was fine. On the weekends, I helped Momma do things to get ready for her classes on Monday. I was fine. At first, Momma and Daddy asked where Charlie was, but then they stopped asking, and I could see them giving each other looks again when they thought I wasn't paying attention. Finally, I got so I just didn't care anymore about our friendship. He went his way, and I went mine. Nobody said anything to me at school, probably because I had beat up Bobby Lee so bad, and that was fine. I did still carry a crush on Lynn, but I kept that to myself. All in all, it was fine. I told myself I had moved on. Thanksgiving break came, and we went up and visited with Momma's folks up in Winn Parish.

While we were up visiting with Grandmama and Grandpapa, I spent some time with my cousins on that side of the family. My cousins on Daddy's side were a rambunctious lot, always daring each other and doing crazy stunts just to prove who was foolish enough to try them. We would run and fish and fight and play all day long. And my aunts and uncles sort of did the same, although they usually added beer, wine, and, late at night, whiskey to the mix. Momma's family, on the other hand, was stiff and quiet. The kids all sat in the living room on the couch in clothes you wouldn't dream of wearing over to Saline Bayou to fish in. They'd sit there all quiet, listening to the adults talk about politics and the weather or, more often, about something someone had done, someone they knew but I had no clue who they were. I figured they had to talk about what other people did because they themselves never seemed to do anything. Momma and Daddy listened as if they were interested, but I don't see how they could've been. The older people did have wine with dinner, and, on occasion, a beer, but it was all done with tremendous reserve. It was the longest Thanksgiving break ever. If Charlie was boring on his best day, Momma's family made him look like Mr. Excitement.

But when we came back to finish the year, I didn't try to find Charlie. That was over. Instead, I would hang around Daddy's "parts" and help him, or at least, that was my plan.

In fact, Daddy's business fell off almost completely. The decline started off slowly, right after the fire, with a few people coming and getting their items they had left for repairs even before they were fixed. The first time it happened, it was a guy Daddy had known from the mill, Mr. Bertrand, who had left his boat for Daddy to fix the motor on. I was out in the yard playing in an old Ford when he came backing his pickup down the driveway. Daddy came out of the workshop, wiping his hands on an orange shop rag.

"Carl?"

"Hey, Ben." Mr. Bertrand said dryly as he got out of his truck.

Daddy glanced over at his skiff, still sitting where Mr. Bertrand had left it two days before. "Afraid I haven't gotten to the . . ."

"It's alright, Ben. I know. My brother-in-law over in Lydia knows a guy and . . ." Mr. Bertrand pulled the trailer towards the hitch since he had not backed up far enough. He seemed like he was in a hurry.

"But, Carl," Daddy started helping him move the trailer. "I can have it for you by the end of the week. Lydia's all the way over . . ."

"It's okay, Ben. I got it." Then my daddy's head nodded back like he suddenly got it. I guess Mr. Bertrand saw him make that nod too. He stopped cranking the jack. "I'm sorry, Ben."

Daddy took back a step and put his hands on his hips. He stood there for a moment, sizing it up. "It's okay, Carl. You have to do what you have to do." Daddy moved forward and helped him nudge the tongue of the trailer over the hitch on his truck. It fell part of the way but seemed stuck. "I got some three-in-one . . ." Daddy turned to get the oil from his shop. I sneaked out from the passenger side of the old Fairlane so I could hear better.

"Nah, I got it, Ben." Mr. Bertrand frowned and looked at the ground. He looked like he had eaten a bad peanut. "Ah, dammit, Ben. It's not like I want to do this. Sally, she . . ."

"It's okay, Carl." Daddy stopped and turned around and put his hands up. "Really, it's okay. Let me squirt a little oil on that coupler." Daddy went inside to get the oil. That was when Mr. Bertrand saw me hiding behind a pirogue that my Daddy had taken in payment one time. It had a hole in it he was going to fix "one of these days." Momma had laughed about Daddy having a hole in his pirogue. When Mr. Bertrand saw me, his whole body slumped a bit. He shook his head and turned around to pretend to mess with the boat trailer. Daddy oiled the coupler, they hitched up the boat, and Mr. Bertrand left. Daddy watched him drive away. Ordinarily, when people picked up their stuff from having it fixed, they waved as they drove off and Daddy would wave back. They were happy their car or boat was fixed, and Daddy was happy to get paid. But no one waved this time. Daddy stood there in the driveway, wiping his hands on the orange rag. He was thinking about something far away, it seemed like. I slipped back out of the yard and around to the side of the house and climbed over the scalloped wire fence. I sat on a root in the side yard under the live oak draped with Spanish moss and thought about how things were changing. Momma and Daddy didn't go anywhere anymore. They didn't take me anywhere either. Christmas was coming, and as far as I could tell, there were no preparations. No lights went up along the porch rail. The Christmas wreath had not been brought down from the attic and dusted off to be put on the front door. We didn't even have a tree yet, and Momma loved putting up the tree. Usually. We didn't even sit out on the porch either. It's true, it was getting cooler, especially in the evening, and it rained just about every other day, but that didn't usually stop us. But everything seemed to be grinding to some sort of ending that I didn't understand. I sat under that oak tree all afternoon, wondering what was going to happen next and feeling alone. Someone's dog barked off in the distance. A train went by, announcing its approach by whistle, then clank-clanking along for a few minutes and fading away. I heard the bells ringing when the drawbridge opened. A gopher frog let out its low, guttural croak somewhere down by the bayou. I heard Daddy clanging his tools as he worked on a car in his shop. I sat and thought.

The mood around the house grew quieter, more sullen. Daddy spent a lot more time in the house, and the yard began to empty out. After a couple of weeks, the only things left in the yard were daddy's parts cars and the holey pirogue. One day, Daddy pulled the broken-down cars one by one to the junkyard and sold them for scrap. He came home that night with a small wad of money, but he wasn't happy about it.

"I sold it all to Sammy for less than it was really worth." He tossed the small pile of money on the dinette table. I was sitting there reading a chapter book Momma had brought me from the school library called *We Were There*. I looked up at Daddy. He was frowning. "But we gotta eat." He shrugged as he watched Momma reach over and pick up the cash. She rifled through it quickly.

"Yes, we do, Bennie." Momma sat down at the table across from me. She looked up at Daddy, and he sat down too. Momma put the cash in her apron pocket. "Sy," Momma reached over for my hand. I lay my book down on the table before me, the pages open. "We have some troubles these days. You know that, right?" Momma took her free hand and folded the book closed so the binding wouldn't break, but she kept looking at me.

"Yes'm."

"Do you know why?" Momma held my hand gently.

"No. Yes. Maybe. People think Daddy did something?"

"What do they think he did?"

"Burned down the mill?"

Daddy started visibly. "Silas, little man, your daddy did not burn down the mill."

I hung my head and looked at the floor below my chair. "I know," I said, but deep down I wondered.

Momma let go of my hand and stood now and started putting dishes away from the drainer by the sink. "Sy, your Daddy is the finest man you are likely to ever know. Don't ever forget that." Plates rattled as Momma slid smaller bowls atop big platters.

"Yes'm."

The room grew quiet except for Momma plunking flatware into the plastic drawer divider. Momma stopped, looked up at the ceiling, and gave out a big sigh. Then she turned back around, and she managed a thin smile. "Sy, what do you want for Christmas this year?"

"Nothing." I was only a child, but I recognized what being broke looked like. It felt like even wishes cost too much. I picked up my book again.

"Nonsense." Daddy stood now and started helping Momma put away glasses from the dish drainer. "It's almost Christmas. What is it you want Santa to bring?" Daddy and Momma went into their "everything is fine" act. I had seen it a lot since Thanksgiving.

"I don't know." I shrugged. I had had cousins long before disabuse me of the Santa Claus myth, and I did not want to ask for anything we couldn't afford. "Socks?"

Daddy gave out such a huge laugh it startled me. It echoed across the house. "Ha! Socks? Really? Socks?"

"I don't know." I felt embarrassed at asking for socks.

Daddy stopped laughing and sat down again next to me. "You're a good boy, Silas. I'm proud of you." He tousled my hair. "Don't you worry. Santa knows what to bring you. Don't even start worrying about that. And my guess is, it won't be just socks."

Momma watched from where she stood in front of the stove stirring red beans that had been cooking all day with a slab of pork knuckle. We had had red beans and rice frequently the last couple of weeks. I liked them, but it was getting a bit tiresome. I said nothing, of course.

Momma stopped stirring and turned around again. She pulled an envelope from her apron and held it up in front of her like it was a train ticket and the conductor was coming by to punch it. "Bennie?" She paused. "Papa wrote me again."

Daddy gave a nod of acknowledgment. "And?"

"He says he can get you on at the Cary mine up near Winnfield." Momma looked sad, just saying it.

Daddy looked sad too. "Sure hate the idea of not seeing daylight all day."

"It's work, Bennie." Momma sounded more resigned that enthusiastic. "And like you said, we have to eat. And Uncle Grif is on the school board so maybe I ..." Momma trailed off.

"Okay. Okay. Let me think on it, Bele." Daddy leaned back in his chair and looked out the backdoor window. I tried to go back to my reading, but I couldn't keep my mind on it.

"Bennie?"

"Yes, Cher?" Daddy looked over at Momma.

"There's more." Daddy raised his eyebrows. "The superintendent came to my classroom today." Momma sat now. Daddy watched her sit, mulled it over, then turned to me.

"Little Man, why don't you go on upstairs and read for a bit?"

I went up the stairs about halfway and tried to listen to what they were saying, but they spoke in very hushed tones. I could hear them talking, but I couldn't make out what they were saying. It was like the conversations I remembered from going to Aunt Lillian's funeral up near Possum Neck. Everyone spoke in mumbles and nods as if words weren't so important in such conversations.

We ate dinner that night in quiet. Afterward, I cleared the dishes, Daddy washed, and Momma dried. It wasn't a happy mood, but there was a feeling something was different. And it felt like to me, change was not a bad thing. It only makes sense if you see a truck heading for you to step aside.

The next morning, Momma and Daddy called me aside as I was putting on my jacket to leave for school.

"Little Man?" Daddy squatted so he was eye-to-eye with me.

"Yes, Daddy."

"We need to tell you something, but it's a secret. You know how to keep a secret, don't you?"

"Yes, sir. You don't tell nobody."

"Anybody," Momma corrected, then she bit her lip a little.

Daddy didn't stop looking at me. "That's right. This is a secret just for you, your mother, and me, okay?"

"Yes, sir." I felt belly trembles. Was it bad news?

"Silas, we are moving over Christmas. We are going to go someplace new and start again."

"Where?" I was curious, but I wasn't sad. In fact, I felt a sense of relief.

"We're going to stay with Grandpapa and Grandmama." Momma chimed in, but Daddy gave her a quick look, and she stopped. I was okay with going up to Calvin. It wasn't great, but it was doing something. It had felt like we had been wading through a silted-up creek with wet boots the last few months. I was ready. I thought.

"Okay." I started processing this news.

Daddy stood now. "Remember, it's a secret."

"Okay, I won't tell no...anybody." Momma smiled. I finished the last few days of school before Christmas break. I found I liked that I had a secret that no one else knew, and I rather liked not telling anyone. I guess I wore it on my face though because my classmates looked at me oddly. Maybe it was the smile I had. I loved knowing what they didn't. Even Charlie came sidling up after school one day.

"Hey, Sy." I have to give him credit: he said it as if he hadn't been avoiding me for the past several weeks.

"Hm." I didn't even look at him.

"What're you doing?"

I gave him the idiot stare. "Walking home from school?"

"Oh, yeah. Ha! Good one." He gave a little forced chuckle. I stopped dead in my tracks and stared at him. He stopped a few steps in front of me and looked at me with sorrowful eyes. I just shook my head and cut across the parking lot towards Bourgeois Avenue. He had the good sense not to follow me.

The Saturday after school let out, we went out to see Daddy's family, but it wasn't the same. Everyone was reserved, quiet. I sat on a tire swing a good part of the day, watching people go up and talk to Momma and Daddy. At one point, Daddy went inside, carried something out to the truck, and squirreled it away in the bed of the truck. He came back, shot me a glance, then stood with his sister and his brother, drinking beer and talking seriously. It did not feel like the normal Saturday celebration, for sure. Even the Boudreaux boys were not cutting up, and I had never known that to happen.

The next day, Sunday, Daddy, and Momma loaded most of what we owned in Daddy's pick-up truck and the trailer he used to cart off junk. When it came time to load the furniture, Charlie's father came over and helped Daddy carry the chifforobe Momma had inherited from her aunt and the dresser that Grandma Boudreaux had given to Daddy and Momma when they married. Charlie's father and Daddy looked at each other intently, but they almost never spoke during the whole day, working in tandem as they moved the heavy furniture the way men who have labored often do. It felt like they were avoiding talking, at times. When they had loaded everything we were taking, Daddy locked the front door with the things we didn't have room for still inside. He shook Mr. Blanchard's hand and joined us in the cab of the pick-up truck. We were lined up across the bench seat, Daddy, me, and Momma. We pulled out onto Bourgeois Avenue and then turned onto Main Street. The only places we saw cars were in the church parking lots. About the time we made the turn towards Coteau Holmes, it hit me: we had moved away from the only place I had ever called home. It also struck me that none of us had spoken since we had left.

"Daddy?" My voice sounded raspy to me since I had not spoken all morning.

"Yes, little man." Daddy kept an eye on his mirror, watching the furniture sway back and forth on the truck bed. Every once in a while, he stared intently into the side mirror, as if making sure the trailer was still there.

"Are we ever going back?"

"No." Momma and Daddy said in unison. They glanced at each other, then continued their gazes out the windshield.

That was the second big thing that happened after the fire. We left our old life behind and went off to start anew. It was bittersweet. I had found myself without many friends this last month, so I wasn't very sorry to leave my classmates. In fact, I relished the idea of being mysteriously gone when the new year started at school. No one would know what happened. Except maybe Charlie, if his Dad told him. But somehow, I didn't feel like he would tell him. There was something very stealthy in the way we had loaded up and left.

As Daddy drove, I slept, leaned up against Momma, for most of the trip, the combination of the rocking truck and the hum of the highway beneath the tires lulling me. Momma and Daddy didn't talk much on that trip. It didn't feel like they were mad at each other, just that they didn't have anything to say. I awoke when Momma nudged me.

"Sy, honey, we're there."

We drove through the gates and down the long drive that led to my grandparents' house. It was something of a mansion, compared to where we had just left, but it had faded a great deal from its glory days. Huge magnolia trees lined the driveway, the thick green leaves making it seem almost like evening beneath them. The driveway itself was bumpy and rutted from the roots. Daddy kept his look out on the furniture and the trailer. When we pulled up before the wide semicircle of a porch, Grandmama and Grandpapa were standing there, waiting. It was always easy to tell when someone was coming; the dust from the driveway was telltale.

We climbed out of the truck and Momma went up and hugged Grandmama and Grandpapa. She held onto the hugs longer than usual, it seemed to me. Daddy came up and shook Grandpapa's hand and gave Grandmama a gentle, quick hug. I was still standing on the steps of the porch watching.

"Silas?" Grandpapa stuck his hand out. I had never been treated like an adult much, so I liked the gesture. I took his hand and gripped it hard since Daddy had told me to give a firm handshake. But I was only six, so it wasn't like I could grip very hard. Still, Grandpapa nodded approvingly. Then Grandmama came over to me, her arms outstretched.

"There's our little Sy-Sy!" She leaned down to kiss me. I hated being called "Sy-Sy", but I didn't want to be rude, so I let her kiss my cheek, although I did rub off the moisture from my face when she turned around. Daddy saw me and shot me a grin.

Inside, the Christmas tree was set up in the foyer, a huge white pine festooned with thick colored lights and glass balls and draped all over with icicle tinsel. It was really pretty, and for the first time that year, I actually felt like it was Christmas. Momma's parents had always liked the holiday. I guess that was where Momma got it.

We spent the next couple of days settling in. Grandpapa had a family that sharecropped a part of the farm and the father, and two of his sons came by to help us unload. Most of the things went into the barn, and with the three men helping, they unloaded in no time. I spent my time reading books from their library. Grandpapa had a wide selection of books, and he loved telling me about them. He had recently purchased a set of books from an encyclopedia company, and he said I would do well to read every one of the fifty-four books, starting with *Homer*. But he also said I needed to build up to that so instead, he gave me a new copy of *King Arthur and His Knights of the Round Table* with a cover that looked like stained glass. So I started reading. I didn't always understand the romance and chivalry and such, but the action riveted me. The books were a godsend to me since the farm was fairly isolated and I knew no one. By the time the following Wednesday came, and it was Christmas Eve, I was into *The Swiss Family Robinson*, which my Grandpapa also gave me, and also looked new. I carried my reading with me everywhere. It was a kind of security for me, something I could delve into and forget about Loreauville and Charlie and the draw bridge and the mill. But it was hard to not think about the mill.

Christmas Eve, cousins came by, and we all sat on the divan in pressed pants and starched shirts. One cousin was named Albert, after Grandpapa. He was always especially fidgety. I sat there on the divan with my cousins, feeling a little inadequate with my hand-me-down Buster Brown's and twill pants from Montgomery Ward, but I sat still and tried to listen to the conversation the adults were having about communists and the president and, eventually, to Uncle Earl, the governor. Grandpapa's chest swelled when Earl's name came up. Earl was a local boy, and he and his brother had made Louisiana a better place. Grandmama pointed out that Uncle Earl was not a very good role model for young people, but Grandpapa would hear nothing of it. Earl was his second cousin twice removed, or something like that, and no one, not even his beloved Amanda, should ever say bad things about him. I suppose I should have been impressed, but I wasn't. I wanted to read about the treehouse. Instead, I sat there with a squirmy cousin and his older sister who, to my knowledge, never smiled. It was a long evening. Eventually, Aunt Rachel started talking about her sepia paintings, which everyone admitted were quite interesting.

The next day dawned brightly, and we all dressed and combed our hair before going down to presents. My two cousins who were there marched dutifully down the steps as if they were about to be punished. I grabbed my book and followed them. The floor under the tree was filled with presents, but they were mostly for the adults and my cousins. It was true, I didn't think we could afford much, but I still was a little disappointed. My Grandparents gave me a copy of *Robinson Crusoe*, which I did look forward to. My cousins and their parents gave me a box filled with Life Savers that I also thought was a good present, but otherwise, the presents were for others. Each couple received one of Aunt Rachel's sepia paintings, yellow, grey, and dark brown scenes of trees and fence rows. I liked them. Finally, when everyone had gathered their treasures and left, I sat there and watched the adults clearing up the wrapping paper. I felt an emptiness. Daddy picked up some paper, then turned around and said, "Hey, this one's for you." He handed me a balled up little package. It was very small, but I was really excited, but when I ripped it open, it was a pair of white socks. Daddy grinned at me. "Well, it's what you asked Santa for, I guess." He shrugged. I just looked at him, trying to understand why he thought this was so funny. Then he turned around again and reached behind the tree and pulled out the most beautiful guitar I had ever seen. It wasn't new, but the colors on it were perfect. It was a Gibson from the 1940s. It caught the light from the front window and sent a flash of daylight into my face. Momma stood next to Daddy now. "Little man, this was my father's. He taught me every note a guitar can play on this one right here. And now, it's yours." Daddy thrust the instrument towards me, and I felt dizzy, suddenly. I knew this guitar. I had seen my Daddy, and his cousins handle it with almost reverence at family get-togethers. I couldn't believe what I was hearing. Mine? It was mine? Momma and Daddy wore huge smiles. Daddy was still holding it because I was frozen in place. "Here, son. It's yours now. Take good care of it." I took it now and held it like I had seen my Daddy hold a guitar thousands of times before. I was too small to handle it with much agility, but I had seen Daddy play a D chord enough that I placed my fingers on the strings and gave it a strum. It came out flat and dead. "It will come,

Silas. Takes practice." Daddy nodded. "You know, some of my favorite songs start off in D." I looked up at him, and my eyes filled with tears. It was without any question the most unexpected, perfect present I would ever receive. Momma shooed me now.

"Go get ready for church, honey child. You and your Daddy can do a lesson this afternoon." I cradled the guitar and carried it upstairs.

That present was the third thing that happened as a result of the fire at the mill that changed my life. We didn't have any money for presents, so instead, my daddy gave me his most beloved possession, his Daddy's Gibson. My world was forever changed.

# Chapter 4

When we are young, we are filled with dreams about what road we want to go down and where we hope it will lead. We are told over and over that we can do whatever we put our minds to. With those reassurances ringing in our ears, we set our sights on what we plan to be, usually before we really know much about the world. The truth is that we often find ourselves looking back somewhere down some different road, standing in some odd clearing, gazing around, wistfully wondering just when it was we made that turn that led us to where we are standing at that moment. When did we take that comfortable, paved highway, perhaps, to comfort and certainty, and abandon the rocky path of adventure and chance our bravado youth once embraced? Or perhaps we got lost down some shortcut we never intended to take for very long and find we have become someone other than we believed we would be in our formative years? Like the clay a potter must work with to achieve what can be turned on the wheel, life presents its own resistance to the images we dare dream. In any case, most of us usually end up in a different spot than we planned. The wistfulness comes from thinking the crossroads are no longer there, that the chance has passed us by, but that isn't necessarily so. It's entirely possible those roads meet again somewhere over the horizon from where we are standing if we care to look. Then the only question is, do we have the courage to change our route this time.

The road we took from Loreauville led us to Winn Parish, where I started in at Calvin High School the following month. At first, I wondered if I was skipping grades, but it turned out, all the grades were in high school. It wasn't a path I had much say in, but I trusted Momma and Daddy, so I marched on. Momma registered me in after the new year started and for the first week or so, Grandpapa drove me in his old Hudson Hornet, a huge vehicle that floated along the rutted roads like they were made of cotton. Then we found where the bus stop was, and Grandpapa said I needed to take it because it was the right thing to do, to ride "with the people," but I think he just got tired of getting up and getting dressed so early. Daddy started at the salt mine right after Christmas, leaving early in the morning and coming home late covered in a white powder. He tried to look happy, but his skin became pallid, and his face became drawn after only a few weeks. Momma taught at Winnfield High and left every morning before I did, driving Grandmama's Nash off in a cloud of dust each day. I spent my afternoons reading and doing my homework. I sat by myself in an old bedroom they rarely used except when the holidays came. Grandpapa told me the house was once used as a hospital during the civil war when a trainload full of soldiers had been hit by cannon fire during the Red River Campaign and that supposedly, the house still had the hauntings of some of those who died. He told me the last part with a wink, but it still spooked me a bit. I would sit in the room that had recently become "my" room, reading, smelling the coal fumes from the octopus furnace, and listening to the thumps and groans it gave out. Daddy told me there were no ghosts, but the sounds still startled me. I wore hand-me-downs from cousins in the area, and we ate whatever Grandmama fixed, which meant not Cajun, but still good food. For a while, Momma and Daddy hoarded all their money, trying to get a stake of some sort. I would have thought it was a tough time, but it seemed like everyone we met in Winn Parish was struggling. There weren't a lot of jobs, evidently, but there also weren't a lot of people. And the land was beautiful, with lots of woods filled with game and lakes filled with cypress stumps and fish. I loved the ride to and from school, just looking out the window at the scenery. It was very different from Loreauville. The kids at school were a little stand-offish at first since I was the new kid, but I didn't mind. At least no one talked about the fire at the mill, at least, not yet. And I had my books to read and, after Daddy's first paycheck, the spongy rubber ball he had gotten for me to squeeze all day to build up my hand strength so I could play my new guitar. Daddy might have been worn out from working in the mine, but he always gave me a guitar lesson each evening. At first, he taught me the strings and notes and how to keep it tuned. We showed me how to find *E* on Grandmama's spinet and then how to do the rest from there. At the end of January, Daddy taught me how to play my first song.

"Now, Silas, you know how to play a D, right?" I slowly placed my fingers, tender from the strings already, into the chord on the guitar neck. "Okay, now hold in hard and give it a strum." I did so, and suddenly I had played music. I gave Daddy a grin. Daddy smiled approvingly. "Okay, now this here is a G." He showed me on his guitar. I studied his hand and tried to copy his finger placement, but I couldn't adjust the left-right conversion. He gently moved my fingers into place. I strummed, and the notes came out dead. "Hold them down hard. Try again." I tried again, and the notes came out, but it felt like my fingers were going to be bloody stumps before long.

"Ow!" I pulled my fingers back and looked at them. They weren't bloody, at least not yet, but they did have deep impressions from the strings, and they were very red.

"That'll get better. I promise. Play a little each day, and you'll build up callouses." Daddy leaned on the body of his guitar. "Now, this is the last one for today. It's an A." Daddy placed his three middle fingers in a row. "Can you do that?"

"Yes, sir."

"Just put your fingers there for now. Don't try to play it yet. Let your fingertips rest."

"Okay." I imitated his fingering and looked up at him. "Like this?"

"Yes, little man, exactly like that." Daddy gave me a smile. "You now know a song, a song written by Jimmie Davis, who was once the governor here in Louisiana. You practice as often as you can, and you'll be playing it smooth as a whistle before you know it. See?" Then Daddy sang "You are My Sunshine" slowly, showing me where the changes were. He played it through then had me follow with just the fingering about a half dozen times. "You're on your way, Silas Lamontaie," he finally said. Then he put his guitar back in its case and put it back under the divan. I was hooked. I tried playing it that day, but my fingers were too sore, so I spent the rest of the night squeezing the rubber ball and reading *Treasure Island*. I fell asleep that night dreaming of pirates, ghosts, and playing guitar.

By the end of February, Momma and Daddy had gotten paid a few times, and they decided to fix up an old sharecropper's house on my grandparents' farm. Daddy didn't like staying at their house for free. He said he felt like a freeloader. Grandpapa had said we could live in the house for free if Daddy and Momma would fix it up. Daddy said we shouldn't since it was still taking from them, but Grandpapa assured him that if we fixed the place up, it would be payment enough. One drizzly Saturday in early March, we got directions and drove over to the other side of the farm in Daddy's pickup and sat in the muddy lane in front of it for a long time, trying to decide if it was worth going in.

"Cher, that's not a house. That's a shack." Daddy shook his head.

"It's sure not much."

"Tin roof needs to be replaced first thing." Daddy ducked his head to see through the windshield.

"Yes, it does."

"Why is the porch leaning like that?" I leaned my head sideways to correct the angle, but it was still crooked.

"That shed roof will need to come off the front and be rebuilt. You're right, Silas." Daddy opened his door and climbed out, still eyeing the building almost as if it would fall down if he took his eyes off of it. Then he saw the pitcher pump standing to the side of the yard. He went over and pushed and pulled the pump handle, and after a few times, some muddy-looking water came flowing out into the dirt. He kept pumping until the water came out clear. "Well, we got water." It wasn't lost on me that he said "we." That sounded like we were staying. "It's got power coming to the house." Daddy pointed to the sagging wire that draped from a short pole behind the house. Momma got out now and started for the front porch, or, rather, what was left of the front porch. "Careful, Bele. Those boards may be rotten."

"I got it, Bennie." Momma tiptoed across the peeling boards, making sure to step where the boards were nailed to the joists below and stood before the front door. The screen door hung to the side, the top hinge broken off and the screen pulled loose from the frame of the door. Momma shook her head and tried the door. The dented brass handle turned, but the door wouldn't budge. By this time, Daddy and I were standing on either side of her, waiting for the moment the door opened. Daddy took over and gave the door his shoulder at the same time he lifted up hard on the handle, and the door groaned open. We stood there for a minute, letting our eyes adjust and waiting to be sure the door had not somehow been holding up the house. Momma went in first, looking around her, sizing things up. "I think the floor's actually okay, Bennie."

Daddy went in and walked back and forth through the room, stopping every now and then, shifting his weight up and down. "You're right, Abella. They aren't bad. And the walls need to be stripped of this old paper and painted, but they're still here. Mostly." I walked in now looked over at the fireplace where a drum stove had been put in. The lathing showed around the edge where a stovepipe flue had been installed into the old chimney. Everything looked dirty and dusty to me. It reeked of mice and urine. There was a broken ladder back chair lying over by a doorway the led into a kitchen. I couldn't imagine we would be staying. Then the room got bright. Momma had pulled the roller shade open on the window. The dingy yellow light coming through the window made the room look worse. There was a pane broken out of the window. Then Momma went out to the truck, reached in the back and picked up a couple of brooms a bucket full of brushes, and a mop. She marched back to the house. I looked over at Daddy, and he looked at me.

"Ready to do some work, Sy?" Daddy gave me a wink. What I wanted to do was sit in my clean if haunted bedroom at Grandmama and Grandpapa's and play guitar and read in the latest book Momma had brought home from the library, a Hardy Boys mystery, *The Tower Treasure*. But we were in this together, so we spent that Saturday cleaning on that old sharecropper's house. We worked until dark, stopping only for a quick lunch on the edge of the porch of sourdough bread and cold fried chicken. It drizzled all day, but the damp, cool weather felt good after working so hard. I washed up every hour or so, pumping the handle and lathering with the bar of soap Momma brought from Grandmama's house. I swept and carried broken fragments of furniture to the yard, and then I mopped the sagging linoleum kitchen floor as best I could using a bucket of well water and a heavy dose of Pine-Sol. The pine scent was a welcome respite from the smells we had first encountered. When the daylight started to fade, we were spent. Daddy sat on the step next to me in front of the house. I could barely move. I felt limp all over.

"You know what a home is, Sy?" He looked out across the yard of bright red clay. I looked up at him, then turned my head to look at the building we had spent the day cleaning. It still looked like a shack to me. I looked back at him. I wasn't sure I knew what he was asking. He hugged me closer to him around the shoulders. "A home is just a box. And like most boxes, in the end, it's not about the box itself. It's about what you put into the box that counts. A home is a box full of memories. Just be sure they are good memories and nothing else really matters."

We spent every weekend working on that old shack. Sometimes, Daddy went there after work to have things ready for weekend chores. Grandpapa paid for materials, and we did the work. Again, Daddy objected, but Grandpapa pointed out the house was still his, and it wouldn't be right for us to sink all our money into it and not get anything from it in the long run. Besides, he pointed out, the work we were doing was more than enough payment. He was right, too. Daddy rewired the house and put plumbing in the kitchen and even added a small room behind the kitchen to be the first indoor toilet the house had ever had. He spent one week putting in a five-hundred-gallon metal septic box Grandpapa paid for. Eventually, towards the end of April, the list of chores grew smaller and easier, at least for me. One weekend,

I was even allowed to hike down the gravel road and do some exploring while Momma and Daddy painted the walls white. Along the ditch, butterweed grew in profusion. Further back from the road, daisies and occasional primroses grew in clumps. The red fields beyond had been tilled, and rows of small peanut plants stretched across the slow hillside. Redwing blackbirds and meadowlarks called out to me. The sun warmed me as I walked, and I closed my eyes to let my face absorb the light as I moseyed along. It was a beautiful morning. When I opened my eyes, I found I had walked up almost to the front of another small house. There was smoke coming from a chimney in the back, and two boys about my size were pushing each other on a tire swing hung from a cottonwood tree. They saw me about the same time I saw them and stopped, looked at each other, and ran towards me. An old woman leaned forward on her rocker on the porch and watched them racing towards me. The boys stopped on the other side of the ditch from me. One of the boys I recognized from school, but I didn't know his name. The other boy was younger. The red-clay dust from their yard contrasted their ebony legs.

"What's your name?" The younger boy asked as soon as he caught up to his brother. His brother gave him a look, but the little one paid him no attention.

"Silas."

"I know you. You're that new kid from down south, ain't you?"

"Yeah." I shuffled my feet a bit.

The younger boy looked me up and down twice. "You wanna swing?" He pointed towards the tire hanging from the tree.

"Sure." I looked at the ditch between us then back at the boys. The younger one was already racing back to the tree. The old woman was standing at the edge of the porch now, shielding her eyes from the sunlight.

"Come down here to the drive," my classmate pointed, and he walked opposite me towards the drive that traversed a battered metal culvert. "I'm Fredrick. You like to read a lot, don't you?" I stopped next to a battered steel mailbox sitting atop a fence post. "Bailey" was hand-lettered on the side.

"Yeah."

"What else you like to do?"

"I'm learning how to play guitar." I shrugged.

"Really? My Grandma plays guitar!" He turned and faced the old woman who had sat back down now, assured I was no threat, I suppose, and called out, "Hey, Grandma! This here is Silas. He's in my school. He plays guitar just like you."

I started a bit. "I'm just learning." We had reached the driveway, and I entered the yard. There were small tufts of grass trying to grow, but the yard seemed too packed down for growing much. Fredrick came over and stood in front of me. He was several inches taller than I but just as skinny. He was all arms and legs and wore only some cutoff jeans: no shoes and no shirt.

Grandma called hoarsely from the porch, "Bring that boy over here so's I can see him. My eyes can't see far away no more." Fredrick led me to the porch. His Grandma leaned towards me in her rocker, holding up her wire glasses to see through them at me. "Your name is Silas?" She had grey hair that curled tightly on her head. She was heavy, but she still looked strong. I could smell black-eyed peas cooking inside, and it made my mouth water.

"Yes'm. Silas Lamontaie."

"Oh, my! Now that's a good name! Your Momma gave you a good name, a name that will take you somewhere, uh huh! That's a name you can carry, and it will carry you. So, you play a little guitar, do you?"

"A little. I'm not very . . ."

She leaned back in her chair. "Fredrick, go fetch my 'box." I figured she was going to play me a song, so I waited while Fredrick ran inside, but when he came out with her well-weathered guitar, she pointed towards me and said, "Give Mr. Silas a go at it. Let me hear what you got, son. Grandma Bailey loves music." Fredrick handed me the guitar.

"Oh, I'm just learning, Ma'am. I don't really . . ."

"Hon, we are all just learning until we die. It's okay. Play something for Grandma Bailey."

I took the guitar and sat down on the porch step in front of Mrs. Bailey, and I sang and played "You are My Sunshine" clear through with only one short pause when I needed to play the A. She tapped her toe to the music and patted the arm of her rocking chair to beat and then she clapped when I finished and so did Fredrick, who had stood next to his Grandma while I played. It was my first performance in front of anyone other than my parents and grandparents.

"I like your finger pickin,' Mr. Silas. Who's been teaching you?"

"My Daddy. He's really good at guitar. He says finger-pickin' works good for a small hand."

"Well, he's teaching you right, I'd say. What else you got?"

"Oh, well, I can play 'O Susanna.'" I was eager to show off my new chord, C. I started playing "O Susanna" in the key of G and Grandma Bailey, as I would forever know her, started singing with me. Her voice had a raspy quaver that

I liked. About halfway through, Fredrick started singing too, and by the end of the song, his little brother was singing as well. I decided to sing and play the chorus another time since we were all at full voice. Grandma Bailey grinned at me when I went into the second chorus. And then she laughed.

"Oh, you are a performer, Silas Lamontaie. I can tell that right away." She rocked in her chair after I had finished. "Here, let me show you a song I think you might like." She took the guitar and handled it familiarly. "I bet you know these notes." She sang and played "Low Down Blues" using a slap strum to create a beat and strumming a long guitar solo in the middle. I watched her hands closely. They were gnarled up with arthritis some, but she still could play the guitar. I had heard my daddy play that beat before, but he hadn't been playing much lately since he started working in the mine and fixing up that old house, so this was a new style for me. When she finished playing the song, she showed me how to do the slap strum, and I played several beats on her guitar. I couldn't wait to practice my new skill at home on my guitar. She took the guitar from me. "Now you boys go on out to the yard and play some." Grandma Bailey shooed us with one hand.

I spent several hours playing on the tire swing with Fredrick and his little brother Jackson. The sun was high when I saw Daddy's truck heading up the road, a cloud of red dust rising behind it. I had been having so much fun, I had completely forgotten about checking in. Daddy saw me in the yard and pulled to a stop in the middle of the gravel road before the driveway. The cloud of dust blew across the road, settling across the field of peanut plants. He and Momma got out of the truck and walked towards the porch. Grandma Bailey stood up stiffly. Daddy took off his straw porkpie hat he always wore when he worked outside and held it in both hands before him. He and Momma stood before the porch looking up at Mrs. Bailey.

"Good afternoon. My name is Benoit Lamontaie. This is my wife, Abella." He waved with his hat towards Momma. Momma nodded. "I think you've met our boy, Silas." Daddy did a half turn as I walked over to his side. He put his hand on my shoulder.

"I have indeed, Mr. Lamontaie. I have indeed." Mrs. Bailey leaned forward and reached her hand out. Daddy stepped forward quickly to shake her hand. "He's a real good boy." She nodded in my direction. "My name is Imogene Bailey, but everyone just calls me Grandma Bailey. Probably 'cause I'm old as Methuselah." She gave out a big laugh and Momma and Daddy laughed too. When she stopped laughing, she added, "I never seen you all hereabouts before, have I?"

"We're fixing up the old house just up the road here." Momma chimed in.

"That old shack? Oh my! You are adventurous souls, you are." Grandma Bailey returned to her rocking chair. Fredrick and Jackson stood on either side of her.

"Well, it's coming along." Daddy offered.

"I'm sure it is. I'm sure it is. Well, we are happy to have neighbors. Welcome. You need anything, you let me know. We ain't got a lot, but we make do. I got some folks around too, you need anything more."

"Thank you." Momma nodded again.

"Your boy seems to take to that guitbox." Grandma Bailey nodded towards me.

"He's a natural." Daddy was turning to go.

"He tells me you can pick a song or two."

"Yeah, well, I enjoy it when I can." Daddy was half turned around.

"I got my 'box. You care to sit a spell and play?" Grandma Bailey waved towards the guitar leaning against a windowsill. "I do love music."

"Maybe not today. But I will. I promise." Then we all three retreated to the truck. That was how I made my newest best friend, Fredrick Bailey.

Within a few weeks, we moved into the old sharecropper's house. The furniture was mismatch hand-me-downs from family and the thrift store in Natchitoches. Momma made sleeve top curtains from some cotton that she and Grandmama had stained with tea and hung them in the windows. We had a rag rug in the living room from my grandparents' attic that Daddy hung on a nylon rope and beat until all the dust came out. That rope became our clothesline. All the cookware and assorted dinnerware we had was from that same attic. Dented and chipped, they still served the purpose. It wasn't a fancy place, but it was clean, and it was where we were staying. I didn't mind it. The right-hand side was the living room and behind it the kitchen. Behind that was the bathroom Daddy had added. The left side of the house included my parents' room and my room. I had to go through my parents' room to get to my room, which also meant, if I had to pee at night, I had to go through every room in the house to get to the toilet. But that was okay.

After we had moved in, we discovered we had a few other neighbors in addition to Fredrick's family. They were all different colors and of assorted backgrounds, white, black, Cajun, what have you, but no one seemed to notice. We were all just folks, poor folks mainly, doing our best to make ends meet by working the land or landing the few jobs around in the mine or the quarry near that. Some folks timbered. Regardless of what people did, they worked hard, and they took nothing for granted. We settled in, developed our routines, and went about our day-to-day lives. We went to Grandma Bailey's house a couple of times, and Daddy played music with her and some other folks who lived nearby. It wasn't like the Cajun music I usually heard Daddy play, though. This was bluesy and sad, and they seemed to change chords whenever they felt like it. Daddy was a good enough guitarist he stayed with them, but I definitely saw him focusing hard. They sang songs about hard times and loving someone who didn't love them back, which I didn't understand yet, but I would. Grandma Bailey's nephew played harmonica on a lot of the songs with them and his wife, Fredrick's Aunt Louella, sang beautifully. I had never heard music like this. The first time they asked Daddy to play one of his songs, he played "J'ai Passe Devant Ta Porte" and they all just filled in on their guitars and harmonicas and an upright bass that one man played. Aunt Louella hummed in harmony the second time through. It was as if they all knew the song ahead of time, although I don't think they did. Fredrick sometimes huffed on an old ceramic jug to keep time. I had taken my guitar, but I was clearly in over my head with these folks. But they cajoled me into leading a song and Daddy told me to go ahead, so I played "You Are My Sunshine" and they all just jumped in and I would've thought I was on stage at the Grand Ole Opry the way it sounded. I could not believe my ears. I beamed with pride when it was over, and they all laughed until they cried at the look on my face.

"Mr. Benoit, I believe you better keep an eye on that young'un. He's got musician writ all over him." Grandma Bailey rocked in her chair, surrounded by kinfolk and friends, and gave a chuckle.

Daddy grinned at me. "Little man, I don't know if you can grow up and be a musician. You may have to choose between them." At that, Grandma Bailey laughed even louder.

The area where we lived they nicknamed Crackletown. It wasn't a town at all, but just a stretched-out row of small nearly fallen down houses, all about a half mile apart or more. Momma said they named it that because everyone made crackling cornbread, but I don't know. All I knew was, we were living our lives just fine, making do with what we had and getting by okay until a ghost from our past came back to haunt us, the burning of Kohler Mill, and a new threat emerged, Operation Plowshares. Odd as it may sound, I am thankful now they did, although at the time I was devastated.

# Chapter 5

School was nearly out for summer when we moved. Once school let out, I spent that summer running back and forth to Fredrick's house, and he often came back with me when I came home again. We played on the tire swing at his house with Jackson in tow, being trapeze artists or calling out like Tarzan. We walked along the grey, gravel road that spanned our families' humble homes, throwing pieces of limestone at cans and bottles and, once and only once, at a hornet's nest up in a persimmon tree. I read books from the public library in Winnfield. Fredrick started reading more too just so we could read at the same time on one of our porches in the afternoon to escape the summer heat. Momma would take us into the library in Grandmama's Nash that seemed more Momma's now than Grandmama's.

Fredrick and I shared books back and forth. We traipsed through the fields so much, I never bothered about sweat bees; they didn't even hurt me. We found mulberries to feast upon and blackberries too, although the attack of chiggers I had after the blackberry feast was a bit of a price I hadn't bargained for. My feet got tough from walking on gravel and through sticker bushes all the time. I still practiced guitar and sometimes we would put on shows for Grandma Bailey or my parents, me singing and slapping at the guitar, Fredrick huffing, thumping, and humming into a jug or sometimes just slapping his knees and clapping. He had a great sense of rhythm, so it actually sounded pretty good, for being just kids, or at least I thought so. We both had chores around our homes, but the fact we had to complete our chores before we could visit with each other made the tasks easier. I flew through the trash removal, the porch sweeping, and the making of my bed. On the weekends, Daddy would sometimes tug an old tired jon boat he had bought into the back of his pickup and take us over to Lake Saline to fish for shell crackers around the cypress knees in the early morning cool while the tree frogs were still calling and the odor of honeysuckle filled our heads. He would scull us around the stumps and Fredrick and I would drop our bobbered lines baited with catalpa worms into the shallow water. More often than not, we would take a mess of fish to Grandma Bailey, who fried them all up and shared them with as many people up and down the Crackletown Road as the fish would allow.

Momma continued working on our tired old house, painting the trim around the windows and adding pictures on the wall; family photos in the bedrooms, prints of birds and flowers in the living room, and a print of a man saying grace before his dinner of bread and soup over the table in the kitchen where we ate. She grew flowers and brought in bouquets to put around the house. She grew squash and tomatoes and beans from seeds she got from Grandma Bailey. Meanwhile, Daddy worked at the mine. He went in early and dug with picks and shovels after they blasted in the rooms full of salt. He was one of the men who loaded up the rail carts that then went up to the conveyor belt. Daddy took Momma and me over by the mine one day so we could see where he worked. While we were standing there looking at the huge processing building, a horn blared, and Daddy told us to get in the truck. Then there was an explosion that shook the truck, and a few pieces of rock fell in the parking area. Daddy told us that was the quarry but that the mine was just about the same, without the raining rocks.

By the time school started in the fall, Fredrick and I had become constant companions. The bus picked up Fredrick first and then me. He saved me a seat, although we were nearly the first kids on in the morning and the last off in the afternoon. We talked all the way to school every day and all the way home. I was only in the second grade, but I was still left to be at home by myself for the half hour or so until Momma got home. I stayed out of trouble, though. I knew we needed no more trouble.

A part of me knew we were poor, but I also knew we were doing better than most of our neighbors, what with Momma teaching and our having no rent to pay. We went over to my grandparents' house every Sunday, and I came to look forward to it eagerly. Grandpapa sometimes gave me another book to read and asked me questions about whatever book I might have just finished. He seemed to know about all of them. He told me more about the Civil War and how it had taken place, in small part, in our area. He liked telling me how the county had voted against secession and sent nearly as many troops to the north as they did to the south. Grandmama always cooked a big meal with Momma at her side, and they would gossip and giggle while they cooked. I liked seeing Momma so happy. While we were there, Daddy would sit and listen to Grandpapa and me talking. He had taken up smoking a pipe, and I can see him clearly to this day, rocking in the big porch rocker, puffing on his briarwood, the bittersweet smoke wafting across the porch, mingling with the smell of a pot roast or a baked ham, then out into the yard. I felt balanced again for the first time in a long while. But that started coming to an end later that autumn.

Daddy came home early from the mine one day looking even more haggard than usual. His face those days always had a pale, drawn frown on it from almost never seeing the light of day, but this afternoon, he was really dragging. He was home when I got there from the school bus. Momma was surprised he was home when she got home a few minutes later. Daddy was sitting in the metal lawn chair shaped like a seashell they had found beside the road one day in Winnfield and had tossed into the back of the truck. He was smoking his pipe. I was sprawled out on the porch, doing my homework, which consisted of math worksheets. I had not really wondered about his being home. I was just glad to see him. But he looked very sad.

"Bennie? Are you okay? What's the matter?" Momma stepped lightly on the porch. She looked tired too, but she always moved lithely.

Daddy looked up at her and didn't say anything at first but just kept puffing on his pipe. Then he stood up and gave Momma a hug. "Bele, they're talking about some stuff at the mine that concerns me. I told them I was sick, but I just needed to come home and be with my family today."

"Are you okay, my love?" Momma returned Daddy's hug.

"Yes, Bele. I'm okay."

"Layoffs?" Momma pulled back to get a good look at Daddy's face.

"No. No, I think the world needs salt. That doesn't seem to be an issue. They're running three shifts these days. But there's this thing they've been talking about doing around the country called Plowshares where they want to see if they can use atomic bombs for peacetime projects. I read about it in the paper over at your Mom and Dad's Sunday. Turns out, they're going to do some tests here, at the mine."

"What?" Momma's eyebrows shot up. "They're going to set off an atomic bomb here? In the mine? That's crazy!"

"No, no, I don't think so. But they want to use a part of the mine we aren't using to see what happens if they set off some big bombs." Daddy sat down again. He looked weary, heavy with fatigue. I was supposed to write down the time a printed clock on my worksheet told, but I couldn't focus on that. Atomic bombs?

"What kind of bombs, Bennie?"

"I don't know, but big ones. To see what happens. See if it can be detected above ground."

"Will they destroy the mine?"

"I don't know, Cher. They say it won't, but it seems risky to me, but they didn't ask my opinion." He puffed on his pipe, but it had gone out. He laid it beside his chair on the porch floor.

"So, they're closing the mine. Well, I'm still . . ." Momma dropped her shoulders and looked off across the yard.

"No, we're still mining salt while they do the tests. They're going to be testing over in the old area that's played out."

"What? They're setting off atomic bombs while you're mining?" Momma whipped her head back around to face Daddy. Her eyes were wide, and her mouth was open with shock. I scrambled to my feet as well. I did not want my Daddy blown up.

"No, Cher, not atomic bombs, no, but big bombs, yes. We blast down there all the time, so it's not like it's something new. They say it will be fine."

"But do you set off blasts like they're going to? Huge ones?"

"Well, no." Daddy looked at Momma. He shrugged. "What can we do? I don't see any options."

"Bennie, how far down do you go every day?" Momma finally put down her satchel she had carried home from school, and she sat on the front step, twisting her body around to face Daddy.

"Oh, eight hundred feet or more, I guess. Long way."

"If they set off a bomb, you could be trapped, Bennie. This isn't a good plan." Momma shook her head. "I don't like it."

"Well, Bele, I don't think they would do it if they thought it was going to tear up the mine."

"You don't? But how do we know?"

"Well, the company still wants . . ."

"They're going to blow up big bombs in the mine, right?"

"Yes."

"And they're doing it to see what will happen? Is that what they told you?"

"Yes."

"So, they don't know for sure what will happen, which is why they are doing the test, right?" Momma held her hands face up as if to say, "Isn't this obvious?"

"Well, yes. I know what you're saying, but I don't want you to worry . . ."

"How can anyone not worry?" Momma's voice went up an octave.

"Bennie!" She shook her head again and started to stand. I watched from where I was standing at the end of the porch. I also didn't like the idea of Daddy being in the bottom of a salt mine while they blew things up somewhere else in the mine. "What do they call this fiasco, Bennie?" Momma picked up her bag.

"Cowboy is what I heard. Project Cowboy." Daddy sat limp in the lawn chair,

"Huh. It sounds like someone is playing cowboy, all right. Sounds like they are playing with stuff they ought not play with." Momma stomped off into the house, and Daddy got up and followed her. He picked up a gunny sack that was lying next to the front door.

"Grandma Bailey brought us some crowder peas and cabbage from the Rossman's garden today."

"Okay, Bennie, . . ." But she didn't sound okay. Then her voice trailed off. I could hear them talking in the house, muffled voices, then periods of silences, followed by more talking. I went back to my homework. I guess they came to an understanding of some sort. A couple of hours later, we sat at the table, Momma having fixed cabbage and sausage for supper, and they kept looking at each other and then at me. I knew there was something up, but I also knew it would do me no good to ask. Whatever it was, they would tell me when they were ready to.

After I went to bed, I heard them talking again. The walls of the house were not thick enough to keep much sound out, so we didn't have many secrets. I had just closed *The Phantom Freighter* and turned off the candlestick lamp to go to sleep when I heard Momma and Daddy in the kitchen talking. The walls were so thin, I could hear the dishes clanking as they put them away from the dish rack.

"Abella, I don't see how we can make it if I quit at the mine. I know what you said, but we need that money."

"Bennie, I love you too much to put a price on you." A glass clinked onto the shelf on the other side of the wall next to my bed.

"But, there just aren't any jobs around and . . ."

"I still get paid." A bowl rattled.

"Cher, you don't get paid enough. What do you get, four hundred a month?" Flatware jostled into a drawer. Then I heard water running.

"Well, it will have to be enough for Silas and me if you don't come home one day because you died in the mine, won't it?" There was a silence now except for the water running, then it shut off too.

Finally, I heard Daddy say, "But what would I do?"

"You still have your tools, Bennie. And you can fix just about anything people need fixed. Maybe open up your shop again? With times the way they are, people need to hang onto what they have. You can help them do that."

The water came back on. "Yeah, but honey, no one has any money. How are they going to pay me? I can't work for free." The water went off, and I heard the cast iron skillet clunk down on the burner of the stove.

"Yeah, I know. I know. But people get by, somehow, don't they? So maybe they pay you with a chicken. Or some green beans. Or a plow, and we'll grow our own."

"Am I pulling or you?" There was another pause in the conversation. "Yeah, maybe I could, Bele. Maybe. Still, have to have parts."

"Most folks will pay with money, Bennie. I just don't want to know you are in that mine when something goes wrong. I can't stand to think about it. It scares me too much. I love you."

"I know, Bele. I know. And I love you, too." I heard the chairs being pulled out from under the table. "Okay, you're right. I'll do it. I need to give them notice, but I will do it. We don't have a lot of bills, and I do miss fixing things. And I miss daylight. I miss you." Then it grew quiet again, and I fell asleep.

By the week before Thanksgiving, Daddy was home all day. They had set off big explosions in the mine while fighter jets flew low above the mine. The newspaper described it as if it were a battle scene. The mine didn't collapse, but I don't think my Daddy regretted leaving the mine. He was happy no one was injured, but he was glad to be setting up his shop again. In fact, he was downright giddy. He talked with Momma about putting up a little pole building to work in and the Sunday before Thanksgiving when we went to Momma's parents' house, Daddy chattered on all afternoon like a happy chicken. He was usually fairly quiet at Grandmama's and Grandpapa's, but not this time. He talked the whole time the three of us sat out on the porch. I got the feeling Grandpapa was skeptical, but he didn't say anything to Daddy about it.

Momma and Grandmama made the whole Thanksgiving meal that Sunday since we were going down below Abbeville to see Daddy's family for the holiday itself. I know Daddy was excited about that too. We hadn't seen them since Christmas the year before, and Daddy was very big on family. After we had feasted on the turkey and giblet gravy and mashed potatoes and yams and everything else, Daddy shooed Momma and Grandmama out of the kitchen, winked at me, and said, "Silas and I, we've got this." We did all the dishes and put away the leftovers, although I did filch a few bites of turkey thigh along the way, and we cleaned up the whole kitchen. Daddy whistled the whole time, some happy tune I didn't know, but I liked it. Finally, when I had dried the last plate and Daddy had dried and put away the antique turkey platter with the blue transfer of a turkey on it, we sat down at the kitchen table to catch our breath.

"You looking forward to seeing Grandma Boudreaux, little man?" Daddy took out his pipe and filled it. "And your cousins, Daniel, Gaston, Lillian,...?"

"And Sophie." I offered. Daddy eyed me slyly.

"Sophie. Yeah, there's Sophie." Daddy got that look like he wasn't paying attention to me when he really was. I knew what was coming.

"Yeah, and even Beau and..."

"Tell me something, Silas LaMontaie. Are you kind of sweet on Sophie?" He grinned at me.

I knew he was going to go there. I should never have said anything. "No. She's just one of my cousins." I shrugged. But the truth was, I did like Sophie. In fact, I was mesmerized by her. She was maybe three years older than me, and she had a presence about her. I think she knew she was so pretty people couldn't stop looking at her, with her black hair and green eyes that she could flash like heat lightning on a summer's evening. Unfortunately, she had no more clue who I was than a lioness knows about a mouse under her paw that she might toss around a few times before swallowing it.

"Right. Okay." Daddy stood up and walked out to the porch where Momma and Grandpapa and Grandmama were sitting in rockers. No one smoked inside at Grandmama's house. I followed him out. Daddy sat on the banister of the steps to the house and lit his pipe. "Little man tells me he's looking forward to seeing Sophie Soulard this week." I gawked at him. How could he?

"Oh, Sophie, huh?" Momma smiled at me as she rocked. She was needle pointing. "She's pretty."

"She's my cousin?"

"Well, maybe twice removed," Daddy mused, looking off across the steps and down the dusty driveway canopied with magnolias. I did not understand their fascination with my thinking Sophie was pretty. Or even if I liked her.

"Can I go read?"

"No," both my parents said, at the same time, Grandpapa said, "Yes." Momma and Daddy looked at each other, then at me, and then Daddy shrugged. "Sure." I took my book into Grandpapa's library and read until it was time to leave. Along about dusk, we loaded into the truck and headed off for our place. Daddy was still talking about heading down to Vermillion Parish.

"You know, Sy, I think if you take your guitar down and play a song for Miss Sophie, I'll bet you she'd like it. A Lot." He nudged me in the ribs.

I looked up at Momma. "Momma, make him stop."

Daddy laughed, but Momma said, "Leave him be, Bennie. Leave him be." Daddy nodded, and we drove home.

While Momma and I were at school the next three days, Daddy worked on cleaning up a place to work in the back yard of the little shack we lived in. They had decided to wait on the shed until Daddy had enough business to warrant it, but they didn't figure that would take long. Daddy could fix anything. When I got home on that Tuesday from school, Daddy was hacking away at some weeds by the ditch that ran beside the road, and a blue racer took off across the yard. I scrambled up onto the porch, but the snake went under the fallen down barbed wire fence and into the field next door.

"Daddy, kill it!" I yelled from the metal chair, my legs curled up under me just in case the snake came onto the porch.

"No, little man, let him go. He's not hurting anything, and he won't even bite you unless you mess with him. He's fine over there in the field." I knew Daddy was telling me the truth, but I kept my eye on the fence row just the same.

The next day as soon as Momma got home, we headed south towards Abbeville in the Nash. I took my guitar, which had come from there anyway. We arrived at Grandma Boudreaux's after dark, and I slept on a pallet Grandma had set up, blankets and pillows laid out on the floor of one of the bedrooms where all the cousins slept. I could hear the grownups talking and laughing downstairs while they drank wine and told jokes. The level of noise was so much louder than Momma's family and took me a bit to get used to it and fall asleep.

The next day, Thanksgiving Day, all the local family arrived, and the entire house and the yard were filled with Boudreauxs and LaMontaies and Cormiers and, yes, Soulards. Sophie was perhaps even prettier after a year. She floated across the yard while the other girls swarmed around her, talking, laughing, and trying to be in her graces. It was as if they thought being around her the beauty would rub off onto them. Not that any of the cousins were especially ugly, except maybe for Johnny, but Sophie was several notches above. I decided maybe Daddy was right. I pulled my guitar out of the Nash and tuned it up sitting on the stump of a fallen black gum tree while cousins gathered towards the hint of music like moths towards a candle. Just as I got it tuned, I saw Sophie come into my peripheral view. I went into "Low Down Blues" just the way Grandma Bailey had taught me, slapping the rhythm on the body of the guitar and on the strings I deadened with the palm of my hand. As it turns out, I would spend much my life in coffee houses and on stages, but that may have been the best performance I ever managed. When I finished, my cousins started whooping it up and clapping. I looked over at Sophie and she moued her lips while she shot me a look, and I thought maybe I might melt away. She moved on, and I played more songs for my cousins, but I had already been paid all the riches I could handle at my tender age. I also learned something important about myself: if I was nervous, it was not a bad thing. In fact, somehow being anxious made me play even better than I thought I could.

I had finished my small list of songs I knew and was putting away my guitar when I saw the car marked "Vermillion Parish Sheriff" already parked in the gravel driveway. I saw the sheriff leaning against it, squinnying the relatives that moved back and forth across the huge yard. I went in and got Daddy and followed him outside to talk to the sheriff.

"Amos?" My Daddy stuck out his hand, and the sheriff stood up straight.

They shook hands, and the sheriff grimaced. "Ben."

"Why aren't you home with your family today, Amos?"

"I am with family, aren't I? We're all family here, Ben. Besides, my wife can't cook as well as your mother does."

Daddy chuckled. "What's up, Amos?" Now they both leaned up against the fender of the sheriff's car. The sheriff looked over at me, then at Daddy. Daddy just nodded.

"Ben, Sheriff Landry over in Iberia thought you might be here. Asked me to check and see."

"Yeah?" Daddy played a lot of poker in his younger days my Momma told me. Whatever cards he was seeing just now, he gave no clue what they were.

The sheriff looked at me again. "Um, Ben?"

"It's okay, Amos. Sy knows I didn't burn the mill down."

"Well, now, I didn't say you did, Ben. Nor did Remy. He did wonder if you knew more than you were telling, maybe."

"I don't have anything to add to what I already told them, Amos. You all need to leave us be on that." Daddy leaned forward and stood away from the sedan. He toyed a piece of gravel with his boot.

"Well, they really need to talk with you. They're pretty insistent."

"I had no reason to burn anything and, in fact, if you want to talk to Johnny and Beau about where I was . . ."

"I already did, Ben."

Daddy looked up quickly at the sheriff. He paused for a moment. "It's Thanksgiving, Amos."

"Yes, it is. Have a good one, Ben." The sheriff walked around the car and opened up the driver's door. He looked over the car at Daddy. "Ben?"

"Yeah, Amos?"

"They know you went up to Winnfield. I don't know the sheriff up there all that well, but you should know."

"Thanks, Amos. My best to Caroline." The sheriff nodded towards Daddy, causing his hat to tip forward. The sheriff drove off, and Daddy looked at me for a few moments, his face stolid, then he put his hand on my shoulder. "Grandma has dinner ready, little man." He led me towards the house.

# The Tetravalence of Jessie May

## Earth

# Chapter 6

Jessie May never saw me coming even though we had been on a collision course since we were eight years old. I met Jessie May when we moved from Calvin that next summer to Carmack, Kentucky. Daddy didn't want to leave, and Momma certainly did not want to leave her childhood home and her Mom and Dad. But the mechanic business didn't take off, first thing, since it seemed like no one had any money. People needed things fixed, all right, but they generally fixed it themselves in some sort of makeshift rigging, or they did without. Daddy did some work, but not enough, and since we couldn't get phone service out along Crackletown Road, and there was very little traffic on the gravel road, there just weren't enough people who knew he was there and was the best mechanic anywhere. After a few months, Daddy tried to get on at the quarry and at one of the timbering operations, but the jobs were too hard to come by. Generally, if people got jobs, they kept them.

Then there was the local sheriff still wanting to talk to Daddy about the mill fire in Loreauville. Daddy told them time and again he didn't do it and that he had no more to say on it. Daddy said we had nothing to worry about, but he also said that while we cannot control the storm clouds rising in the distance, but we could make sure we get in a safe place before they arrived. I couldn't believe we were moving again. I had made a spot, small as it was, in the world to play and be happy. Fredrick and Grandpapa had a lot to do with that, and I didn't want to leave them. It wasn't fair, and I told Momma that. We were sitting on the front edge of the porch, Daddy's tools in boxes, our clothes in one footlocker and a few necessities and some of Momma's favorite books in another, and our two guitars in cardboard cases and all of it loaded into the back of the very tired pickup truck Daddy still drove. The one good thing about Daddy having so little business was he could tinker with that old Ford. Daddy was out there now, checking the fluids and belts before we took off.

"I don't want to move." I pouted with my back turned towards Momma. "We just got here, it feels like."

"I know. I don't like moving either, honey child, but sometimes, you have to strike out and do something different if you're going to make things work. Daddy needs us to be strong with him. Can you do that?"

The idea that my Daddy needed anyone else to be strong for him seemed almost a sacrilege. "But I don't want to go. Can't I stay here with Grandmama and Grandpapa?"

"What would I do without my Silas, though?" Momma scooted over next to me and hugged me around the shoulders. "We are a family and families help each other and stay together. Remember the lesson of Silas Marner?"

"Yes. Love conquers all." I rolled my eyes.

"Yes, well, it's love that redeems us all."

I wasn't interested in a lesson. I was busy sulking. "But I have Fredrick too. He's my best friend. What about Fredrick?" I heard the whine in my voice, but I didn't care.

"Well, you have his address. You can write him, and he can write you. That'll be fun." I thought I heard doubt in that last part.

"I will never have another best friend like Fredrick. Never." It was somewhere between complaint and defiant prediction.

"Oh, honey, you'll make new friends. I promise." Momma hugged me around the shoulders.

"What's the point of making friends if we're just going to move anyway?"

Momma went silent. Daddy came over, wiping his hands on a rag that had once been Momma's tea towel. I saw just the tiniest wistful glance from my Momma. "Ready, Cher? Little man?"

We left just before Memorial Day. Momma and Daddy sold it to me as a vacation of sorts. First, we were heading to Memphis to see the sights and maybe listen to some music. I think Daddy secretly hoped he would be able to play music at Sun Records, but he never said anything much about it. I did notice him practicing more lately. And it was the only reason I could figure we went to Memphis. We headed up to Monroe and then over to Vicksburg. Grandpapa had filled me in about the siege there, and Momma and Daddy stopped for us to look around. Despite my desire to sulk about leaving, I was intrigued. At the park, we ate a picnic lunch that Grandmama had prepared for us then headed north towards Memphis. I wished I could talk to Grandpapa about the battleground site. And I wished I could tell Fredrick all about it.

When we drove into Memphis, I was agog. I had never been to a city this size before, and Memphis did not disappoint. Tall buildings lined the city streets. The library was one of the most impressive buildings I could imagine. We drove down Beale Street, and we even stopped by Sun Studios, but the door was locked when Daddy tried it. He pulled on it a couple of times, looked at the door, and pulled it again. I thought I saw his posture sag just a tad. We drove off, and Daddy kept glancing in the mirror until we were out of sight of the studio. We went to a couple of churches then, just to see the stained-glass windows, the likes of these I had never seen before. Again, I wanted to tell Fredrick about them. He would have loved them. If I was the guitarist, Fredrick was the artist. He could draw anything, and I knew he would have been intrigued by the colors and the artistry. But I couldn't share it with him and knowing that made me sull up again. Momma noticed it, but she let it go.

Then that night, we stayed in a motel. That was a real first for me. I had really never even considered staying in a motel. I figured only rich people stayed in motels. The motel was after we had left the city, the sun setting behind us over the tops of the big buildings. Alongside the highway, several cabins lined up behind a main office building. A metal sign said it was The Alpine Cabins Motor Lodge. I decided I liked this traveling idea if it meant staying in motels. These new adventures were making leaving a bit easier, I would have to admit. That evening, we ate at a diner next door. This was also something of a rarity for me – eating out. We had eaten a couple of times at The Goat Castle in Winnfield, but, since this was on the road, this felt exotic. My plate of thin slices roast beef on white bread with mashed potatoes and a heavy coating of brown gravy seemed glorious. We retired to our cabin and watched television sitting on the double bed that Momma and Daddy would sleep on. This was also new. We watched "The Jack Benny Show" and then the "Ed Sullivan Show." I liked television. Momma and Daddy had saved up their funds for this trip, and I was not disappointed so far. I fell asleep watching television and awoke on the sofa across the room, covered up with a knitted blanket.

The next day, we left early heading towards the sun. Daddy had bought some country ham on white bread sandwiches at the diner, and we happily munched down the road towards Nashville. Somehow, I did not think about my pouting and Fredrick that morning. We never made it to Nashville. We made it to Johnsonville, and we crossed over the bridge that traversed the lake and Daddy was ready to stop. Daddy loved water, and he loved fishing. And, what was more, Daddy knew how to fix motorboats. We stopped at a grocery and Momma went in to get picnic supplies while Daddy and I stayed in the truck. We drove around the little town some, but Momma said she didn't like the big power plant that seemed to dominate the skyline everywhere we drove, so we headed east again, and Daddy said he too wasn't sold on Johnsonville. It was nice, just not the place for us. But it was clear Daddy had changed his mind about where we were going. Just seeing the big lake had gotten his attention. Momma had bought me a spiral notebook at the market when she went in, and I sat in the truck between Momma and Daddy, writing a letter first to Grandpapa and Grandmama and then one to Fredrick.

The hunt for a place to settle into soon became one of finding a place where there were lots of fishing boats. We went on over to Dover, but Daddy didn't see what he wanted there either, so he decided Dover was not our resting place. Then Daddy saw a road sign telling us the road north went to a place called Grand Rivers. Daddy was excited.

"Look, little man. Les Grandes Rivieres. Les petits ruisseaux font les grandes rivières." It was an adage his father had told my father many times and one he often repeated to me. "Either way, there have to be boats in a town called Grand Rivers." Daddy turned and headed north.

Momma laughed at him. "I doubt this is a French town, Bennie."

"Maybe not, but who knows? But it could be folks from the old country. C'est comme revenir à La Rochelle, la terre de mes ancêtres. Peut-être."

"Peut-être. Peut-être pas."

Daddy drove on, the road twisting and turning, sending us leaning back and forth on each other in the cab of the pickup. Momma looked out the window quietly. I couldn't help getting a feeling she was a little sad. She had made up her mind to go wherever Daddy went, but that did not necessarily mean there was never any difficulty leaving behind what she had built even if it only a small spot she had cleared. It was still her spot.

It was the middle of the afternoon, and the day was getting warmer when the truck broke down. By Daddy's accounting, we weren't that far away from Grand Rivers, but when Daddy got out and opened the hood of the truck, the steam hissing up told us all we were not likely to be making it to Grand Rivers tonight. We all climbed out of the truck, and I sat under a hickory tree reading *We Were There at Pearl Harbor*. It was a going away present Grandma Bailey gave me. She had written inside the front cover, "Wherever you travel, Silas LaMontaie, Grandma Bailey will be with you." I liked reading that inscription each time I opened the book. A luna moth was on the ground, stretching its wings and I watched it, its wing eyes looking like they were opening and closing. I wondered what Fredrick might think of this beautiful moth. Momma sat on the tailgate of the truck which Daddy had lowered to retrieve his tools and to give Momma a better place to sit. When the truck broke down, Daddy allowed the momentum to take us around a corner onto a road marked 58 and off the shoulder. Daddy climbed into the engine from above and then from below, getting himself dirty and sweaty in the process. Momma was writing a letter, her legs crossed and dangling from the tailgate. Finally, Daddy walked around the end of the truck, wiping his hands on that same now very dirty tea towel.

"Well, I do believe she's thrown a rod."

Momma looked up at him. "That sounds serious."

"Well, it can be fixed, but not out here and not today."

"Oh." Momma put down her paper and used her hands to lift herself off the truck and onto her feet in one fluid motion. She looked up the road we had turned onto, but there were no houses around. In fact, other than the blacktopped road, there was not a sign anyone lived here. "Bennie, what are we going to do?"

Daddy looked around too. He glanced in the back of the truck, although he knew everything that was in there. "We didn't bring any camping gear." He scratched his head. "I don't know, Cher." Then a farm truck turned the corner from the road we had been on and the driver, a man older than Daddy and wearing a straw hat, did a quick double take and pulled off in front of our beat-up old truck. I got up from my shady spot and went over to where the two trucks were parked next to the road.

The man climbed out of the farm truck. There were wooden slats along the bed of the truck, and fragments of hay were everywhere. An earthy odor permeated everything. "Broke down?" The accent was very different from what I had heard before. The words were drawn out like they had extra vowels in them.

"Yeah." Daddy extended his hand and the man took it, and they shook. "Name's LaMontaie." The man gave Daddy a quizzical look.

"Duncan," the man said.

Daddy turned around to face the dead pickup. "Think it threw a rod. Going to need a new rocker arm, I'm sure. I just hope the valves are okay." Mr. Duncan came over and also stood there, staring at the old Ford. It was as if the two men staring together at the old pickup would revive it better than one man staring at it.

"Well, if the rod threw, something caused it." The man rubbed his chin whiskers.

"Yeah."

"Need to take it over to Homer's. See if he can fix it."

"Homer's?" Daddy put his hands in his back pockets.

"Yeah," Duncan turned around and pointed up the road we had turned onto. "You go on up here a couple of miles, take the third left past the new school, and you'll see him a little ways on your left. Can't miss him. Big garage."

"Yeah, I'm pretty good at cars, but this is going to need more than I can do out here. Plus, I don't have any parts." Daddy twisted his torso to see where the man was pointing. "Does he have a tow truck? Homer?"

"Oh." Duncan looked like he was stuck with a pin, he started so quickly. "Ha. I don't suppose you can get there in a truck that won't run, can you?" He went up to the passenger side of his truck, reached behind the seat, and pulled out a logging chain. "I can tow you there if you like."

"Oh, wow, yes. Thanks." Daddy slammed shut the hood of the pickup, and the two men hitched it to the old hay truck. Momma, me, and Daddy all climbed back into the Ford, and Mr. Duncan towed us slowly. Daddy took the truck out of gear and steered while Mr. Duncan pulled us. I was nervous being so close to the back of the farm truck, especially when we went down hills and it felt like we were gaining on him. But we made it, and Daddy talked to the man who owned the repair shop, Mr. Ray, and we sat on a rugged little bench in front of the shop with our guitar boxes and a footlocker of clothes. Daddy said it would take a few days. He had told Mr. Ray he was a mechanic and was looking for work and Mr. Ray said he'd keep in mind, although he didn't need anyone right now. So we sat on the bench, wondering what to do. Then Mr. Ray came out and told us he had called the preacher over at Sardis Church which was just down the road, and they were going to put us up for the night since we were stranded. Momma and Daddy looked at each other, and I think that might have been the seed that started our move to Carmack, Kentucky. That everyone seemed so helpful and friendly made us feel welcome. And the fact that we were so far off the beaten path it seemed no one would ever find us probably played a part as well, although they would eventually.

Carmack, Kentucky, was as far away from anything as any place I could imagine, but then, where we lived near Loreauville and later in Calvin weren't close to much either. But those places were more familiar to me, because of family and friends, and this area, people called it "Between the Rivers," was strange and different, at least to me. I didn't know anyone, and school was already out, so I didn't meet any other children for at least a week. It was a farming area, with corn shooting out of the ground in rows and fields of bright green wheat. There were a few cars, but mainly trucks, tractors, and horses. It was every bit as warm and humid as Calvin had been, but the soil here was different. In Louisiana, everything was red clay. This dirt was dark brown. People were friendly in their demeanor, but it didn't feel like we belonged, at least to me. I think our accent and Daddy occasionally slipping off into his Cajun French put people off. And we looked different, especially me and Daddy since we were both dark complexioned and everyone here seemed fairer. But Daddy got work right away helping with the haying with local farmers. In reality, it seemed like there were always jobs if a man was willing to work hard. We moved into a house that no one was living in, paying rent to a Miss Rowena who also owned a grocery store across from the church. The house was a bit rough but was better than the sharecropper's house we had fixed up on Grandpapa and Grandmama's farm. The truck repair took a week, due primarily to the parts not being available, but after we got the truck back, we took the ferry Miss Rowena's husband ran over to Kuttawa, which was a bigger town, but not a lot bigger. It was, at least, a town, while Carmack was really just a smattering of houses and small stores spread out along a gravel road like Grandma Boudreaux's dominoes tossed along her front porch. Over in Kuttawa, we bought seeds and sets, and Momma put in a garden after Daddy turned the soil with Mr. Duncan's draft mule and an old steel plow. Mrs. Herrin, the pastor's wife, went out of her way to help us get started and even got the school superintendent to let Momma borrow books from the consolidated school over on the crossroads once she found out Momma was a teacher. It was a new style of life, for me, not making a friend for a while. But it wasn't too bad. It's true, I missed Fredrick and Grandma Bailey, and I especially missed Grandmama and Grandpapa. I did send letters to them at Miss Rowena's Store and got some in return from Fredrick and my grandparents. I hoarded my letters. I read and reread them to try to recapture what it felt like when we lived there where I belonged. I stored them in a small wooden box I had nailed together from old tobacco spikes I found along the road.

I spent my free time playing my guitar and reading, although with my own books all read, I had had to switch to some of Momma's collection, including Middlemarch and, to my delight, Huckleberry Finn, which I could not put down. Otherwise, we just worked on settling in. We went to the Methodist church across from us once a month, when the circuit brought Reverend Herrin back around. Daddy said it would be good for business, once he opened his business. Momma and I weeded the garden and talked about the books we were reading. A couple of neighbors dropped by to say hello, bringing us gifts. One older woman gave us some homemade pickles that were so tart, they made our mouths pucker. Another woman brought us a loaf of homemade bread. Mrs. May brought us a peck of blackberries she and her daughter Jessie had picked, but when it came time to bring them, her daughter had run off on some new adventure. So we developed our patterns, our new rhythms in this new place. I confess, I felt a bit like a nomad, moving around so much, always being the new kid, but there were lots of people moving around, especially itinerant workers moving with whatever harvest was in. At least we had a place to stay.

Although I did not yet feel like I belonged, life was not all that bad. I remember sitting on the front porch with my mom and dad late at night. My dad was worn out after working all day long, and my mom was also bushed from working in the garden all day long, keeping the house up, and keeping me more or less occupied. The katydids screeched until it got dark, but after the sun set, the crickets and tree frogs took over, and we would sit out there on the front porch of that little house between the rivers. My daddy would bring out his old guitar and play that thing like nobody you ever heard. Daddy liked every kind of music, and he had blended the Cajun music he had learned as a child with the southern blues he had picked up from Grandma Bailey and her family, and then Daddy threw in a dose of the bluegrass music we heard once we came to Kentucky. I never heard such a marvelous concoction before or since.

I played along as best I could, but there were times, I was just lost in the fingering and the chords. But he played, and Momma sang. The words were songs I knew, old French songs and sometimes blues, but with melodies I didn't know. My daddy sang in a high tenor, and my mama sang harmony, picking up on the third as natural as could be. I learned to play the guitar from my daddy, but I never learned to play as well he could. He could make it do things nobody else could. When Momma and Daddy started singing, they sounded like the sky itself opened up. Often, they made the song into three-part harmony, Momma and Daddy and that old guitar. Years later, when I was older and ready to move on down the road, he said that guitar of his Dad's was my destiny. Maybe he was right. I still have it, and I still play it all the time. I just wish I could make it make the sounds he made.

Daddy opened up his repair shop on route 522 in Carmack in a shed behind Aldridge's Store. It was set up on shares, Daddy agreeing to give Mr. Aldridge a percentage of his fees in exchange for the space to work. There was a fair amount of traffic there heading towards the ferry. Daddy was good with his hands and had a knack for figuring out how things were put together. It wasn't a big business or anything, but Daddy built a reputation for fixing things, and before long, the place started filling with lawnmowers and radios and toasters and what have you. I might not fit in that well, but Daddy did. His real calling was boat motors. He was soon in good demand to fix them all around the area. Daddy tried to tell me about fixing boat motors. He said there were only three things you had to think about to fix them: gasoline, air, and fire. If it wouldn't run, it had to be one of the three. It was a process of elimination. But he had a knack and could tell pretty much just by yanking on the rope what the problem was. Not me. It just wasn't in me. Daddy and Mr. Ray had an agreement. Mr. Ray worked on the cars and trucks and tractors, and Daddy worked on everything else. Sometimes, Daddy went over and worked for Mr. Ray if he had a lot of work, but mostly, Daddy ran his shop.

It wasn't far from home to Daddy's shop, and I was walking there one hot June morning, dragonflies darting around the edge of the road, traipsing down the dusty highway with a lunch Momma had packed for me to take to him, when my life changed, although I would not know just how dramatically for years. I crested a small hill, swinging the metal lunch pail Daddy had used when he worked at the mine. It was a mystery to me why that pail made the move and not my cigar box of pencils and crayons. I tried not to think about it. But just as I came over the hill, I saw two boys kicking a small brown puppy and laughing like it was great sport. The dog was cowering, whimpering, looking like it trying to melt itself into the ditch where it was stuck. His tail was curled under him, and his eyes were filled with confusion. I was immediately incensed. Both the boys were at least as big as me, but I didn't even think about it.

"Hey!" I yelled at them, and they turned around to face me. "Leave him alone." I hoped the dog would take the reprieve as a moment to run off, but he just sat there, squatting in the ditch.

"Make me!" The bigger of the two boys turned around and kicked the dog again, and it yelped pitiably. He turned around and faced me again, grinning.

I marched towards him. I had gotten into a few scrapes before, but this was different. These weren't my cousins or anyone I knew. I was anxious, but I could not let them kick that puppy again. The bigger boy set himself, and I dropped the lunch pail and balled up my fists. I might take a whipping, but I was determined to make him stop. I got the first blow in, but it went downhill quickly. The boy was stronger than I was and taller. He landed blows, and my nose started bleeding, but I didn't let up. I swung and kicked and fought, but the boy was able to grab me and wrestle me down, and then he sat astride my chest, sneering at me.

"Now what, boy?"

I squirmed, but I couldn't get my arms free. He sneered again. "Tommy?"

"Yeah, Joey?" The other boy stood gawking at me.

"Get that log over yonder and kill that damned dog." Joey sat on my chest, and I tried to buck him off, but he was too heavy.

"But, Joey, . . ."

"Do it!"

Tommy walked half-heartedly towards a tree branch. I was so angry I was nearly in tears. I could not stand to think of them killing that poor puppy. Just then, my face was showered with dirt and Joey fell off of me, grabbing his nose and screaming. Tommy stopped and looked just as a clump of hardened dirt hit him in the eye, and he also fell, screamed, then gathered his feet and ran off down the road towards the river. I scrambled to my feet and saw a tall, skinny girl in cut-off jeans and a filthy tee shirt pull back her arm and throw another dirt clod, not at me, but at Joey, who had managed to stand up and was spitting blood, when this one hit him squarely in his left eye. She threw straight and hard, and she was ready with another missile when Joey turned tail and ran.

"I'm telling on you, Jessie May!" He yelled as he scampered off the opposite direction of Tommy. She kept her dirt clod half-cocked in her hand, I suppose just in case I was going to be trouble, but I was so grateful, I guess she saw it right away and dropped it.

"Thanks." I wiped my bloody nose with my palm.

"That's okay. Pinch your nose like this, and it will stop." She pinched the bridge of her nose, and I did as she did. "Those boys are just bullies. Don't pay any attention to them." She stuck her hand out. "My name's Jessie. Jessie May." I shook her dirty hand with my bloody hand.

"Silas LaMontaie." My nose stopped bleeding. I was filthy with dirt and dust and blood, but I felt okay. The little dog came limping out of the ditch towards me.

"Looks like you just got yourself a dog."

I turned to pick up the puppy, and when I turned back around with the dog to say it wasn't mine, I saw her marching up the road away from me. I had had good friends in Charlie and Fredrick, but this was a whole new category. I stood there holding the puppy and watched her walk away, as I would far too many times in my life.

# Chapter 7

I fed the puppy the fried bologna sandwich meant for Daddy. It had been rather badly tossed about, so I told myself Daddy wouldn't want it anyway. It's true, it could have been reassembled, but the puppy needed food. He gobbled down the chunks of sandwich I tore off until it was gone. The dog was not hungry enough to eat the pickle, however. I took a bite of the pickle, and my jaws clenched shut. They were the sourest pickles I ever tried. When I arrived home, the first thing Momma noticed was that I was covered in blood and dirt. The second thing was that I was carrying a small brown puppy. The last thing she noticed was I was carrying Daddy's lunch pail, which should have been left at Daddy's shop. I told Momma what had happened, and she was proud of me for standing up to Joey and Tommy, but she said we didn't have enough to take on a puppy. Mostly, we got by on whatever we grew, and the produce people traded with to Daddy at his shop. Sometimes, we got other items in trade, like pickled venison, which looked atrocious but tasted great. Daddy would bring home a chicken from the market sometimes, and Momma made it go as far as she could. She would fry up the liver and heart and gizzards for a meal. She made chicken gumbo with the bird, then roasted the bones and made stock out of them. Whatever meat we had she served with lots of vegetables, since those we had in greater abundance. I knew we did not have much to take on a pet. I suppose my sorrowful look told her my feelings. I didn't beg; at least with my words, I didn't. Momma also wanted to know more about Jessie May, who had rescued both the puppy and me as it turned out. I did too.

I kept thinking about Jessie. She seemed very different from anyone else I had ever met, more confident, somehow. She had a bit of a swagger about her. And, I realized, I had immediately been struck by how pretty she was. Now that I was home and Momma had washed my cuts and scrapes and yanked off my grimy pullover shirt, I saw Jessie in my mind's eye. Her hair was the color of an acorn, brown and shiny, and very curly. The sunlight had glinted off it when she turned her head. And her eyes were the bluest eyes I had ever seen. They were the color of bachelor buttons growing wild alongside the gravel road. She was several inches taller than I, and she was slender, but she also could throw a dirt clod straight and hard. When she had smiled at me, her whole face smiled. I liked that part a lot. I was intrigued, to say the least. I wanted to go out and see if I could find her, although I had to be careful. I did not want to get nailed with a rock or a hunk of dirt just for walking down the road. This was a challenge. I also figured I had to be on the lookout for Joey. I decided Tommy was not likely to challenge me, but Joey might be looking for revenge. And there were not so many people between the rivers that I could avoid him for long.

Momma made Daddy another lunch and took it over to him. She was gone a while, and when she got home, she said they had decided I could keep the puppy since I had rescued it and I had not made any new friends and, what was more to me, if the puppy was my friend, if we ever had to leave again, he could go with me. She said she hoped the dog would eat turnips. We had lots of turnips. She suggested I name it Argos and she told me the story about Odysseus coming home from war and the dog being the only one to recognize him. I agreed that was a good name for the dog. I had already taken to Argos anyway. Once he was free from Joey and Tommy and got a little food in him, he was very friendly and liked to roll around on the floor chasing my rubber ball I squeezed to be better at playing guitar. And if I got down on the floor with him, he licked my face all over, which made me laugh because it tickled and felt like he really liked me. By the time Daddy came home from the repair shop, Argos and I were good friends, one of the best friends I would ever have. Daddy came in, tired, but smiling.

"So, what's his name? Fried Bologna?" He sat heavily on the ladder-back chair in the living room. It was the only piece of furniture in that room so far. He put his hand down low so Argos could sniff it, then he scratched behind the puppy's ears.

"His name is Argos. Sorry about your lunch, Daddy. He was starving."

Daddy laughed. "It's fine, son. I was only joshing you. Your mother told me what you did. I'm proud of you for saving him. Argos, huh? I like it. Makes you into a Greek hero, right?" He got up and carried a bag of summer squash he had received in payment for fixing a radio into the kitchen where Momma was working. I didn't follow his thinking. We were Cajun, right?

Over the course of the next few days, I took Argos out several times a day, and he was beginning to be housebroken. I didn't have a collar or a leash, but he always stayed with me, so I didn't need one. It was as if he knew I had saved him. I hoped so. About the third day after Argos and I found each other, I was outside with the puppy one morning, walking beside him as he did his business in some volunteer hairy cats-ears growing next to the road when I saw Jessie standing there, splitting a piece of straw absently with her fingernails. She was standing behind the corner post of the fence that once ran along the property next door, and although I don't think she was trying to hide, I didn't see her at first. When she spoke, I jumped, not expecting to see anyone.

"Nice dog." She acted as if she just happened to be standing there when we came by. I wondered. She reached down, and the puppy wagged his tail over to her. "What's the matter? Feeling spooked?" She looked up at me, her eyes looking serious. "What are you afraid of?" At that particular moment, it was a lengthy list, including Jessie May.

"No, nothing. I just didn't see you at first." I shuffled my feet a bit. Jessie had on dirty tennis shoes, no socks, a pair of shorts that had once been green, I think, and a blue tee shirt that made her eyes stand out even more.

"What's his name?" The puppy rolled over, and she stooped over to rub his belly.

"Argos." I watched her process that for a moment, waiting for her to ask, but she never did.

"Pretty tiger lilies." She stood and nodded towards the small gulley that ran in front of the house where a patch of flowers had shot up. "Your Momma plant those?"

"No, they were there, I guess. Want to pick some to take home?" I knew I was being transparent, but I always figured, isn't every man who brings flowers?

"No, I don't like to kill them." She sauntered over towards the burst of orange flowers, one hand outstretched, just touching the tips of the blooms.

I shrugged. "They're going to die anyway, aren't they?"

"Yeah." She looked over at me, her face a little glum. "But this way, they die after they've had a chance to live their lives, and, really, that's all any of us can ask for." I stared at the ground. It was something I had never considered. Then her mood brightened suddenly, and she turned quickly to face me. "Hey, you like to fish?"

"Yeah, I do." I nodded.

"Got any fishing line? Hooks?"

"Um, yeah, Daddy has some in a box around back. No poles though." I did worry about using Daddy's tackle, what little he had.

"That's okay. We can make poles." Jessie pulled out a small brown knife from her shorts pocket and started towards the back yard where some water sprouts were coming up from the roots of a sugar maple. "You get the fishing line and a can and a shovel, okay? I'll cut us a couple of poles." She flipped open the thin, curved blade and marched on back. Argos and I watched for a second, then both of us scurried around to the back steps where Daddy had a little bit of tackle he had brought with him. I felt guilty taking pretty much the entirety of Daddy's gear since we had left most things back at Grandpapa's and Grandmama's, but this was to go fishing with Jessie. I thought he might understand. There was a spade leaning against the house, and I took it out to Momma's garden where I figured there would be both easy digging and a good chance for worms. I pushed the blade into the ground between two rows of cucumbers and turned the earth. A couple of red wrigglers were evident right away. Jessie was standing over me by the time I crumbled the dirt clod to release the worms. Argos watched me digging.

"You got a coffee can?" She reached down with both hands as I handed her the bait.

"Oh, no, I don't think so."

"That's okay." She dropped the worms into one of the pockets of her shorts. "Dig some more." I dug several more holes, and we got a good handful of worms and Jessie picked up a small clump of soft dirt and crumbled it into her pocket as well. "Helps them keep alive," she said in reply to my curious glance. She leaned over and picked up the two sticks she had cut. Momma was now standing next to the back door, leaning against the post that held up the meager shed roof.

"Fill in the holes, Sy."

"I did." We walked towards Momma to lean the spade up against the house. Argos walked just behind me.

"Hello, there," Momma spoke to Jessie. It was her way of reminding me to do introductions.

"Momma, this is Jessie May." I waved with my hand that held the remains of Daddy's fishing tackle. "Jessie, this is my Momma."

"Mrs. LaMontaie, I'm real pleased to meet you." Jessie walked up to Momma and stuck out her hand. Momma stood up from her leaning and shook Jessie's hand that still had worm dirt on it. If it bothered Momma, she didn't show it. Momma shot me a knowing glance that I refused to acknowledge.

"We're going fishing, Momma."

"So I gather."

"Is it okay, Momma?"

"Where are you going to fish? In the river?" Momma cocked her head to one side.

I looked over at Jessie. I really didn't know where she had in mind.

"Yes'm." Jessie answered for me.

"Oh, I don't know."

"We'll be safe, Mrs. LaMontaie. I promise." Jessie held her dirty worm hand up in a girl scout pledge formation.

Momma suppressed a chuckle. "Well, okay, I guess. Please be safe. Don't fall in. The river's got currents, you know." Momma did not sound completely convinced.

"We won't fall in, Mrs. LaMontaie. I know a place where the water pools into a spot and there's lots of places to stand."

"Well, okay." Now Momma felt better about it. "If you bring them home cleaned, I'll cook them for you. Be careful." She went inside.

We sat on the back porch and tied the fishing line and hooks to the sticks Jessie had cut, and the three of us walked off down the road, Jessie, me, and Argos. We went all the way down to the ferry landing. Trees hung low over the current and everything had the smell of the river, clinging and a little bit fishy. The ferry was across the river in Kuttawa, loading a couple of cars. As the ferry pulled away, the big bell rang next to the ferry.

"Do they always ring the bell so folks know the ferry's coming?" I watched the boat pull away from the bank and into the current.

"No, only if there are revenuers on it. They tell them they always ring it when the ferry crosses, but it's just to let folks know so they can hide their stills and all."

"Stills?" I turned to look at Jessie.

"Yeah. You know, moonshine."

"Huh." I turned around to look at the ferry again. There was a big sedan on it, and a couple of men all dressed up standing next to it. "Huh," I said again.

"Come on." Jessie waved for me to follow her and she showed Argos and me a path that curled around to a bend in the river where the water did indeed eddy up into a pool. We found footholds on the bank that looked like a number of people had fished here before. It was easy to stand and fish. Because of the eddies in the current there, cans and bottles had washed up along the far bank. Jessie handed me a worm from her pocket and watched me thread it onto the hook. She seemed satisfied that I knew how to bait a hook. She baited up as well and moved a few feet away and swung the line out into the water. The line immediately started tugging around with little fish nibbling at the worm. I moved closer to a log that ran from the bank out into the water and flipped the worm right next to the log as far out as I could get it. The line sank slowly, then went taut and pulled hard. I yanked back, and the fish splashed against the log. I walked backward up the bank a few steps to land the good-sized bass without breaking the line, as my Daddy had taught me. The fish flopped on the clear spot I had been standing on. Jessie was standing there too, now, admiring the fish. Argos was under my feet. Jessie looked at the fish, then at me, and then she smiled a big smile.

"You know what, Silas LaMontaie? I think you just might do."

We fished the rest of the morning until our bait was gone. We cleaned the fish on the log that ran into the water, rinsed them off in the river and threw the entrails into the water, and placed the handful of fish, one nice bass and several little bluegills, into an old coal bucket we found washed up on the shoreline. The handle was missing off the bucket, and it had pin holes all through it, but it worked for carrying the fish we had. The three of us pranced home with our catch. Momma wasn't surprised when we came home with fish. Daddy and I usually did. Jessie and I washed up, and Momma coated the fish with cornmeal, salt, pepper, garlic powder and paprika and just a dash of cayenne. Then she fried it in some bacon grease she had sitting in a can by the stove. Jessie and I ate our fill and Momma had a fish as well. She saved a couple for Daddy too. Jessie said it was delicious and that she'd never had fish that tasted like this. Momma told her that was how we cooked fish down in the bayou. Jessie looked out the back-door screen at something far away.

"Bayou? Where's 'Bayou'?"

"It's where we're from." I volunteered. "Louisiana."

Jessie looked back at me now, and her eyes sparkled in the afternoon light, and she shot me that smile of hers that went all over her face. "Maybe you can show me 'Bayou' someday, Silas." I don't know if that was the first time I ever blushed, but it may have been the most I ever did. My face was so warm, I actually felt beads of sweat form on my brow. Momma laughed out loud and put the fish she had saved for Daddy in some foil for us to take to him for lunch.

Jessie, Argos and I went everywhere together that summer. She took me to Dead Horse Crossing by Mr. Ray's house where someone was building a barn on the hill. A pile of dirt had been left from when the posts had been set, and Jessie and Argos and I dug a fort out of it, hiding in the dusty soil from anyone who came down the road as if we were in a hideout spying on them. We were usually given away by Argos barking happily at the passers-by. They would look up, see us crouched down behind the pile of dirt and then wave to us. We went over to Carmack Church and picked paw paws behind the picnic area and gorged on them. Argos only watched that feast. They made me sick all that afternoon, though. One day, Jessie and I carried Argos up into the loft of Mr. Lady's hay barn. It was hot in the loft and had a rich earthy smell. The three of us lay in the hay, sweating, taking in the golden glow of the sunlight shining through the door for the hayfork and bouncing off the drying fescue. Jessie lay in the hay, her hands behind her head, her dark hair strewn over the hay. It was the first time in my life I ever wanted to kiss a girl, but I didn't try. I didn't want to make her mad. I knew how she could throw a rock, and I also figured she could whip me pretty good, if she chose to. But I definitely wanted to kiss her. Her take on everything was different from anyone else I knew. That fascinated me, and I wanted to know what she was thinking about everything. She once told me that the colors in the oily puddles along the highway after a rain were her true medium. She took a stick and made the colors flow and divide and come back together. We spent hours that day playing in the puddle, making art. In the evening, when Venus would just begin to show herself in the evening sky, she would suddenly stop as we were traipsing along and say, "Wait. Listen. The stars are coming out." And then the frogs and crickets would start chirruping as if on cue. I had never met anyone like her.

I usually read my books in the morning before either I went over to her house or she came to mine. I played guitar for her too. She liked that. She would often sing with me, and the truth is, she was just awful singing. She sounded like a hound dog caught in a trap. The only thing worse than her rhythm was her pitch. I don't think she could hear herself, to be honest. No one would sing that bad on purpose. But I just let her sing because, really, if singing makes someone happy, what difference does it make what they sound like? And singing did make Jessie happy. I would play the guitar, and she would hold a hairbrush as if it were a microphone and she would sing at the top of her lungs. Then she would stop and dance a crazy, rubber-kneed gyration that followed no beat at all, but she was having a blast. And, honestly, she maybe couldn't dance either, but I loved seeing her so happy. We usually had our 'concerts' in the living room, since it still had so little furniture, although we did now have a cane-bottomed rocker Daddy had rescued and replaced the runners on to go with the straight-back chair we already had. There was another chair too, but the seat was missing from it. Momma was doing a needle-point pattern for it, someday. Momma would come in and out while we had our shows, shaking her head and smiling. Momma liked Jessie. I think there was a part of Momma that thought of Jessie as the daughter she might have had.

Sometimes, of course, we also went over to Jessie's house. Her mother was a busy, chatty woman who loved to have people come by. Jessie always acted like it was a bother to stop and visit, but Mrs. May knew everyone and what they had been doing. I was fascinated but usually wasn't in her company long enough to find out any of the good details. Jessie had two older brothers. One was maybe three years older than Jessie and I. His name was Cliff. He wasn't very friendly and liked to tease Jessie and me, singing in a singsong, "Jessie and Silas sitting in a tree, K, I, S, S, I, N, G." Jessie said to not pay him any attention, but it did annoy me, mainly because I wished it were true but dared not admit it. Her other older brother was Edward. He was in high school, and Jessie loved it when he was around. He always seemed to have time for us and even played with Argos in the front yard. Jessie said it was Edward who showed her how to do everything: throw rocks, fish, climb trees, you name it. When we told him how we met, Edward was impressed that I had taken on Joey Simmons, since he was a well-known bully and a few years older than I was. That's when Edward gave me a fighting lesson out in front of the May house. He had me spar with him first. He was a lot taller, so there was little danger of my ever hurting him, so I went fast and furious, the way I usually did in fights.

"Whoa!" Edward backpedaled, but I kept coming. "Okay. Okay. Slow down." I stopped my impersonation of a tornado. I was winded from the exertion. I stood there panting. "Okay, so you're quick, and you're aggressive. But you need to use those more like weapons."

"What?" I gasped for air.

"Okay, so I'm bigger than you. Well, that means I can hit you before you get close enough to hit me. Right?"

"Yeah?"

"So, when someone is bigger than you, you have to get them to swing first and miss. Then, when he's all stretched out with his swing, that's when you get him with your quickness. It's called a counter punch. Watch, we'll do it in slow motion. If you just pretend like you're going to throw a right, then bring your arm back and step to your left, Joey Simmons will think he's got you where he wants you and take a swing, probably with his right. Now see? If I took a swing with my right and you had moved, look how exposed I am. Then you use your speed to nail him with your left hand as many times as you can, right in his ribs." I did see the logic in it. I liked having a strategy. "Also, make your punches land four inches into him, not just on the surface. Punch through your target. Okay?"

"Okay."

"Let's try it for real this time." We squared up, I feinted with my right and stepped left then, when Edward lunged, I got him with three hard lefts, only remembering to punch through on the last one. "Ouch!" Edward held his side. "Dang, Silas. That hurt!" But he was grinning at me. He had let me land the punches, of course, but I think the one had surprised him a little.

"You kids knock it off!" Mr. May walked into the yard. We had heard the tractor pulling up behind the barn, so we knew he was home for lunch. "Ed, I need you to help me run the rake this afternoon." Jessie's father had a serious limp. It looked like everything he did hurt him, but he still worked hard every day.

"Yes sir," Edward called to his father then turned back to me and put his hand out to shake. "You're okay, Silas. You're okay."

# Chapter 8

There's something about watching a campfire that lets people get caught up in what might be or what might have been. We had lots of campfires that autumn, Momma, Daddy, Argos, and I. Sometimes, Daddy and I would play guitar and Momma would sing, always with the backdrop of tree frogs, crickets, owls and the occasional whippoorwill. Daddy would show me new techniques and fingerings, and I would try them out with him. Sometimes, we simply sat there in tristful reflection, staring at the campfire, listening to the soft crackle of the fire, smelling the hardwood smoke, and letting our minds wander. Argos would lie next to me, his chin on his paws, facing the fire, looking like he, too, was lost in thought, occasionally snooping off into the woods after some stray sound then coming back to the circle and his place on the ground next to the stump I usually sat on. The musings would continue unabated. The time he came back after investigating a skunk, however, broke up the party fast. A few times, my parents would sip on liquor made by a neighbor after Momma had soaked hard candy in it to make it more palatable. Daddy would get up, stir the fire with a long, charred stick he kept for that purpose, sending up a stream of sparks like miniature fireworks. Then he would add logs to it and return to his seat, one of the kitchen chairs brought out after dinner, next to Momma, who rocked in the repaired rocker. Momma would give him that look that said she adored him, and the four of us would sit quietly again. The red-yellow light of the woodfire made everything gentle. Shadows danced around the yard like whimsical drunkards. I don't know what my parents thought about when we pondered before the flames, although I could hear the murmurings of their conversation later in the house, soft sounds of a man and a woman sharing the thoughts that they shared only with each other. When I gazed into the fire, I wondered about Grandpapa and Grandmama sometimes, and Fredrick. I still wrote them all letters, and I even told Fredrick about meeting Jessie and how she could fish and throw rocks and even climb trees better than anyone else I knew and how she also liked to read. I mostly got letters only from Grandpapa now, missives about things he remembered from his childhood or a tidbit about local history in Winn. Many times, the letters just seemed to be Grandpapa writing down whatever thoughts came to mind, starting from nowhere. But each letter ended with notes written at the end from Grandmama, telling me she and Grandpapa loved me. I loved getting them, no matter how random the subject would be. I also received some pictures Fredrick had drawn for me. He was getting better and better at it. He sent me a picture of the fence row along the field next to our road, with the gravel road disappearing around a bend in the lane. I knew exactly where he was standing when he drew it. I tacked it to my bedroom wall. There were times when I stared at the campfire, and I thought back on Loreauville too, seeing the cemetery I once played in, watching in my mind's eye as the drawbridge went up, retracing my path to the school with Charlie. I found myself wondering what happened at the mill that night that had changed our lives so dramatically. And I thought about Jessie, wondering what she was doing at that moment. Sometimes, I thought about the fun things we did, like getting in battles using the spiky balls from the black gum tree, the balls sharp enough to bite a little but too light to throw with any force. Or the time we were fishing in Miss Rowena's pond and the hail storm broke out, sending us to a tiny tin-roof shack for shelter while the ice banged and hammered on the roof so loud we could yell at the top of our lungs and not hear each other. And sometimes I let myself think about being in Mr. Lady's hay loft with Jessie that time and how her eyes were so set off by the hay. But all that gazing into the flames didn't change anything. In the end, it was all just hot air and Momma and I would go inside to prepare for bedtime while Daddy extinguished the by that time dying embers and brought in the chairs.

School started late between the rivers since many of the kids were needed to help with harvest on the family farms. It wasn't only the older children that worked. Entire families worked together, and each member had chores that played a vital part in the daily operation of the farm. Even Jessie was too busy to play for a while when the fall came. She had to mow the second cutting of hay so Edward could rake it. Cliff ran the bailer. Cliff was always a little mean to Jessie and me, but he could outwork most grown men. He was big and strong for his age, and even in the sixth grade, I swear he had a five o'clock shadow by the end of the school day. Since we didn't farm, that left me and Argos to our own devices during the days that grew shorter and shorter.

I read all of Momma's classics, including *Wuthering Heights* and *Tom Sawyer*. Sometimes, Momma would ask me to sit at the dinette table and tell her what I liked and didn't like about the books. She would ask me questions that were hard, too, like why is revenge so important in Wuthering Heights and why was Judge Thatcher so important to the story of Tom Sawyer. When I said the most important thing about the judge was he was Becky's daddy, Momma smirked and shot me a look that said, "I see what's going on," but she let it go. Sometimes I used my crayons to draw scenes from the books on flattened out paper sacks, but I never had the skills of Fredrick. I explored the Carmack area a lot with Argos, wandering through the fields and woods, watching the activities of all the farms in high gear before the first frost. I had boundaries, such as not to go to the river or past Carmack Church, but that left a lot of ground for us to cover. Saturday mornings, sometimes Daddy and I hunted squirrels in the trees behind our house using his single-shot .22 Grandpapa had shipped to him. We had squirrel gravy and rice whenever we brought back enough squirrels, a meal I savored. Argos learned to be quiet in the woods with us and even learned to stop cowering each time the rifle popped. Daddy would see a squirrel that scurried up a tree, racing to the opposite side of the tree when it saw us. Argos and I would walk around the tree, sending the squirrel back around and Daddy would shoot him. Other times we fished, usually in someone's farm pond. Daddy had replenished his tackle some, mainly by getting a fiberglass fishing pole and a bait-caster reel that I could never cast without creating a knot around the spool that would have sufficed for Gordias. But Daddy had a deft hand at it, and he liked to throw a red and white spoon across the pond and reel it back. I used worms and a bobber, and my long stick Jessie had cut for me usually. Game and fish were staples of our meals during that time.

The harvest period did not last long, maybe three weeks, but it seemed longer. Towards the end of September, we put Argos in the house, and all three of us took the ferry over to Kuttawa to the dry goods store, and I got some new khaki work pants, just like Daddy's, some new oxfords, and a couple of new shirts as well. We also got me my first loose-leaf notebook, since that's what we were told would be needed at school, and some pencils.

I don't think I mentioned before that I went to Yale. I did. I attended The Yale School with about forty other kids from various communities between the rivers. The county school system had consolidated the assorted one-room schools into one four-room school at the crossroads that led to the other ferry across the Cumberland on highway 58 That ferry took people to Eddyville. The

Cumberland River was dammed at Eddyville, so the current was different. We weren't allowed to fish in that area, but, although it was not actually far, we weren't really tempted. It seemed like the other side of the country, no more often did we go over there. Eddyville was a bigger town and where the penitentiary was. The penitentiary towered over the landscape like a fearsome castle, and just knowing it was filled with the worst offenders in Kentucky made it even more foreboding. One of the schools they closed between the rivers when they consolidated was Harvard. I think they liked the high ideals of the names. Momma liked it that I was going to Yale and she said someday if I worked hard enough at my studies, I might even make it to the real Yale. But that never happened.

The Yale School was maybe a mile from our house, and I walked it each morning unless it rained extra hard or, later, if it snowed or iced up. Daddy took me in his truck then, although in snow and ice, the rear end slipped and slid so much there were times it felt like we were going sideways. A few of my classmates rode horses to school and tied them out behind the building, but they had to tie them away from the lunchroom. Most of the kids walked though including Jessie and her brother Cliff. Her oldest brother Edward took the ferry each day over to Kuttawa High School unless the river flooded, then he stayed over in Kuttawa at friends' houses. When school started, I saw Jessie in a whole new light. Since she was not allowed to wear cut-off jeans or overalls to school, she wore a dress. I had not seen her in a dress before, and it made her look different. She looked more refined, somehow, more grown up. She looked even prettier, but I didn't say anything, of course. She was almost dainty in her dresses, but I always liked the way she looked in overalls better. They just suited her, somehow. We arrived at school that first day at different times, Jessie arriving maybe ten minutes after I did, but I had hung around the front door, waiting for her while pretending not to wait for her by fiddling with my notebook and repeatedly dropping and picking up my pencil until I broke the tip off. When she and Cliff came up the steps, Cliff gave me a goofy look but kept walking inside. Jessie came up to me in her blue gingham dress and stopped. She had a loose-leaf notebook in one hand at her side and a small, zippered bag of pencils in her other.

"Hey, Silas." She twisted a little in her dress. Was she flirting, or adjusting?

"Hey, Jessie." I tried to think of something to say, but my mouth was suddenly full of cotton, my thoughts twisted around like a dust devil, and I could not speak. Instead, I stood there gazing up at Jessie. Jessie looked at me for a moment, waiting for me to say something. Then she shrugged and started walking into school when Greg Thomas, a fourth grader who lived near the school, came up behind her and flipped the back of her dress up high enough we could see the backs of her legs.

"Hey, Jessie. Didn't you hear? Today's 'Dress Up Day'," Greg sniggered, elbowing Tommy Griffin who was standing next to Greg. Tommy laughed nervously. I think he had a strong recollection of what Jessie could do with a dirt clod. I was immediately enraged and dropped my notebook and pencil. Greg had no right to do that, and I was ready to go after him, but it was too late. Jessie had dropped her zipper bag, turned, and slapped his face so hard, Greg's eyes rolled back in his head. Then Jessie balled up her fist and hit Greg in the nose, hard. Greg stumbled down a couple of steps, gathering his balance.

Before anything else could happen, Mrs. Jenkins, our teacher, came out. She took one look around and barked at me, Jessie and Tommy. "Get your things and go take your seats." Then she turned and looked at Greg. "Keep your hands to yourself, Gregory Thomas." He looked up at her in disbelief, as if he thought he was the victim. As we walked into the building, I saw Cliff looking out the door at Greg, and he had a face that was so angry, it almost made me sorry for Greg. Daddy said he didn't want me to hang around with Greg, not that I was tempted. He said the rumor was his grandfather had been a night rider back a number of years and that was a bad thing.

I liked Yale. Mrs. Jenkins was a strict teacher who maintained a very orderly classroom, which I appreciated, since, with only four classrooms, Joey was bound to turn up. He did, although it took a while. Also, Mrs. Jenkins let me read books other than what other kids were reading. In fact, all the pupils seemed to read a whole range of books, either because they read at different levels or because the collection of books was a bit meager, or maybe both. One corner of the shelf space, the corner under the pencil sharpener, had been designated a "library" where we could select any book we wanted when there was time. In fact, there was never a lot of unscheduled time for Mrs. Jenkins, but I still found there an old set of Excelsior Readers from 1904 that someone had donated to the school and they were a very welcome read while some of the others went through *Adventures with Dick and Jane*. Jessie also liked browsing through the old collection, and we would switch books sometimes so we could both have read the same ones. Since I had been reading for so long, I was pretty far ahead of the other students who were in the "third grade," although saying it was the third grade makes it sound like there were distinctions about levels that really were fairly fuzzy. At any rate, I was ahead in my reading compared to the other children of my age. Where I was not ahead was math. I had not really worried about numbers that much. I knew my numbers, of course, and could count fine, and tell time, but multiplication tables were something I had to spend considerable effort on and word problems were always a bit baffling to me. I could read well enough, of course, but it always seemed like they asked a question at the end that had little to do with the information we were provided to formulate an answer. They perplexed me. Fortunately for me, Jessie was great at math, and she sat next to me and showed me how to read the problem backward, so I knew what was being asked before I read the lead-in and then I knew what information I needed to solve the problem.

I usually walked back home with Jessie as far as Sardis. We would amble along and talk about school and Mrs. Jenkins and the other kids and all. Each day, I looked forward to the walk home when I had Jessie's undivided attention. And evidently, Cliff had decided I was okay since I had been ready to take on Greg that day, so he always walked on ahead. He usually had a number of chores to do before dark. I felt emboldened that day in late October when we were walking home, and the wind was blowing. We had to actually lean forward to make headway. I had thought about it for a long time and had mulled it over the entire walk towards home. Today was the day.

"I think it's going to blow up a storm." Jessie held her dress down with her books at her side.

"Yeah, maybe." I had to squint into the wind. Her hair was blowing straight back, and I realized it was longer than I knew, just really curly.

"I hope it doesn't wash out the road to my Granny's. She lives over near Woodson's Chapel. We're supposed to go see her Saturday."

"Can I carry your books?" My question was completely out of the blue, I realized, but when I got up the nerve, I had to ask then.

Jessie stopped in her tracks. "To Granny's?" She cocked her head to one side, trying to make sense of my offer.

"Oh. No. The rest of the way home." I nodded towards our destination.

Jessie started walking again, grinning, leaning into the wind once more. "Silas, don't be getting all gushy on me. You know you're my best friend, right?"

"Yeah, I guess." I liked that she said I was her best friend. It made me feel warm inside, and my stomach did a quick flip.

Jessie stopped again and looked at me hard. "Well, do you know it or not?"

I felt a small panic. "Yes. Yes, I do."

"Am I your best friend?" She started walking again, and I hurried to keep up.

"Uh, yeah. I thought you already knew that." I wrapped my thready jacket around me tighter. It was one of the few clothing items from last year and a size too small. Spits of rain started pelting my face, driven hard by the wind.

"Okay, you can carry my books." She stopped, handed over her three books and her notebook. I nearly dropped all of it but managed to juggle them into something resembling a grasp. She took four more steps, then turned and said, "There. Thank you very much." She grabbed her books back and turned to go to her house, and I looked around and realized we were already at Sardis. I watched her walking away, again, the wind whipping her dress sideways now. I turned and went to our house where Argos greeted me gleefully on the sagging porch. While I knew Jessie had thought it was a funny trick to pull, since we were much closer to the crossroads than I had realized, but I still liked that she let me carry her books. And she had confirmed we were best friends. I rested in the warm glow of that information all afternoon while a heavy rain pinged off the tin roof. By the time Daddy got home, it was dark from the shorter day and from the heavy rain.

"It's a toad-strangler out there, all right." Daddy came sprinting through the front door. He had parked right out front, so he didn't need to go far, but he was still drenched. I was splayed out on the floor doing a mimeographed worksheet, a picture in purple ink followed by blank lines so I could spell the word out. They were easy words, so I was going through it pretty fast. I was working in the light from a gooseneck lamp Daddy had salvaged and repaired. He said all it had needed was a new cord. Daddy had also built a small wooden desk from two-by-fours and a piece of plywood for me to do my homework on, and the lamp was on it, but if I moved the lamp to the side, I could do my homework on the floor and play with Argos at the same time. Momma came in with a dishtowel and handed it to Daddy. He dried his face and arms, but he was still dripping.

"Why don't you go change, Bennie?" She looked at him and then the floor. A loud clap of thunder made the old house shudder. Momma and Daddy looked at each other quickly. "You think it'll flood the shop?"

"Maybe." Daddy kept wiping the rain off, looking out the window, but it was too dark to see much outside. "I put everything up high, so the tools and people's stuff should be okay. But I may not be able to get there tomorrow."

"Well, I've got half a bushel of apples from Mrs. Herrin we need to can. If you're stuck here, we can do it together."

"Sure, Cher." Daddy sat at the stiff seat that had now become my desk chair, although I usually found the wood floor better to my liking. The grain in the boards did sometimes make lettering harder. He pulled off his boots and placed them next to the wall. He gave out a sigh as Momma turned to go back to cooking dinner.

Momma looked over her shoulder and stopped. "What is it, Bennie?" I sat up and watched too. Daddy stared at the floor.

"It's just always something." He shook his head and sighed again. "It's always something."

"What?" Momma turned all the way around and came back into the tiny living room.

Daddy paused a minute. "I was over at a meeting at Homer's Garage, and that dam they're building downstream on the river?" Momma nodded. "Well, not only is most of the area around here going to be a lake one day soon, now they're talking about making all of between the rivers into a big park or something." I liked parks. I didn't see the problem at first. "They're talking about making everyone move, from Grand Rivers all the way down into Tennessee."

"Move? Off their family farms? They can't do that. Who is doing this?"

"TVA is doing it, and apparently they can do that. No one is happy about it, and people want to fight it, but I don't see them stopping it."

"They're just taking people's land?" Momma crossed her arms.

"Well, they are buying their farms. But it's not like they have any choice on whether to sell."

"What? We're going to move? Again?" I thought immediately about Jessie. I was so tired of losing best friends, and Jessie was special. Just today, I had carried her books, if only for about eight feet.

"Everyone is, I'm afraid." Daddy leaned his elbows on his knees, looking from me to Momma and back. "Eventually. Thing is, we don't own any of the property, so we'll just have to move on our own."

Momma stood still, her arms still crossed, staring at Daddy, but not really focused on him, thinking. Then she put her hands on her hips, the way she always did when she was resolved to get to work. "Well, if we have to, we have to. Let's start thinking about it. Maybe we should go back to Calvin, see if there's any work there."

Daddy stood slowly. "No, Cher. We can't go back there either. I got a letter from your father," Daddy stopped short and looked at me. I knew what he wasn't going to say. It was about the fire at the mill. Again. Or still. I picked up my homework and folded it into my notebook, then took it to my room. Argos came with me. Momma and Daddy watched me leave but said nothing. I just couldn't understand why they kept pestering Daddy about the fire. He said he didn't do it and Sheriff Landry in Iberia Parish said he believed him. Why did they keep making us move? Maybe Daddy didn't do it but knew who did. The thought hit me like a rock in the head. Maybe Daddy knew who did it and wouldn't tell them. Perhaps that was why they kept after Daddy.

# Chapter 9

I wasn't going to say anything to Jessie or anyone else about having to move, as if it were only our burden to move yet again. Somehow, I felt ashamed. And I felt like I didn't matter. But soon everyone was talking about the TVA coming in and moving us all out. Folks had known about the dam making the big lake and that lots of people would have to move for the lake. That part was expected and the reasons for doing so made sense to people: flood control, hydroelectric power, shipping. There was already a "New Eddyville" where many of the people from "Old Eddyville" were moving, although the penitentiary wasn't going anywhere. The same was true of Kuttawa. There was a "New Kuttawa" and an "Old Kuttawa" just a few minutes away. In fact, in Kuttawa, some people were moving whole houses out of the way from where the water would be, hauling them slowly with trucks to lots above the highwater line when the dam started holding back the river. Momma and Daddy had told me months ago that Daddy's shop behind Aldridge's would be under water. Everyone knew that the ferry would be gone. But folks also believed the lake would be a big economic boost for the people who lived between the rivers, what with the tourism and the new shipping capabilities. And although there had been rumors about the government taking the land between the rivers and making a nature preserve out of it, I don't think most of the population thought it really would happen or that they would take it all. Momma and Daddy had been scheming to save enough money to build a little place farther up highway 522 where he could have a real shop, maybe near Carmack Church. But the TVA had already started buying land, and now it was all people could talk about.

It had never come up at school before, but now it did. Mrs. Jenkins, who usually talked about the United States as the lone beacon of goodness and righteousness in the universe, talked scornfully about the TVA, Franklin Roosevelt, John F. Kennedy, the United States Army Corps of Engineers, and

Governor Bert Combs. All of them were personifications of evil. She did introduce the concept of "personification" to us, so it was actually a lesson plan, strictly speaking. When Greg Thomas offered that his family felt like they were going to be rich after the government paid them for all the barns and outbuildings on their place, I thought Mrs. Jenkins was going to cry.

"Gregory Thomas, money cannot replace memories. You would be well off to remember that lesson, if you remember no others, as I suspect." Mrs. Jenkins shook all over she was so angry. "And you cannot buy a family." She stood over him, glowering. Greg was smart enough to keep his head down and remain quiet. Then Mrs. Jenkins read Kipling's "Rikki Tikki Tavi" to us and talked about perseverance. That lesson was about the forced removal as well.

When Momma and I went to Miss Rowena's store for canned goods and some borax for Momma to make detergent with, and to see if we had received any mail, the store had lots more customers than usual, all standing around, talking, gesturing in big, sweeping motions. The words I heard rise above the din of voices were "generations" and "livelihood" and "communism." While we were somewhat disconnected from the loss of property these people were talking about, I certainly felt no less impacted by the effects of the move, and I sulked. I felt that every time I found a niche in a new place, every time I made a friend, every time I started to feel at home, the bottom fell out from under me. It wasn't fair. There was one thing different this time. At least this time it wasn't about the mill, although that had prevented us from going back to Grandpapa and Grandmama's. If anything, though, that made me feel even more like a helpless victim. The powers at work here were far away, in Washington and in Frankfort, and there was seemingly no recourse. In that way, my parents were victims too. There was nothing we could do to stop this, evidently. We were flotsam.

Reverend Herrin preached about the government taking people's farms at church, taking as his starting point that Jesus and his disciples were the first Christian community and the model for how communities should support each other. Sardis and Carmack were a Christian community, Brother Herrin avowed, one that could not and would not be broken. He also pointed out it takes only one Judas to tear at a community, but that even losing Jesus couldn't tear apart that first Christian community, which continued to flourish unto the present. He actually said, "unto." He urged all of us to pray, but to also work together to keep our community strong, no matter what happened. I listened to his sermon, and I wasn't certain if he was urging people to resist or to accept what they seemingly could not change but to keep in touch afterward. Perhaps he was hedging his message for either eventuality. In any case, the congregation left muttering and grumbling when it was over, so he had definitely made an impact.

Daddy attended a few community meetings held at Ray's Garage where they worked to plot strategies to combat this affront to our population, but Daddy said it was hard for people to come up with real plans because it usually was more expressions of anger and resentment, sometimes dissolving into yelling, tears, and even cursing. Eventually, calmer people rose to the front of the fray, and in the end, lawyers were hired, petitions started, and meetings held with lawmakers. There were times it seemed that maybe there was a chance to forestall the compulsory removal of people between the rivers. Rumors would circulate that changes were afoot, that some would be spared the taking of their land. The mood of the area swung from depression to hope to anger to resignation.

There is always one person we feel perfectly comfortable lying to, and that's ourselves. Sadly, those are the lies we fall for most often. We fall for the lie because we want to believe it, just as we do most lies we fall for. We tell the lie to ourselves because we cannot accept what we already know. Unfortunately for the people of Sardis and Carmack and all of the rest of that area, the lie they had told themselves was that they could beat the government. Gradually, farmers sold out, tired of the fight, no doubt, or willing to take the money, since land prices between the rivers had not been that high to begin with. Since we didn't own any property, Daddy attended only a couple of meetings of those trying to fight the TVA. He told Momma he worried some of the people were going to turn to violence, but they never did. Momma and Daddy saw the clouds on the horizon, and they started looking around for someplace to move. Each weekend, the three of us would climb into Daddy's battered pickup, and Argos would climb up into the bed, and we would drive around, looking for yet another new place to move to while Argos ran back and forth in the truck bed, his tongue wagging in the wind. I went, of course, since I had no choice, but I could not feign interest. What difference would it make where we lived? No doubt we would move in a year or two anyway. I think Daddy had set his mind on a small community, perhaps thinking it was easier to remain hiding in plain sight that way. I started resenting that, too. If Daddy knew who burned down the mill, why not tell Sheriff Landry and let whoever did it suffer instead of us? Then we could simply move home to Louisiana. I felt unjustly persecuted.

Underneath it all, of course, I was most angry to be leaving Jessie. I had

had best friends before, of course, in Charlie and Fredrick, but somehow, in ways, I did not yet understand, Jessie was different. I had certainly never had a crush on my best friend before, and I most certainly had a crush on Jessie May. She brought a sense of wonder to my world I did not realize was not there. So when we drove through the tiny village of Iuka, I could not care less about the huge store that stood there that sold everything from animal feed to men's suits to plows. I didn't care that they also had a ferry there that went across the Cumberland River, just like we did in Carmack. I didn't care and couldn't be made to care. I know Daddy's patience was wearing thin, but Momma just said, "Okay. We'll look someplace else." And then we drove on. We had checked on Grand Rivers, of course, since at one time that had been our destination, but it was more of a railroad town, and Daddy did boats, not trains. We drove to Salem, no river, and to Marion, too big. Before we started these forays searching for a likely home, I had looked forward to drives with Momma and Daddy, but this felt more like work. Momma and Daddy tried hard to see each place through the eyes of living there, rather than merely passing through. But I could see only darkness through my sullenness.

In fact, it was autumn now, and the weather was pleasant, and the bosky countryside was ablaze with yellow, red, brown, and orange. Great fields of soybeans had turned golden in the fall. Barns weathered grey had columns of yellow-green tobacco hanging in them visible through the open doors. Sometimes, the doors were closed, and smoke seeped out from every edge of the barn spreading a woodsy scent across the hillsides. One little town was having a fall festival, and we were delayed in the middle of the highway while a parade went through the town. From what I could tell, the parade consisted of a couple of floats on flat wagons pulled by tractors, some old cars that had been redone in bright colors and chrome, a band, boy scouts and girl scouts marching, a convertible with the mayor sitting on the backseat top, and a dozen folks riding horses, which they knew to put last, I guess. I liked the parade and watched it keenly, almost forgetting to sulk for a few minutes. When the parade was over, we were allowed to drive through, and Daddy said it was like we were part of the parade, so he honked his horn and waved at people. Momma laughed so hard she could barely contain herself. Then Momma and I both started waving, and people waved back too, some of them smiling with either greeting or understanding the joke, others looking at us curiously, wondering if they knew us, maybe. We were still driving slowly, which got Argos excited, and he barked all the way through town. When we stopped for a hotdog at a place called The Dip, a woman there told Momma there was a large Amish community in the area. Momma was curious, and we headed off to find it. It turned out, the community was much more spread out across farms in the region than it was an actual town, but we did see buggies and people dressed in Amish clothes, and there were places to stop and get things if we had wanted to or had the money, which we didn't. The roads were not marked all that well, except for an occasional sign advertising a saddler or farrier. Otherwise, the roads met and stopped or came together at odd angles along some long-ago property line and before long, we were lost.

Momma laughed. "Bennie, admit it, we are lost. Maybe you should ask directions."

Daddy looked at the gas gauge, as he had been for several minutes. "Bonne idée, Cher. You see anyone to ask? I haven't seen a living soul for miles. And we're getting low." Daddy raised one hand on the steering wheel to check the gauge he had just checked.

I was worried about running out gas, but Momma just laughed again. "We'll be fine."

"Look!" I pointed at a black wagon being pulled by a single horse just visible over the next hill.

Daddy sighed, very relieved. He slowed the truck as we drew near, and I could see the man driving. He had a long grey beard growing from his jawline, and he wore a white shirt, a black jacket and pants, and a straw hat on top of his grey hair. He was lost in thought at first and didn't take notice of us until our window was right next to him. When Daddy called to him across the truck, the man startled a little.

"Excuse me, sir," Daddy called.

"Yes?" The man pulled the reins, and the wagon stopped. Argos watched from the bed of the truck.

Daddy stopped too and leaned across Momma and me so he could speak with the man. His left hand was draped on the steering wheel as he propped himself far across us. "I wonder if you could help us?"

The man didn't answer for a moment, as if he was trying to decide. "I suppose that depends on what you need help with." He looked at Daddy intently.

"Well, we're lost."

"Ah!" The man nodded. "Where are you trying to be?"

"Well, we were just driving around aimlessly, really, and . . ." Daddy held his hand up and shrugged.

"Well, if you aim at nothing, you're bound to get there." The man flicked the reins and the horse, who had turned his head around to see why he had been stopped, faced forward and started at a slow trot.

"Wait!" Daddy glanced at Momma, who suppressed a smirk with her hand. "Is there a gas station nearby? We're almost out." He let the truck idle alongside the wagon.

The man didn't stop this time. "Straight ahead. When you come to Rebecca's mum farm, turn left at the end of the garden. That'll take you to Tyner's." The man said nothing more and seemed clearly finished.

"Thank you," Daddy called, and Momma echoed him, and we drove on. In fact, we were not far from the tiny town of Tolu, although I'm not sure we would have ever thought of going there.

We drove past the small sign announcing we were entering Tolu and pulled into a combination grocery and gas station at the top of a hill on the edge of town. The metal sign atop the pole said it was an Esso station called Tyner's Market and there was a cutout of a tiger next to the gas pump. A man about Daddy's age wearing bib overalls sauntered out to fuel us up. Momma opened her door, and she and I climbed out while Daddy told the man we wanted two dollars' worth, then came around to our side of the truck. The store itself was weathered wood, covered in metal signs advertising Nehi, Marlboro, Colman mustard, Prince Albert, Bunny Bread, and a dozen other products. In places, there was more metal sign than beat up old wood. We went inside, and Momma said I could have a soft drink, which was exceedingly rare for me, so I had a peach Nehi, a drink so sweet my teeth were on edge. I loved it. Momma and Daddy each got an RC Cola and we went outside to stand in front of the place and take in the town of Tolu. Daddy filled a metal bowl with water from the hose by the gas pumps and gave it to Argos.

Tolu was tiny. There were a dozen or so houses lined up on three or four streets. There was a First Avenue but no Second Avenue. There were two churches, a school building, a tiny post office, and a bridge over Caney Creek.

"That'll be two bucks." The man in the overalls wiped his hands on a small rag and stood next to Daddy, who pulled his wallet from his khakis and paid him.

"This is Tolu?" Daddy pronounced it "Tow-loo" and handed the bills over.

"Too-lu." The man corrected Daddy then turned and walked back in the store. Daddy looked at Momma and shrugged, which made her giggle. Daddy could always make Momma laugh. Another car pulled into the lot, a green Fairlane with a white top, and Momma stood back to admire it. The young woman who climbed out nodded acknowledgment of our standing there and started for the door of the store.

"Nice car." Momma nodded, then took a drink from her cola.

"Thank you." The woman stopped and smiled at Momma. She had on a white and red polka-dotted blousy dress. Momma knew how to start a conversation.

"Excuse me, but we just drove in here, and we're a bit turned around." Momma looked up and down the road.

"Where are you trying to go?" The woman turned and faced Momma.

"Well, if we could get to Marion, we would know where we were."

"Oh, well, that's easy enough. Head up this way until you get to the ferry road, turn right." She smiled and started to go inside.

"Do you live in this town?" Momma stopped her again.

"Tolu. Yes, I do." Now she seemed a little bit put off by the delay, so Momma stopped asking questions. The woman went in and came back out with a package of Tareyton cigarettes. She paused next to the door of her car long enough to open the pack and pull out a cigarette.

"So, where does the ferry go?"

"Illinois. Cave-in-Rock, Illinois."

"Cave-In-Rock? The rock caves in?" Daddy cocked his head to one side.

"No, Cave-In-Rock as in a cave that's in the rock on the banks of the river. You can go into the cave, even, if you're of a mind to." She opened her car door.

"Do you like Tolu?" Momma asked.

"Yes." The woman shot Momma a quick smile. "Yes, I do." Then she got into her car and drove off. Momma looked at Daddy and then at me. It was one of those conversations they had where no words were needed. Daddy took our empty soft drink bottles back inside and was in there for a while before he came back out, and we headed back to Sardis.

It was nearly Thanksgiving, and the farming operations had returned to more steady rhythm of maintenance rather than the seemingly frenetic pace of the harvest. One day after school, Jessie had been picked up by her mother to go shopping in Paducah and I was walking alone towards home when Joey Simmons stepped out from behind a cedar tree directly in my path. Tommy was there too. Other kids were walking behind me and in front of us, but I was by myself.

"Hey, Tommy," Joey pretended to be addressing his sycophant behind him. "Look, it's Sorry-Ass Le-Monkey!" Joey grinned an antagonizing smirk. Tommy puzzled over the name, then gave a "hyuk" in support of Joey's taunt.

"And he ain't with his sweetheart today. What's the matter, Sorry-Ass, Jessie break up with you? She's probably off getting another pair of granny boots to wear tomorrow."

I was not ready to get in a fight over Joey making fun of my name. I didn't care. But as any guy will tell you, start talking about my girl, and that's a different story completely. The other classmates who had been walking behind me caught up with us, and they stopped to watch. A couple of the kids who had been in front of us returned to see what the commotion was. I stood there fuming, Joey walking towards me. I dropped my books and balled up my fists. Tommy walked up beside Joey like he was going to get in on the fight. I was not at all sure I could take Joey. I knew I couldn't fight them both. Then Cliff May stepped in between us.

"Tommy, you stay out of it, you hear?" Cliff towered over Tommy. Tommy was visibly intimidated and wilted backward silently. Cliff looked back and forth between Joey and me. We stood there, staring each other down. "Well?" Cliff held his hands before him. "You going to fight or make goo-goo eyes at each other?" I admit I had hoped he would keep this fight from happening, but that hope was now dashed.

I remembered what Edward told me and faked a right, stepped to my left, and when Joey threw his right cross as predicted, I landed three hard lefts to his side. The rest of the fight was more of a blur, but I remember Joey's eyes getting big when I nailed his ribs. In the end, we both had black eyes and bloody noses. I had landed as many shots as I had taken, and I was still standing. So was Joey. We were both a bit winded and had stepped back, and I realized my classmates were cheering loudly every time I landed a punch. I stood facing Joey, both of us panting. I would have never admitted it, but I was done. I had been hit as many times as I wanted to be for one day. We faced each other, fists at the ready next to our faces waiting for the next advance, when Cliff stood between us.

"Okay, it's a draw." He announced loudly. A murmuring came forth from my classmates, who immediately started drifting away to their homes. I think they were disappointed, but I wasn't. Cliff looked at me. "Draw, Silas?" I nodded. "Draw, Joey?" He nodded. "Okay, then. Shake." We dropped our guards and shook hands. Joey gave me a look he had not given me before, maybe one of respect. Cliff was standing behind him and nodded towards me with a smile. That was my first realization that while Cliff might not be the best student in school, which he wasn't, he did know about the workings of day-to-day life. Joey turned to leave, and Cliff blocked his way. "Now, Simmons, I let LaMontaie fight his own fights. That's his business. But if you ever again in your life talk about my sister, that will be my business, and you will find out for sure who has the sorry ass. Got it?" Joey gulped and nodded. Cliff let him pass, and Joey took off at a run.

"You did good, Silas." Cliff turned and sauntered off towards home.

Momma was very upset about the fight, but Daddy just shrugged about it. "Boys get in fights sometimes." Of course, by then, I had cleaned up my injuries a good deal. Momma got the whole picture when I got home covered in blood and dirt, again. Even Argos had looked perplexed when I walked into the yard all battered, but the truth was, I felt victorious. After that fight, Joey never bothered me again. He even acted as if he rather liked me, although I had no interest in being friends with the guy who had kicked Argos and had wanted him killed. Still, not having to look over my shoulder any more was a welcome change.

Momma was sick over Thanksgiving, lying in bed coughing and sweating. When I went in to see what I could do to help, she looked awful. It scared me. She told me she had the flu, and I was not to come in and catch it. I was not sorry to be told not to see her looking like that. Daddy made Thanksgiving dinner, and Daddy knew how to cook Cajun style. We had a turkey stuffed with andouille dressing, and we had dirty rice and boudin. The andouille was sent to us by Grandma Boudreaux. Daddy had wanted to make gumbo, but he couldn't find the shrimp, and he said the crawfish around where we lived were too small and too few to make a reasonable gumbo. He made a persimmon pudding for dessert that was incredible. Momma wanted to come in to eat, but she said just the smell of cooking food made her sick. Daddy made her some chicken soup and took it to her.

By Saturday, Momma was feeling better. Daddy took the truck and was gone all day. I didn't know where he was off to. I spent the morning playing in the yard with Argos until he decided he had played enough and lay down on the mat next to the front door and went to sleep. I was feeling a bit all alone when I heard Jessie behind me.

"Hey, Silas." I spun to see Jessie standing there, smiling broadly, and wearing a new blue dress that was different from her school dresses. In fact, she had been out of school sick for a week, and I had missed her. I had not seen her since the fight with Joey, and I still had the yellow-purple remains of my black-eye. I ran over to where she was standing.

"Hi, Jessie!"

She reached up and touched the remnants of my shiner. The feeling of her finger just touching my cheek sent a thrill up my spine. "Cliff told me you stood up to Joey for me, Silas."

"Uh, yeah, well, . . ." I had never felt so at a loss for actual words.

"Thank you." Then she leaned over and kissed my cheek. My knees became jelly. "See you at school." Then she turned and bounced away. I stood watching her skip off, again, and reached up to touch where she had kissed me. I focused on what that felt like. I wanted to remember, forever, the gentleness of her kiss, the softness of her touch, the sparkle in her eyes. I stood there like a statue, my hand up to my cheek, looking down the road towards the path Jessie had taken but she was out of sight now. Argos ventured from the front porch, perhaps to see if I was still among the living. In truth, I was just as bewitched as if I had heard the songs of the Sirens.

# Chapter 10

The next few months went by quickly. Christmas came and went. We were not able to go see family because of finances. Grandpapa and Grandmama sent me books for Christmas. I got a Zebco rod and reel from my parents, my maple twig having gotten brittle. Momma and Daddy had saved up a little money, but most of it had gone for doctor bills and medicine when Momma had been sick. We had a cedar tree Daddy cut down from a neighbor's field decorated with mostly homemade ornaments, including construction paper chains and "cookies" made from flour, salt and water that Momma and I painted. I made Momma a wooden box for her recipes and for Daddy I made a wooden toolbox that was a little tilted at one end. The wood for both I had salvaged from a shipping pallet that had washed up next to the ferry. The hardest part of making the gifts was hauling the waterlogged wood home to take it apart with one of Daddy's brown-handled hammers. The nails I used were all salvaged from the pallet itself, or from some other piece of lumber, straightened carefully on a cinderblock that served as half of the back-porch step. I did some cleaning chores for Daddy at his shop to earn some money and got Jessie two blue ribbons for her hair. It was the most perfect gift I could imagine – blue ribbons to match her blue eyes. She got me two new guitar picks, one grey plastic, the other a tortoise shell color. I loved them. We exchanged gifts after school the last day before Christmas break, sitting on the steps of the Sardis Church, and she told me her family was moving after the first of the year to just outside Marion where her mother had relatives, and they had the opportunity to continue farming on family land. They were taking the TVA money and leaving. Her father was tired of the squabbling and the anger people expressed with so little hope for a more satisfactory outcome. I was, of course, devastated. Jessie was sad as well, but all of us between the rivers had gotten kind of beaten down, so our sadness was dampened by a more overwhelming feeling of defeat. When she told me, her blue eyes were filled with tears, but she did not let them spill. She hugged me, and I hugged her, and then she walked away, one more time, towards her house. We saw a lot of people over the course of the next few weeks and months giving similar hugs of friendships and families rending. When I told Momma Jessie was leaving right away, she hugged me too and said she was sorry things were so hard, but that she and Daddy had a new plan that they thought was going to change our situation for the better and that they wanted to finally settle down. I hoped so. I was much too tired for a boy to be. I was tired of losing friends, tired of being poor, and tired of feeling rootless. We had never been rich, but living between the rivers was the first time I had felt truly poor.

The fact that Jessie was moving did at least allow me to accept our own departure a bit better. I no longer could consider that if we could somehow stay, I would have more time with her. I couldn't. The Mays moved before school started back up. January was bleak, cold, and miserable for me. I went to school, came home and did my homework, played guitar, read, and played with Argos. That was it. I had been so focused on Jessie, I had made no other friends. I had not even considered making other friends. And because it was cold and windy, I wasn't tempted to stay out trying to make friends. But we were all leaving anyway, so it made no sense, really, to try to make friends. Everyone was pretty much just going through the motions. Daddy's business fell off to nothing since people were trying to scale down their belongings rather than trying to keep them. There were lots of yard sales, but when Momma and I went by the one at the Simmons, Momma stayed only long enough to appear not to be running off. She shot me a couple of looks that said, "This is nothing but junk," then we walked on home. That winter, I did a lot of moping about Jessie being gone. I focused my mind's eye on seeing the cheekbones in her face when she had hugged me that last day at Sardis Church, her curly hair blowing straight in the wind, her crisp blue eyes every time she looked at me. Again, I pictured her in the hayloft in Mr. Lady's barn. I relived in my imagination, her kissing me on the cheek that day after I had stood up for her. I saw her tear-filled eyes telling me she was leaving. I wanted to write a song for her, but I didn't really know how, so I made up words that were about Jessie for the songs I did know. I discovered "Jessie May" was fun to think up rhymes for. Of course, "Camptown Races" with the line "I sure miss my Jessie May, doo dah" was perhaps not great lyricism, but I did like it. I didn't play any of those songs for Momma or Daddy though. I knew I would get a ribbing from Daddy especially. Often in February and early March,

Daddy was gone all day. Sometimes when I got home from school, neither of my parents were there and I would go through my routine on my own: walk Argos, do my homework, sweep the porch, take out the trash, practice guitar, in that order, waiting for them to come bouncing up in Dad's old truck. I would see them sitting in the cab of the truck, talking, then, usually, kissing, and they would come in, and I would act surprised by their arrival. I felt a little like a spy, seeing them when they didn't know I could, and watching them without letting them know. Momma and Daddy talked about whatever they had been up to later, I think, when I could hear muffled voices coming from their room, but I didn't know where he was going on his trips or where they went together. Then one Saturday in late March, Daddy and Momma said they had a surprise for Argos and me. They smiled so broadly, I could not help but be excited as well

Winter had finally released its hold, and it was a beautiful morning, with the grass dewy and the daffodils blooming beside the house. Robins hopped around the yard, finding worms which crawled out to escape the damp earth. We piled once more into the pickup and jostled across the yard and onto the road. Argos was in the back. The shocks and springs in the old truck were no longer any help. The body was rusting through visibly in a number of places. Daddy could keep the engine running, but the rest of it was falling apart from around the motor. We took the Eddyville Ferry this time and drove past where the new town was being built. There was already a courthouse and a drug store there, houses were being built, and the town seemed to be rising from the ground itself. We drove up through Fredonia, and when I saw the sign announcing we were in Marion, my heart skipped a beat, but we drove on through, all the way up almost to the Ohio River Ferry, and then we turned left.

The house in Tolu we stopped at was a two-story house on Orchard Street. There was a tall wooden slat fence around the back yard, and the porch was freshly painted. There were actual steps up to the porch instead of concrete blocks. The screen door was intact, and the windows were not covered in plastic. Compared to where we had been living, it seemed posh. Daddy let the tailgate down, and Argos jumped out of the truck, and the four of us walked up to the front door. I had no idea who might live here. Usually, when we visited people, Argos was left in the pickup, since Momma said it was rude to show up with a pet. But here we were, walking right up to the door. Momma and Daddy seemed quite happy. Then, instead of knocking, Daddy took out a key and unlocked the front door. He pushed the door open, and with a sweeping gesture, let me lead the way.

"Our new home, little man." I walked in, Argos just behind me, and marveled at the space in the new house.

"We're going to live here?" I looked at the shallow coal fireplace with its tile filler panels and painted wooden legs. It reminded me of Grandmama's and Grandpapa's house.

"Yes, we are, Sy." Momma came up behind me, stooped down and put her hand on my shoulder. "Things are going to be better now. You'll see."

"Huh!" I looked around the room, and there were already a few pieces of furniture there: an old buffet was against one wall behind a scratched but solid looking cherry table with six matching chairs around it.

Momma marched into the kitchen. "And look at this, Silas. There's a brand new refrigerator and electric stove in here too." It was true. There were matching coppertone appliances and a big white double sink. There was still room for our dinette set in the kitchen. I was confused. Had we struck gold or something?

I looked out the back door, a half panel door that led to a porch that went across the entire back of the house. The yard was completely fenced in, which meant Argos could play outside when I was in school. I turned around and looked at Daddy.

"Your room is upstairs, little man."

I had seen the steps going straight up from just in front of the front door and raced back to go upstairs, Argos hot on my trail. He slipped a little on the steps but still beat me to the top. The second floor was mustier than downstairs from the house being closed up, but it was so far superior to any bedroom I had had other than the haunted bedroom at Grandpapa's that I was beside myself. At the top of the steps was a bathroom with a big claw-footed tub. To one side of the steps was a hallway that led to Momma and Daddy's room. On the other side was the doorway to my room. Argos and I went in and looked around. Actually, Argos sniffed around. There was no bed yet, but the walls were freshly painted. Along one wall was a set of bookshelves. There was even a closet for me to use. I went over to the double-hung window. I could see the little town of Tolu spread out down Broadway Street. A block away was the school building, a new structure that had brick walls and a row of classrooms. I turned around, and Daddy was standing in the doorway.

"This is my room, Daddy?"

"Yes, it is, Silas." Daddy gave a half happy, half sad smile. "I know it's been hard on you, little man. Things will be better now. Things are going to be a lot better."

Momma came into the room now and leaned up against Daddy. He put his arm around her shoulder. "Daddy got a new job, didn't you, Bennie?"

"I did indeed, Bele. I did indeed."

"What are you going to do, Daddy?" I couldn't believe we were moving into such a nice house. Of course, the fact was that the upgrade in housing had much to do with where we had been living as much as anything. The house in Tolu was quite serviceable but compared to the hovels we had been living in, it was as nice as I could have imagined.

Daddy leaned over to brace himself, then sat on the floor. Argos and I sat next to him. Momma shifted her weight in the doorway and leaned on the frame. Daddy waved with one hand. "Well, it seems there's a low flow dam just up the river here," Daddy started.

"What's a 'low-flow dam,' Daddy?"

"It's a dam they only use when the water flow is low when there's not much water in the river."

"What's its name?"

"Uh, well, 'Dam 50' I believe is the only name it has."

It wasn't much of a name, I thought. "Why do they have a 'low flow dam,' Daddy?"

"Okay, that's the Ohio River there, and it's a big river, and they use it for sending stuff up all through the country."

"Like what?"

"Oh, coal, gravel, corn, things like that."

"In those big barges?" I had seen long barges before on the Mississippi when we had lived in Louisiana.

"Yes, exactly. Only sometimes, especially in the summertime, the water level gets too low, so they have to raise the wickets on the dam so the water level will go up and the boats can take their goods through."

"Wickets?"

"Uh, yeah big sections of the dam. Actually, it's more of a weir, but . . ."

"Bennie." Momma chimed in.

"Yes, well, anyway, they take this barge with a crane out on the river, prop it against the dam, and raise the wickets one by one until they get the water flow high enough for boats to pass."

"Oh." But I did not really understand. "So you raise and lower the dam?"

"No. No. Those fellows who do that work for the corps. I keep the crane running." Daddy cocked his head to one side. "That's what I do, I keep things running, little man."

This part I understood. Daddy was the mechanic. That made sense. I didn't know who the corps was, but that didn't matter. Daddy had a job as a mechanic, and that meant we had an honest-to-goodness house to move into.

"We don't want Daddy out there playing with that dam, anyway." Momma stood away from the door, and Daddy climbed to his feet. "It's too dangerous." They walked through the doorway and down the hall holding hands.

Argos and I followed. "When are we moving?" I called after them. For someone who had sulked for weeks about moving, it was quite the reversal.

Momma turned with a smile. "When do you want to move, honey child?"

"I'm ready."

Daddy laughed, and his laughter echoed in the mostly empty house. "Then we'll get right on it, won't we, Cher?"

"Mais ya, Bennie. Mais ya."

We moved the next week. In fact, most of the heavy moving, we did not actually have much, occurred while I was at school on Wednesday. By the weekend, we had loaded up our last few things and left much of the makeshift furniture and moved to Tolu, Kentucky, a town of maybe eighty people with a store, a school, a post office, and two churches. It was a move up for us since we had struggled to make it in Carmack.

I finished what was left of the school year in Tolu. I was the new kid, and most of the other students had grown up together, so I was a bit of an outcast. I wasn't reviled, or anything, I was just forever the new kid. I wasn't from around here. Plus, my Daddy still had a habit of tossing in Cajun words from time to time when he talked to people, so that really made us different.

In fact, the local men started calling him "Frenchy" when we went into Tyner's Market or sometimes when they walked by in the evening with their families and wave to us on the porch and call, "Hey, Frenchy. How y'all doing?"

Daddy would wave back and call, "Bien! Bien!" I knew he was putting on, talking in Cajun, since they called him "Frenchy" and all, but no one else seemed to notice. Whenever he did that, I could see Momma suppressing a giggle. At first, he seemed to not like the nickname, but I think he decided it was better than some he could have been labeled with.

I spent the summer hiking down River Drive to the long flat area where Hurricane Creek emptied into the Ohio River, Argos by my side. I would put heavy sinkers on my Zebco line and drop a hook filled with red wrigglers deep into the current to catch catfish. Sometimes I would hike down the farm road to where Caney Fork and Hurricane Creek joined. There was a deep swimming hole and Argo and I would spend hours wading in the muddy water. Those days, I usually wore cutoff blue jeans that worked for me as universal clothing. However I spent my days, I did it with Argos and the evening began with my taking a hot bath in the big tub upstairs before supper. Nighttime was time with Momma and Daddy, talking about our days. Daddy always wanted to know what I had done with my day. Momma would talk about her chores she had done: canning, making quilts, picking cucumbers and beans in her garden. Momma worked hard all day every day, it seemed to me. Daddy would tell us about what happened at the dam. His main job was to keep the crane running, but he also worked on anything else that needed fixing from the government trucks to generators to lawn mowers. Sometimes they asked about other children who lived around us, but I always told them the same thing: I didn't see them. It was true, I did not go try and make friends. I had my dog and my guitar and my books. I had plenty.

My bookshelves filled slowly with the books I had received over the years and with new ones I collected. I organized them by the series they were in: Hardy Boys, We Were There, Whitman Classics, and so on. Having them all arranged reminded me of Grandpapa's library. But gifts alone could not feed my edacious reading habits. I did odd jobs for people around Tolu to earn spending money: mowing, raking, picking up trash around Tyner's. Every few weeks, we would go into Marion and go to the Sureway, and I would head over to the drug store where they sold paperbacks on a rotating display rack. There were books about Dr. Fu-Manchu and mysteries by Agatha Christie. There was science fiction by Ray Bradbury and James Bond books. My library grew, but I also went to the public library there in Marion and the librarian, Miss Scott, soon recognized me when I came in since I visited so often. She was the one who had me read *To Kill a Mockingbird*, which I read in a single sitting, poring over it all night. I had read to escape for a long time. I believe my reading about Scout was the first time I was ever changed by a reading. It was amazing to look around at the world around me after reading it and to have it somehow changed, colored in a manner I had not known possible. I saw myself in a new way, and I saw others differently as well. My tastes in reading started changing because of it too.

When we went to town from Tolu, we would sometimes eat at the Marion Café, the chicken noodle soup being my favorite, although I strongly suspect it was canned soup. Still, soup with individual packets of saltines, what was there not to like? And after Daddy started getting ahead a little, we even got to see the movies occasionally. Momma liked Doris Day movies, but Daddy and I liked the westerns. That fall, Momma got hired to teach English at the county high school, and then we actually were doing better than we had ever done before. We certainly weren't rich, but we did not have to scrape by anymore. Daddy even traded in the old truck for a newer although still a used one at the Ford dealership in Marion.

We took the new truck and went back to see Grandma Boudreaux and Daddy's cousins, and they made the usual wonderful fuss over us all. This time, I had enough skill on the guitar to play along with the adults, although I quickly learned there was much I did not yet know. On the way home, we visited Grandpapa and Grandmama and picked up Momma's Chifforobe and dresser from where it had been in storage in my grandparents' barn. I went by and visited with Grandma Bailey and Fredrick one afternoon, too. It's a funny thing about old friends: it seems like we always pick up right where we left off. We were too big for the tire swing, but after sitting down with his grandmother for a bit, Fredrick and I just ambled around the Crackletown Road, saying hello to people and catching up with each other. I realized as we said goodbye just how much I missed his friendship.

The gaps between times I thought about Jessie May grew. When I thought about her, I still missed her, but I found that between doing odd jobs, fishing, swimming, reading and playing guitar, I just did not dwell on it as much. I've heard that you can't really remember pain. You can remember that you had pain, but you cannot remember the pain itself. Perhaps that is why everyone is not an only child since mothers don't remember how painful the childbirth was. But I think love is like that too. You can't really remember the feeling of love that you had, only that you were in love and that you liked it. It's only when you're in love you know what it feels like. Perhaps that was why I found it so easy to retreat into my own world. My parents thought that since I was just a child, my depth of emotion was not that great with Jessie. But I had a deep, deep crush on her, and she was my very best friend, my only friend, really, the entire time I had known her in Carmack. I was captivated by her laughter, by her view of the world, and by her beauty. There were many ladies in my life thereafter that I would believe myself to be in love with that never held all those levels of esteem for me. Was I too young to be in love?

I went to school at Tolu for the remainder of elementary school. Life became more settled as I became comfortable in my surroundings, and the years marched on. I went to school each morning after Momma took Daddy to work and went off to her teaching job. After several months of that, Momma got her own car, a white Buick Special. Momma really liked that car. She had never had her own car, and she babied that car like it was made of gold. I liked it too. It was far more comfortable than even Dad's new pickup truck. But I still walked to school. It was only a couple of blocks. Sometimes, I would take my lunch money and go to Tyner's Market and buy a bologna and cheese sandwich on white bread, a bottle of RC Cola, and a small bag of salted peanuts. Then I would go across the road to the small knoll and sit in the shade and have lunch with other students who did the same thing. We didn't sneak off from school. It was an option instead of the cafeteria. By the time I was in the eighth grade, I knew all the kids. There was still a sense that I was the new kid, even though I had been there for years, but they did at least talk to me. It helped that with Momma and Daddy both working, we were able to get me the clothes that helped me fit in. Yes, I sought out bleeding madras shirts, and I wore bass weejuns and white jeans. Fitting in was all I aspired to at the time. Momma could not understand buying a shirt that you knew the dye would bleed on. It made no sense. And we were able to get a new radio. We had not had a radio since Loreauville. I listened to WLS out of Chicago late into the night, when its signal was stronger, and kept up with all the music. I liked Motown most, but the British invasion was also influential on me and my direction in guitar. I had practiced for years playing rhythm guitar and fingerpicking tunes. I liked to slap strum now and then but listening to the radio made me want to add lead guitar to my skills. It was a little hard to do with my Gibson, at least the way the songs on the radio sounded. I received a small phonograph for one of the Christmases and bought and hoarded records. I spent hours playing and replaying songs, copying the lead riffs on my guitar. Sometimes, I found myself adding some extra fingering to the leads, since I didn't have any other musicians with me, and I found I could add another line to the riff if I hammered on the frets while I was playing the lead, although I didn't know exactly how it sounded without an audience besides Momma and Daddy. Daddy said I was getting better than he was and he couldn't teach me much more, but I think he was being nice.

One Saturday in the summer, Daddy said he wanted to take me to meet a man. We drove until we got to a bigger city an hour and half away and went to a clothing store in the downtown. The place was packed with used clothes, piles of suits, jeans, coats, shirts, all tossed on tables without any order that I could discern reaching up past where I could possibly reach. There were lots of young people there buying old army jackets and vintage clothes. The anti-Vietnam War movement was strong and, somehow, old army coats and such were a part of the attire for that movement. I liked the idea of maybe being ahead of the pack in fashion than my classmates for a change and started to look around, but Daddy put his hand on my shoulder.

"That's not why we're here, Silas." He turned and led me towards the back room. There in an office not much bigger than a closet was a huge man, darker even than Grandma Bailey, smiling and talking to all these young people who had come by the store and were crammed into this little office with him. It was as if he was holding audience. When Daddy and I walked in, he gave Daddy a nod, as if he knew him. The man was really big, a good foot taller than Daddy and twice his weight. He would listen to the young people talk, mostly guys a little older than me, in their late teens and early twenties with long hair and wearing vintage clothes. He would nod his head, then give his take on whatever they had asked about, much of it about music, but also about old times and his days on the road with a blues band back when there were separate clubs for white people and for people of color. There was one kid a few years older than me who sat right at his elbow, tall, skinny, with dark hair and piercing eyes, who hung on every word the man said. The tall skinny kid was leaning on a guitar, and I wondered why Daddy thought I should meet this other boy who played guitar. What could I learn from him? Then the kid started playing his guitar, trying to employ some technique the big man had just described. He was scary good. He played guitar like I wanted to play but had not figured out how to. Everybody got quiet when he played, and the big man nodded his head in time and tapped his huge foot, at one point correcting something he had heard amiss.

"No. No. Take the bottom, drop it out, Bobby, you play the top, then you say, 'Boom!'" Then the other young people, there must have been seven or eight of them, started imploring the big guy to play.

"Come on, CD. Play something."

"Show us how it's supposed to sound."

CD grinned, seeming like he had been waiting for this moment, and pulled out an old National steel body Resonator guitar. I had never seen such an instrument. It was gorgeous and gave out a loud, reverberating sound when he played.

"Now, y'all, this is how you swing them blues so's people can dance to it. Now watch." He played mainly with his thumb to fret chords and play leads. He had tuned his guitar different from the usual. The sound mesmerized me. It was like Grandma Bailey's music, but this had a steadier if languid beat. While he was playing the short lesson he was teaching, Bobby retuned his guitar to match CD's, and he started picking up on the melody CD was playing, but with a different chord line. The two of them sounded like a whole band to me. I could not believe what I was hearing. It was beautiful, sad, rhythmic, lilting, funky. I stared at the two guitarists. The Resonator sounded like CD was playing in a cave, the notes folding up on top of each other. I guess I was sitting there with my jaw dropped because, at the end of the melody, CD looked at me and started laughing.

"So, Benoit, your boy looks like he's seen a haint or something."

Daddy gave a chuckle. "He's never seen a resonator before. I think he thinks it's from Mars, maybe." I gathered myself together enough to flash a sheepish grin. Bobby was putting away his guitar, and a couple of the other fellows were leaving too. "CD, this is my son, Silas."

"Pleased to make your acquaintance, Silas." I put my hand out, and it was enveloped in the man's mammoth paw. "You like this piece, huh?" CD rested his massive body on the instrument. "This old guitar has seen a lot, Silas. Oh yes. Her name is Marie. Old CD used to play in every juke joint from Cincinnati to Memphis, and Old Marie has been with me every step of the way. She was much in demand. Lots of those places didn't have amplifiers or things like that, so I had to use Marie to be heard above the drums and the piano and all. Yeah, Marie was always faithful to me. Except in '37 when there was the big flood. Then Marie went sailing down the Ohio without me. I came home, and everything we owned had washed away in the flood, but the worst was losing Marie. I pined and mourned for her for weeks. Then, this fellow in Evansville I knew found it and he knew it was mine and brought it back to me. Everybody knew me and Marie belonged together. Sweet Marie, back in my arms again." He shook his head with delight. He said the last line almost like it was a song. Daddy shot me a look as if to say he wasn't sure we weren't being shined on, but I didn't care. It was a great story. I left more determined than ever to get better at guitar. I wanted to try the Resonator out, but CD did not let go of it.

That last year at Tolu, I did try to develop a passing interest in one of the girls in my class. I knew there was going to be a dance later in the year and I decided I might just try to find a new girl, although she could not replace Jessie. The girl I decided on was pretty though, long blonde hair and a freckly face that I found cute, but I guess I was still the new kid. I talked with her after school one day until her bus arrived to take her off to her home, but she didn't seem at all interested. I tried and I tried to thaw her icy attitude, but it was like the sun shining on a freezing day. Some of the ice went away, but there was no melting. I could see I was getting nowhere and went on home. If that last year at Tolu passed ever more slowly because of it, the next year, when I went to the high school in Marion, would make up for it. My life was about to shift gears. I was about to be reunited with Jessie May.

# The Tetravalence of Jessie May

## Fire

# Chapter 11

Attending the consolidated high school in Marion was a whole new world for me. First of all, it was by far the largest school I had ever attended, although it wasn't huge by most standards. But the schools I had attended before had maybe twenty-five or thirty kids in the entire school. I had three times that just in my grade. We were all put into tracks based upon test scores, so I was in the highest English class but a lower math class. I had improved in my math, but I just didn't care about solving for x. We had some options as well, and I took Mr. Carter's shop class, figuring that having been around the best mechanic in the country all my life, something would have rubbed off on me. It wasn't actually so, of course. Daddy liked fixing things. I was far too distracted by girls, guitars, and novels, pretty much in that order. Besides, Daddy just knew how to make things. I didn't, and going through puberty made me impatient and restless. Still, I liked the smell of the shop class with its mixture of sawdust and oil.

There was also something about going to high school rather than elementary school that let me plow new fields. For one thing, I wasn't the only new kid. We were all new kids, of a sort. And I knew my former classmates from Tolu and a few of the kids who had moved from between the rivers, so I had some grounding already, and we were all seeking to define our space in the bigger setting. But we were immediately the little guys at school too. One of the first former acquaintances I ran into was Joey Simmons, who acted like we were old buddies when I saw him getting off the bus in front of the school. I still didn't like him of course: he would have killed Argos if I had not stepped in and that was a crime I thought I would never forgive. But I did let him think we were friends if only so we would not have to fight again. In fact, I had my Daddy's Cajun stature, thin, sinewy, and not very tall. With my dark hair and olive skin, you might have thought I was from another world compared to my fellow students at Crittenden High. Meanwhile, Joey had kept growing and was already trying out for the varsity football team in the ninth grade. He was a solid young man. I decided it was fine if he believed we were old chums.

When I ran into Jessie, the world stopped turning normally for a moment. Instead of the world keeping its usual path, it suddenly started rotation horizontally around Jessie May. When I saw her the first day of school, we were in the cafeteria. She was surrounded by a gaggle of boys and girls who buzzed around her like drones attending the queen. The cafeteria was a cacophony of teenaged voices, thin metal cutlery, and plastic trays. I was looking for a place to sit, seeking mainly a moment of quiet when there she was. I stopped in the middle of the room, my tray in one hand, my glass in the other. I stopped dead still and gazed. I don't know what I thought the intervening years would do to my Jessie May, but they had been beyond kind to her. Her hair was still curly, but longer now so that ringlets of her acorn-colored hair dangled around her shoulders. She had on a teal dress with a red belt, and she had developed curves where there had been none before. Kids behind me pushed me aside so they could find a seat and jostled me out of my torpor. I moved towards a long chrome-legged table, the end of which was empty to put my tray down. The swirl of the pack of classmates surrounding Jessie kept her attention for the moment. The clanking of utensils and plastic trays faded into a distant backdrop. She laughingly joked with the kids, and they laughed as if she had said the most incredible thing. I wanted to go sit with her, but I didn't want all those courtiers there, and, to be honest, I feared very deeply she had moved into a world where she no longer saw me in the same light. She seemed to be the high priestess and I the hanged man. I set my tray down, still looking over at Jessie, when, somehow between the flurry of attendants, Jessie saw me and her eyes blazed azure, and her face broke into the most magnificent smile I had ever encountered. It was incandescent. She stood up slowly, and the crowd of kids fell silent for a second and traced her line of vision over to me.

"Silas," Jessie called out to me. Her voice had grown breathier. "Silas LaMontaie?" It was almost like she could not believe she saw me. I could feel my face blush. In fact, I felt the warmth go through my entire body.

"Hi, Jessie," I managed to croak. She swung her legs over and stepped over the bench seat, picking up her tray. A girl sitting next to her jumped up abruptly.

"I'm taking mine, Jessie May. Want me to take yours?" The girl was nearly snatching it from her hands.

Jessie looked at her for a moment, confused by the sudden action, then she let go of the tray and came over to where I was sitting. "Silas. I didn't know you were coming here." She sat next to me on the bench seat, facing outwards. I twisted around on the bench to face her. My tuna noodle casserole and canned apricot halves did not hold my attention.

"Yeah. I've been in Tolu." I shrugged.

"Tolu? Why, that's not that far away at all, is it?" The breathiness of her voice made every sentence sound like she was excited to say it. And that made me excited to hear it. The other students she had been sitting with passed by with their trays, eyeing me closely, wondering, perhaps, who was this kid who garnered her attention when they had been so faithfully circling the flame before I arrived. One boy, tall and blond, gave me the skunk eye as he walked by. I didn't care. "I can't believe we've never run into each other these past years."

"I don't know. Guess we just didn't get out that much." I was trying to gather control of myself. We had gotten out plenty. I don't know why I said that. "How's Cliff?" I wanted to turn the conversation.

"Oh, Cliff is great. He's a senior this year, you know." Jessie swung her head as she looked out across the cafeteria, and her hair bounced around her shoulders. She looked back at me. "He's captain of the football team. Plays fullback." She nodded. That did make sense. He had always been a stout kid.

"Edward?"

"Oh, Ed. He's in the marines now. And he wants to be called 'Ed' now, by the way. He's off fighting a war." She nodded again. "What have you been doing all this time, Silas?" The glow from her face was nearly iridescent. I stumbled again, looking for words that would have been easy five minutes ago. "Still reading?"

"Oh, yeah, sure." I nodded.

"Still playing that guitar?" That was a bit coyer.

"Oh, yeah. I play a lot, really." I was happy to have something to say to Jessie. I nodded enthusiastically. "In fact, I wrote you a song." As soon as I said it, my face flushed again. I could feel it. I know she saw it too. I actually did not mean to confess that; it just sort of popped out. I knew what was coming next.

"Did you?" She cocked her head to one side. "Sing it for me."

My armpits grew moist, and my hands were clammy. "Here? Now?"

"Why not?" Her voice was soft and clear.

"Well, I need my guitar." I shrugged. A bead of sweat formed on my forehead.

"Oh." She was visibly disappointed, looking down at the floor. Then she looked up again brightly. "Bring your guitar tomorrow?"

"Sure." Again, I have no idea why I agreed to do that. I was speaking in tongues, perhaps, possessed by the spirit that was Jessie May. I was immediately taken back to when we first started being friends, how she could turn from sad into ebullient on a moment's notice. It was both endearing and unnerving, leaving me completely at the mercy of whatever she had in mind.

Jessie stood now and leaned over and said into my ear. "See you tomorrow, Sy." She straightened, shot me a wry grin, and bounced off. At the doorway was the tall blond-headed boy, waiting for her. I couldn't help but think that whisper into my ear was for his benefit. I turned back around and looked at my tray, and the bell rang, signaling the end of lunch. I skewered an apricot and shoved it in my mouth, placed my tray on the huge pile of lunch trays in the window, and went off to civics class.

Daddy let me borrow his guitar case, and I loaded up my Gibson. Neither he nor Momma was sure about this plan, worrying no doubt about the well-being of both me and the guitar, but I feigned self-assurance and headed to school with Momma, my guitar in the back seat.

Momma had to get to school early as a teacher, so I was always one of the first students at school. I found a folding metal chair leaning up against the row of lockers in the hallway and set it up outside the gym in the parking lot where the other kids gathered to smoke. I pulled out my guitar, tuning it carefully. My stomach was tied in a dozen knots. I didn't know exactly where I would be presenting my song to Jessie, but I wanted to be ready. A few other students arrived, awkwardly smoking cigarettes, and set up a semicircle around me. They waited for me to play something, urged me on, and peppered me with questions.

"What can you play?"

"Where are you from?"

"Come on, play something for us."

"Can you play 'Louie Louie'?"

"Play us something."

I figured a little loosening up wouldn't hurt so I played "Walk Away Renee" using a combination of slap strum and hammer notes. I missed a few notes, but I didn't let on, and I suspect no one noticed. I did not sing, however. After I finished, the kids around me clapped and murmured approval. Then I realized Jessie was standing there with them with the tall blond boy next to her. She was smoking a Virginia Slim cigarette and grinning at me between draws and exhales. "Oooh!" She yelled when I finished, throwing her right hand with the cigarette in it up over her head in a victory stance. "Oooh!" She pushed her way past the other kids. "Go, Silas!" The boy with her made his way forward too, and he was clapping, but he looked dubious. "What else you got?" She let out a long stream of smoke and dropped her cigarette to the blacktop. The entire area was a designated smoking spot and carried a stale cigarette smell at all times. I looked up at her, standing right in front of me now. She was wearing a navy-blue skirt that did not quite come to her knees and a white blouse. She was also wearing the blue ribbons I had given her, and I nearly melted on the spot. "Got anything you wrote yourself?" Her eyes were filled with mischief. She reached into her purse and pulled out another cigarette. The blond fumbled in his pocket a moment, pulled out a lighter, and lit it for her.

"Yeah, I have something you might like." The crowd had grown some now to maybe fifteen. I saw Joey Simmons in the pack as well as the freckled faced girl from Tolu, but I paid them no attention. I thought about how Grandma Bailey had said I was made to be a singer, so I broke into my song about Jessie, finger-picking slowly in the key of D. I played a few notes, then said, "This one is called 'Sitting on the Steps'." That really was only half the title, but I didn't want to give it away.

"Been fishing in the bayou.
Picked peanuts from red clay.
Fished along the muddy river bend.
Listened to the katydids.
Flipping skipping stones.
Dragonflies a-dancing in the wind.

"I walked along a gravel road while rain washed cares away,
Wishing I could change the things what may.
But nothing quite prepared me
For the day I sat alone,
Sitting on the steps with Jessie May.

"Living in a tin shack
Sleeping on the straw
Sitting all alone on a log.
Waiting for the sunshine
On a cold hard winters night,
No one there to love me but my dog.

"I've been around long enough to know you can't go back
And try to change all the things what may.
But nothing quite prepared me,
For knowing I would never
Sit again on steps with Jessie May.

"Say goodbye.
Say goodbye.
Say goodbye on the steps with Jessie May.
Say goodbye.
Say goodbye.
Alone on the steps with Jessie May".

When I finished, I looked up at Jessie, and her eyes were open wide and filled with water, although they again did not spill. The boy who had been with her the whole time was red-faced, and I think he would've come at me, but Joey saw him too and stepped between us and simply gave him a look. The rest of the kids were quiet at first, then started talking in low voices and drifting away. The tall boy bit his lip. He clearly wanted me. Jessie pulled his arm back. "Oh, Donnie, stop it. Silas is my brother from different parents. Don't be acting so silly." Then she looked down at me, sitting on the metal chair. "That's a very nice song, Silas. I love it. Maybe someday you can make a million bucks on it." Then she giggled and led Donnie away, but before she turned the corner of the building, she shot me a look, one like the looks she gave me back between the rivers, genuine and tender. The bell rang, and I hurriedly put away my guitar and hustled off to English class. *Lord of the Flies* was up for today's lesson. My knees were still shaking when I went inside, but I had done it. I had sung my song for Jessie May.

The autumn was a succession of high school football games, school dances, cruising through The Dip, and impromptu concerts. I confess I did not know all that much about football. We, of course, had a television and could watch sporting events on it, but my attention had been intermittent on the game itself. I watched on television now so I would know what was going on, but it soon became apparent that if I thought that would rekindle everything with Jessie by being knowledgeable about football, I was wrong. It's true she went to all the games, surrounded by an entourage that was mesmerized by her every word. She would laugh and throw out some witticism, and everyone would convulse in laughter. But she rarely paid attention to the game itself. I was happy that I knew more about the game, however, since I was relegated to sitting three rows below Jessie, far from those who had her immediate attention. By understanding the game, I at least could focus on what was happening on the field and be entertained by that, the chilly autumn air, the yellow stadium lights, and the smell of hotdogs from the concession stand behind the bleachers. I soon grew tired of trying to move up the bleachers to be able to talk to Jessie. That was the process it seemed. If you fell into her graces, Jessie May would invite you to move up closer, to the row directly at her feet, and, if you were truly in her good stead, alongside her on the same level. I don't want to imply that Jessie was haughty. She wasn't. She was just the one girl everyone wanted to be around. Still, I confess, it put me off some, and I stopped going to the games. It took a couple of games for her to even notice I was not there. I decided it was time I find someone else to focus my attentions on.

Her name was Susan, and she was in my homeroom class. She was cute enough, with short brown hair and dark eyes. She dressed stylishly, and she carried herself with self-confidence. She was no Jessie May, of course, although she didn't know that. In fact, I never met anyone who described herself in more glowing terms. But then, I never met anyone with such blurry vision. Nonetheless, she was there, and the homecoming dance was approaching, and I wanted to go, so I went up to her desk before the first bell rang one day.

"Hi, Susan." I tried to be nonchalant as if I happened to be passing her desk on the way to mine, although my desk was on the other side of the classroom and near the front. It was a sorry ruse.

"Hi, Silas." Susan blinked her eyes at me. She had witnessed this scene before, starred in it, in fact.

"So." I swung my arms awkwardly. "Would you want to go to homecoming with me?" Now I knew she had set herself to go with Jimmy, but I also knew Jimmy wanted to take Kay. Ninth grade society was always hierarchical.

"Oh, well, I don't know. Um, . . ." She looked around at her friends who sat near her but let herself peer over to Jimmy who even now was leaning across his desk solicitously towards Kay in front of him, who giggled just then. Susan sized it up pretty quickly. "Yeah, why not?" Now it wasn't exactly a resounding yes, I will admit, but it was better than "No."

"Great. Pick you up at 6:00?" I watched television, so I knew the banter. I did not, however, drive. But I would figure out the details later. Better to be nonchalant cool at this point.

"You going to write a song for me, too, Silas?" She returned to her eyelash batting.

"You never know." Then I walked away.

When word got around that Susan and I were going to the dance together, and the ninth grade rumor line being faster than the local paper in sharing the latest news, my status changed in ways I had not expected. Suddenly, I was part of a "couple," although we were only going to a dance together. When Jessie heard about it, she stopped me in the hallway and stared at me rather fiercely. It was a rare time she had no traveling sideshow around her. "I think you and Susan make a cute couple, Sy." Her tone was a bit more accusatory than congratulatory. She was baiting me.

I shrugged. "Just going to the dance."

"I heard you were writing her a song, too." It was the first time I ever saw Jessie jealous. I took a certain pleasure from it. Jessie May, who was said to have multiple dates on the same day with different boys, the boys passing each other on the sidewalk in front of the May's house, was jealous of the attention I showed Susan.

"You never know." I walked on and gave myself a little smile.

The dance came and went. Momma drove me, and we picked up Susan, and then Momma picked us up after the dance and took us back home. If it wasn't exactly the dashing approach James Bond would take, it would have to do. It turned out, I was actually pretty good at dancing, Daddy's impromptu lesson before we left having helped tremendously. Susan was an enthusiastic dancer who seemed to know every move ever done on *American Bandstand*. We had fun, laughing and dancing and talking. I liked her. I decided maybe we could do some other things together if she wanted to as well, and she agreed. At that point, we did become a neophytic couple, although I was pretty green at the entire process of being a couple. When we dropped her off at her house, Momma had to give me a nudge to remind me to walk her up to the front door of her house.

Susan and I being a couple lasted about two weeks. As it turned out, Kay actually had a crush on a boy from the tenth grade who finally asked her out, so Kay and Jimmy were no longer an item. As a result, Jimmy asked out Susan, who immediately said yes and then let it be known to me through the rumor mill by friends that I had been "dropped." That was the word that was used. "Dropped." I suppose I should have been upset, but in truth, it was so convoluted, I had to be mildly amused. Oh, it stung a little bit, but not enough to send me in some kind of spiral. Only one girl had the power to do that, and she was keeping busy.

Jessie was always on the go, and everyone kept up with her escapades as if she were a pop star. She went out with juniors and smoked cigars and drank gulps of whiskey from bottles in brown paper bags. She went with Cliff and his friends over to Mexico, Kentucky, to the fluorspar mine and collected blue crystals, even though the place was supposed to be dangerous and off limits. In fact, what Jessie seemed to like the most was taking dares. It's true she cultivated a following of kids who seemed to idolize her, but their worship was not so much nurtured by Jessie as it was by the other kids' envy of Jessie's lifestyle. She did all the things no one was supposed to do, but they wanted to do, if only once. And she was doing them as rapidly as if she thought there was a schedule and she was late.

Jessie soon dropped Donnie in favor of an angular junior named Hank, who had a certain swagger about him, due primarily to his having a black Oldsmobile 442 with a shiny Hurst shifter that he loved to drive fast down back roads throughout the county. And Jessie loved the fast lane. Donnie had the temerity to come up and ask me to teach him to play the guitar. I figure he thought that was his ticket back to Jessie.

"You have a guitar?" I asked him.

"No. But I can get one."

I figured his interest was only passing. "Well, it takes time. And a lot of practice. A lot of practice."

His gaze dropped to the floor. His desire was a quick fix. "Oh."

"You know, anyone can build a raft. That doesn't mean they can cross the river." It was a saying Grandpapa had taught me that I only understood completely that moment. And I think Donnie got it too.

My guitar playing made me something of a novelty at school now. I didn't take my guitar every day. I was too worried about breaking it or something, but when I did take it, the other students clamored around me, shouting out songs to play. I found I liked the attention, although all the yelling of suggestions was disconcerting. I found it hard to focus on just what they were asking for sometimes. It was like when I went out fishing on a jon boat on Hurricane Creek in the summertime, and I would start to get hot, and the black flies would start buzzing my head. All the swatting and waving I would try to do never slowed the flies down a bit; they just kept buzzing me. Everyone yelling song titles at me felt a whole lot like a black fly swarm. Instead, usually, I just played what I had been working on at home, and they generally liked that. I did sing more now with my playing, although my voice still had a tendency to crack at times. There were songs by British groups and a few Motown songs, but I found myself drawn more and more to blues songs, which most of the other kids at school did not know. I liked the rhythm of the songs, and they suited my style of guitar playing as well. And they reminded me of Grandma Bailey. While I didn't play them in public, I continued writing songs of my own too, jotting down lyrics on the back of returned homework and loose-leaf notebook pages and once, when a phrase came to me suddenly, and I did not want to lose it, on the inside cover of a novel I was reading, *Of Mice and Men*. It was the beginning of another song about Jessie, although I decided this time to keep her name out of it so it might be about anyone. Of course, I would always know better.

# Chapter 12

When I turned sixteen, I could not wait to drive. Dad taught me on a manual transmission, but I already had the knack of the rhythm of it all, since Dad never had an automatic transmission in his life to that point. I knew the concept pretty well. I practiced driving to school with Momma in her Buick, which was an automatic, and Dad would let me drive him down the back roads around Tolu and down through Sheridan and even down to Levias. With Dad, we always took his truck, with the windows rolled down and the galoshes he wore for work wedged between the truck cab and the top of the truck bed and Argos in the back, looking into the wind, his tongue out. I had to be careful since the roads were twisty and we often came across horse-drawn carts along the country roads. I learned to parallel park along the streets of Salem and Marion. I passed my test easily. Of course, I still did not have a car of my own, but Momma often let me use her Buick after school after I dropped her off.

I landed a job as a stock clerk at the Sureway to pay for my gas and to make myself a bit more independent. I saw pretty much everyone in town at the Sureway, from teachers to Miss Scott the librarian to even Susan, my brief experience-with-being-a-couple back in ninth grade. In fact, I seemed to see Susan more often than I expected to since I wouldn't have anticipated her to shop for groceries that often. The first time I saw Susan, she was with some of her girlfriends, and they all giggled as if they had never seen someone load cans of lima beans on a metal shelf before. After that, she would occasionally saunter into the store with Jane Powers, her best friend, and no matter what task I had been assigned to, she would end up on that aisle, shopping, comparing prices, picking up the box of raisins or the jar of bean salad, turning it in her hand and perhaps discussing it with Jane, before seeing me and saying, "Oh, Hi, Silas!" as if she had no clue I would be in the store. I admit I liked seeing her there. She was always friendly to me, and I don't think she had a crush on Jimmy anymore. I think it may have been my uniform, a green full-length apron with a plastic badge on it that told my name. Perhaps not. In any case, we started dating some, although I did not consider us as "going steady." We went to some dances, and occasionally she would ride with me to a football or basketball game. We had been out often enough that we did do some kissing in a spot behind a barn we found off Aunt Jane Tabernacle Road, but nothing more.

I started hanging out with a couple of guys from my class too, after school, when I had gone home first and taken care of Argos. I would go home, feed him and water him, throw a stick for him to retrieve for a bit until he grew tired, which seemed to take less and less time. Then I would borrow Momma's car and drive over to Mark Cason's house, and we would cruise The Dip for a few hours before I had to go back home to complete my chores and do my homework. Mark was interested in music also, which is why we became friends, I guess. He played piano, having taken lessons from an older woman in Marion for much his life. She had him play more classical stuff, sitting very upright with his hands held just so above the piano keys. The music was very interesting and complicated, and Mark was fairly good at it, but he had taken more interest in popular music as well, figuring out how to play rock-and-roll the way I did, by listening to the songs and imitating the melodies and adding harmonies, and he was very good at that. He had the advantage of knowing the theory behind the music as well as the practice of playing. He could pick out the chords to a song from the radio in one listening. We played songs together at his house, and he helped me fill out some of the songs I had written, showing me how the harmonies worked and how to always find a minor chord and how to make a sixth chord. We were going to start a band and spent considerable time discussing various names for our someday band. Because of my Cajun heritage, I leaned towards something kind of "French-y" like The Lagniappes, but Mark was more into the experimental groups and wanted to be called Celestial Underworld. I thought that was too mysterious for what I wanted to play, which was softer, more acoustic than electric. As it turned out, they were idle discussions since we never did form an actual band together.

I was with Mark at The Dip when I heard the news. Momma had laundry to wash and hang in the back yard, so she let me take the car to go cruising. Despite the various places we had lived, and the sometimes difficult times my family had endured, I never knew just how insulated my life had been up to that point. I had even dared to see myself as somewhat worldly, compared to my classmates, many of whom had never lived anywhere other than Crittenden County, but that vision of myself was washed away in one quick sentence that Joey Simmons said. I was sitting at The Dip with Mark, discussing what other instruments we would need for our band, when Joey walked up. He looked like he had been punched in the stomach or something when he leaned over into the driver's side window of Momma's Buick and looked me in the eye and said, "Did you hear? Edward May was killed in Viet Nam. They just found out today." He blinked. His eyes were beet red around the edges. For the briefest of moments, I wondered if it was some sort of sick joke Joey was pulling. Or perhaps, I only wished it were so. My stomach churned. He kept looking at me but now with an unfocused gaze, looking somewhere ten yards behind me.

Mark leaned over and said to Joey, "Who is that? Is that Jessie's brother?" Joey stood and walked away. Then Mark looked at me. "Is that. . . ?"

"Yes." I started the car and drove off fast. I drove too fast, and I didn't speak. I couldn't speak. My throat was as tight as a knot.

Mark was confused. "Where are we . . ." I pulled up in front of his house.

"I have to go, Mark." I looked at Mark, and I'm guessing my face spoke volumes. He got out of the car and didn't say another word. I drove home and walked into the house and started crying. I leaned against the living room wall and let gravity drag me down to the floor where I sat and bawled. How could this be real? Edward? I kept seeing Ed, teaching Jessie and me how to climb the mulberry tree behind the Carmack church. I pictured him teaching me how to fight. I remembered how he smiled at Jessie so big, I could just tell he adored his little sister. I saw him letting her walk up his legs and onto his chest while he held her hands, and then she would flip off his chest while he held her. They called it Skinning the Cat. Jessie loved it. The more I thought of all of it, the more I cried. The concept of Edward being gone was overwhelming. Argos came over and put his chin on my knee and didn't move.

Momma came in the back door with a basket of clothes the same time Dad came in the front door. I looked back and forth at both of them and cried some more. Dad made a motion to Momma, who was standing there, frozen, trying to figure out what was wrong, I'm sure. The two of them went into the kitchen, and Dad whispered to Momma, and they were both quiet for a moment. Then they came back into the living room. I had found a lull in my crying.

Dad reached his hand down, and I took it. He helped me up. "It's awful, Sy. It's just awful. I'm so sorry. Sorry for you, that you lost someone you admired so much, and very sorry for the Mays, who have had their world wrecked." He pulled me into his chest and hugged me. We watched the news. We had seen the war correspondence about Viet Nam, but it still somehow seemed like it was happening on a different planet. We saw no evidence of anything like war in our little world. "Silas, I'm so very sorry." Dad hugged me close, and I felt wrapped in his embrace. Then he pulled back and looked at me, his hands still on my shoulders. "Are you okay?" I nodded. "How is Jessie?"

"I don't know." I choked on the words. I sounded like I was ten, my voice cracking and unsure.

Dad set his mouth in a straight line. "Think you should find out?"

"But I don't know what . . ."

"You'll figure it out as you go, Silas. You can't fix it. But you can be there for her."

"But what can I do?" I shrugged.

"Silas, even the slightest breeze can move a tree. Just be there. If you're hurting this much, try to imagine how she feels."

I could not even begin to imagine how she felt, but I knew it was terrible. I nodded, turned, went back out and got into the Buick and drove over to the Mays' house. There were cars parked everywhere. Some people were standing around outside in small groups, huddled against the news of untimely death. I got out of the car and started walking towards the house.

"Silas!" Jessie came around the side of the house at a full sprint. She wore a face of confusion, deep sorrow, and anger. She was still wearing the flowered dress she had worn to school that day. She had no shoes on though. I stopped walking, and she ran straight into me and threw herself around me in a desperate hug. I held her for a long time. She sobbed onto my shoulder and held me so tightly, I could not see her face. Some of the people in the groups standing around watched for a few moments, then they turned back around, letting her cry, and letting me hold her. She finally ran out of snuffles for a few minutes and pulled back from me enough to look at me. Her face was streaked with tears, and her hair was matted from the heat of her despair. I saw the same Jessie who had thrown a dirt clod hard enough to bloody the noses of both Joey and Tommy, and if I could have, I would have taken on the world right then to make her not feel the pain she felt. At that moment, my self-sorrow disappeared, and I wanted to make Jessie feel better, somehow.

"Thank you, Sy. Thank you." She started tearing up again and lay her head on my chest. "They took Edward from me, Silas. They took him. It's just not right. They killed my brother. Why did they kill him, Silas?"

"I don't know, Jessie. I don't know." I held her close to me, wishing my hugs could erase her pain. She sobbed again deeply, then she caught her breath and shuddered, trying to gather something inside of her.

I saw Mr. May limp slowly out the screen door of their house and onto the porch. He looked just awful. His arms drooped at his sides, and his entire body was slumped, like a man who had taken the worst beating a man could take. "Jessie?" His usual commanding voice was faint, defeated.

"I'm okay, Daddy. Silas is here. My Silas is here." She turned to look at her father and patted my chest with one hand. Mr. May nodded at me, and I saw a glimmer of gratitude in his eyes. He shuffled stiffly back inside the house.

"Do you want to go inside, Jessie?" I looked down into her face.

"No. No, I can't stand it in there. All those people. They mean well. It's just too much, though. I can't stand it. I can't take it anymore, Sy." She glanced around at the front porch again. Everyone had gone inside now. "Let's find someplace else. Can we? Can we, Silas?"

"Of course, Jessie. Of course." She pulled away from me and took my hand and started walking away. I let her lead me around the house, the direction she had run from, and we made our way back into the Mays' barn. We passed a gathering of cows, who raised their heads to watch us with blank stares. The air was thick with the smell of cows and hay and mud from the pond beyond the fence. The barn was grey and battered, but still very solid. We went inside, and Jessie climbed up the ladder to the loft, and I followed her. The floor of the barn had been bumpy with rocks and clumps of dirt, but in the loft, it was smooth wood with a scattering of hay. Rectangular bales were stacked neatly along the back wall and up to a side near the hay door.

Jessie found a clear place to sit in the middle of the loft, and she sat cross-legged, spreading her dress as she sat so that it furled out in a cascade of blue and green flowers and leaned back with her arms behind her. She reached for my hand and pulled me down to sit next to her. I held my knees up to my face, my arms folded to rest my chin. I watched her face the entire time. She looked then out the hay door toward the pond where the cattle were now wading. "Where did our childhood go? Everything is changed. Everything is different now. Sardis seems a million miles away now, doesn't it, Silas?" I nodded. It did seem like an entirely different lifetime to have only been a few years before. She folded her hands onto her lap. "Do you remember when we climbed up into Mr. Lady's barn that time?" She gazed out onto the field.

"I do." I followed her line of sight, but she wasn't looking at anything in particular, so I looked again at Jessie. "The first cutting was in. It was hot."

"It was. July maybe."

"Yeah. You had on cutoff blue jeans and a striped tee shirt."

Jessie whipped her head around, and a small smile came across her tear-stained face. "What? You actually remember what I was wearing?'

"Well, . . ."

"I can't believe you, Silas. Who would remember that?"

"I remember everything about that day, Jessie. I remember carrying Argos up the ladder, me handing him up the last part to you so I wouldn't drop him. I remember you lying on the floor, hay all around you, your hair spread out from your face like some kind of sepia painting."

"'Sepia painting'? Who are you, anyway, Silas LaMontaie?" Now her face changed. It was not the mischievous smile she wore so often at school, but a tender, soft smile. "You know what I remember, Silas?"

"What?"

"You wanted to kiss me so bad it hurt." She reached her hand out, and I took it, and she gave me a squeeze.

I nodded. "That is very true, Jessie. I didn't know you knew that."

"I did. But you were very chivalrous."

"Well, I was also afraid you'd beat me up."

"I might have." We fell silent a moment. She looked over at me. "Silas?"

"Yes?"

"Do you want to kiss me now?" Her smile was gone now, replaced by a face of earnestness. She looked like she wasn't sure what the answer would be. I had never known Jessie to have any self-doubt. She looked alone, frightened.

"I want to make you feel better, Jessie. I want to make the pain stop if I only knew how. I just want to be here for you." I reached over and brushed her hair back from her face. Her tears had dried. I pushed her hair back, and her penetrating eyes stared back at me.

"Silas?"

"Yes?"

"Kiss me?" She leaned forward, and I reached my arm around her shoulders and kissed her. I wanted my kiss to make her stop hurting, if only for a moment. It was a long, slow kiss, and it felt like neither of us wanted to let go of it. When we pulled apart enough to catch our breaths, she threw her arms around my neck, and we kissed again. We leaned backward onto the floor of the loft, our embrace unrelenting. Her lips were salty from crying. I kissed her cheeks where the tears had left a trail, because kissing the tears would make them stop, perhaps. I kissed by her ear, the ear that had heard the terrible news. And then I kissed her neck and then where her neck met her chest. She raised her head so I could reach her neck and chest and kiss away her awful aching. She pulled my shirt tail out and ran her hand up my back. Her touch sent a tingle up my spine. I pulled the zipper down the back of her dress and touched her back, her skin smooth and soft. She was lying on the floor of the loft, and I was leaning over her. I pulled back long enough to look at Jessie's face. She looked at me intently, her eyes so blue they almost hurt to look at. Then we made love, my Jessie and me. It was tender and slow, and I wanted her to feel how much I wanted her and how much I wanted to make her sorrow better, somehow. I think she did. When we were done, I lay flat on the floor of the loft, and she braced herself on her elbow to look at me.

She traced my jawline with her finger. "Silas?"

I turned my head to look at her. "Yes, Jessie?"

"You know you will always be my Silas, don't you?"

"Yes, I do. And I always will." There was a sense in which I saw her for the first time that instant. She was not a little girl, and I was not a little boy. Jessie was right. Somewhere in the intervening years, we had become different people than we had been. She was my Jessie, but she was grown. I was her Silas, but I was no child. I heard a car door somewhere in front of the house, and it reminded me we weren't in the absolutely most private place. I reached for my jeans and pulled them on, and Jessie sat up and straightened her hair. She pulled on her underwear and stood, smoothing out her dress. I also stood and zipped up the back of her dress. I pulled on my shoes, and we climbed back down the ladder in silence.

I walked her around the house, then she turned and looked up at me. "Silas, I need to go help my Mom and Daddy. They need me, and I need them too." She glanced towards the front door. "Thank you, Silas. Thank you for being here."

"Of course, Jessie." I looked into her face. I wondered if I should kiss her again but quickly dismissed the notion. "Always, Jessie. I am always your Silas."

She gave me a somewhat rueful smile, then turned and walked to the porch. I watched her walk away, again, and I realized that every time I watched her walk away, she stepped a little deeper into my heart.

# Chapter 13

After Edward May's funeral, Jessie was different. She was still as much a flame as she had been before, but the spark before had seemed to be focused inward. Now she seemed determined to use her energies outwardly. She still came across as a daredevil, but she also held a lot of anger. She was angry at her father for letting Edward go into the army, although I pointed out that Ed was making his own decision. She was mad at her mother for not standing up to both her father and her brother when the discussion had come up before about his enlistment. She was upset at our classmates for treating her with more deference after her brother died. I argued that they were just trying to be good friends, but she would have none of it. She said it made her into some sort of pity case. And she was livid about the whole Viet Nam war effort in general. That was the biggest change, I think. Jessie became very opposed to the war. She had not been exactly in favor of it. I don't think any of us were. We were simply disengaged. We just avoided thinking about it, I think, despite the reminders on the news every night about battles and about the protests across the country. But now we knew what the effect of war was and how real it all was, and Jessie embraced that knowledge as a clarion call to action. And I was with her for much of it. I also wanted to protest. In fact, my parents, even my Grandpapa, whom I spoke with on the phone when Momma called him on Sundays, thought the war was a huge mistake and that no one should be over there dying for it.

Our reading habits changed, as well. Jessie also loved books. We had always shared that. Now we shared a different reading list. We moved from classics and the occasional genre piece to the literature of the times: *Catch-22*, *Slaughterhouse 5*, *Johnny Got His Gun*, and *Night*, and pretty much anything that portrayed the horrors of war. I think facing the horrors was a first step for us. We had denied that reality far too long.

As protesters, we were surely lightweights. There was not much opportunity to protest much of anything in our small community, and, much as we had been before, most folks were trying hard to not see it, going about their daily lives as if no one was dying on the other side of the planet. But Jessie and I were determined, if inexperienced. For starters, we wanted to make some noise. We took a two-fold approach to being more visible. In the first place, we started speaking out at school about it, which was pretty safe, since virtually everyone was opposed to going over and fighting, and the army was drafting guys only slightly older than we were to go fight. But we spoke up in classes, making the injustice of it all a salient point in the discussion, whether the class was history, English, or even algebra. That last one was a stretch, but we found ways, such as the impossible numbers the American government released each week wherein ten U.S. troops died that week, a hundred fifty South Vietnamese troops, and four thousand six hundred and sixty-three North Vietnamese and Viet Cong had died. It obviously could not be true, we argued and was why the calculus of combat was flawed and evil. We even held a protest rally in the school parking lot once, although, again, it was an already converted crowd. But we didn't worry about that. And we made the Crittenden County Press with our protest, a photo of Jessie standing on the hood of Chuck Strong's Chevelle gracing the first page of section B with the headline: Local Students Strive to End War. We felt like we were raising awareness and gaining a few converts, in our own small way. At first, Jessie had been afraid her brother Cliff would have to go fight too since the draft was in full sway and they were doing away with college deferments, but the irony was that because of Edward's death, Cliff could not be drafted. As it turned out, he had received a football scholarship at a small college in Tennessee and was working on a degree in agriculture. He wanted to return to the family farm when he was done and take over from their father, who seemed to have lost a lot of steps since Edward's death. I don't think Jessie had any notion of returning to our little community once she busted out. She was far too combustible for small-town life.

Poor Don, her beau of some twenty minutes back in the ninth grade, seemed frozen by his once star-like quality of having been Jessie's boyfriend. He hung around and waited in every spot Jessie seemed to be. Finally, one time when we were at The Dip in Momma's Buick, and Don sauntered over in an awkwardly forced nonchalance and stood in front of our car, trying to look like he was interested in some goings on nearby, Jessie said, "I need to help Don, don't I?"

"Help him?" I picked out another French fry from the order we were splitting.

"Oh, just cut him free once and for all so he can get on with himself." She opened the door and climbed out. Don tried to act surprised to see her. "Don?" Jessie walked up to him.

"Oh, hi, Jessie. I didn't see you there." Don's fib was transparent.

"Don, did you know, you can catch a cat once, but not twice? Even a kitten will remember a trap once she's been in one. And if you try, odds are good you are going to shed some blood over it."

Don's jaw went slack. "What?"

"Don, you're a nice guy. I like you. But you need to stop worrying about me. I'm your friend, but that's all. Okay?"

It was odd to see Don's face. It was a mixture of disappointment and relief. He was quiet for a moment, looking at the ground. I thought he would pretend to not know what she was talking about, but instead, he looked back at her and found a wan smile. "I like being your friend, Jessie." Then he walked away towards his car.

Jessie came back to our now cold fries and settled into her seat. She sat there munching a moment, then looked out the window. "He's a good guy."

"Yeah." I dug into the bottom of the bag the food had come in and found one last crunchy French fry.

There was a second way we tried to stand out, which was to look the part. We, of course, had seen all the protests on television, and we wanted to wear the look. Even then, the irony of standing out by looking like every protester we saw on television was not lost on me. Jessie and I both let our hair grow out. Jessie's long, dark ringlets were of course stunning. I looked more like a poodle. Dad only smirked at my haircut, shaking his head and saying it was my decision, and Momma laughingly called me a "hippie" although in truth my hair was not all that long by counter-culture standards, if it was pretty shaggy by small-town Kentucky standards. One Saturday early in our senior year, Momma let me borrow her Buick and Jessie, and I went over to the used clothing store Dad, and I had visited before so we could get the old army clothes that were appropriate for the anti-war movement. It turned out, I was the one who ended up wearing the vintage clothing. Jessie instead had started wearing long flowing maxi dresses. They were still different than what most of the kids wore at the time, so they suited her desire to stand out. The dresses also had the effect of making her even more exotic. Still, we had permission to go to the city, so we took it. I put my guitar in the backseat in case CD was there with his resonator guitar, and off we went.

I picked up Jessie early for a Saturday. We took U.S. 60 through Morganfield and Henderson and got to the used clothing store early in the afternoon. Before when Dad and I had visited, the place was full of kids, but it was mostly empty now. We found CD in his office, sorting through a pile of old woolen suits. I stuck my head in first.

"Mr. CD?" Only my head was in the door.

"'Mr. CD'? Nope. No one here by that name. No, sir." He went on sorting. The suits were rumpled and threadbare. "Now, me? I go by just CD. No 'mister' for me, thank you." He was so large his presence occupied the entire office.

"Oh." I pulled Jessie with me, and we went inside. "Um, CD, this is my friend Jessie." Jessie came in and gave CD a smile and a nod. I could tell she was also struck by his size.

CD dropped the suit coat he had been inspecting and broke into a wide grin. "Jessie!" He said it as if he knew her already and was seeing her again after a long absence. He stood now and walked the few steps across the room and stuck his hand out. Jessie shook his hand. "Jessie, it is my honor to meet you." CD bowed slightly at the waist. Then he turned to me. "And remind me who you are, young man."

It had not occurred to me that having met him only the once he would have no clue who I was. He had made an indelible impression on me, but I was one of dozens and dozens of kids who came by the store. "Oh. Yeah. I'm Silas. Silas LaMontaie." I put my hand out, and he took it in his massive grasp. I fully expected my hand bones to be crushed by this man, but instead, his grasp was light, almost gentle.

"Silas." He seemed to be turning it over in his head. "Silas LaMontaie." Then his face lit up. "Oh. You're Benoit's boy, aren't you?"

"Yes, sir."

"Yes, yes, I remember you now." He turned and shuffled through the piles of clothes back to his chair. "What can I do for you kids today?" He sat heavily.

"Oh, we're just here to get some clothes, Mr., ...I mean, CD." Jessie spoke up. "Silas said he wanted me to meet you."

"Well, I'm glad about that. Yes, sir. I am. Clothes are on the tables in the front, folks. I wish I could tell you where things were, but no one knows. No one knows." He laughed.

"I was telling Jessie about your steel guitar . . ."

"Ah, my sweet Marie. Yes, everybody loves Marie." CD leaned back in his chair. "Marie is taking a nap right now. You kids find yourselves some clothes, and we'll see if she wants to wake up here directly, okay?"

"Okay." I pulled Jessie's hand, and we went out into the shop again. There were more long-haired kids around now, so we dove in, sifting through the piles of coats and shirts and pants. Some were army green, but there were all kinds of clothes there: gabardine slacks and pea coats that looked like they were made of hopsack. There were twill jackets and cotton work shirts. The pile was daunting, but also fun. We found an old army coat that was a bit too big for me but decided an exact fit was not likely in any case, especially since I weighed all of a hundred forty pounds at the time. We also found some green-grey BDU pants that looked like the previous owner had walked on the back cuff for several years and worn it to a frazzle. They too would be too large for my waist, but we picked up a web belt with a tarnished brass buckle that would let me essentially cinch the pants to whatever size I needed. I felt ready. I couldn't wait for school Monday. We took our treasures back to the office to pay, and CD was sitting there with his resonator guitar, smiling.

"You want to play?"

"Yes, sir. Let me get my guitar." I turned to go out to the Buick.

"I got a guitar." CD picked up Marie with both hands and held it out for me.

I turned and looked at the guitar then at him then back at the guitar. "Really?"

"Sure. It's tuned to open G already, so just bar the frets to make different chords." CD handed over his resonator. I took it and sat at the molded plastic chair next to CD. I was agog to simply be holding it. I strummed it once. It was a G all right, and it was loud, and it echoed. I fingerpicked a few notes, went up and down the neck some and strummed some. "Add a seventh right there on that last string, three up." I tried it, and it worked. "Yes, sir. You got it."

"How do I make a minor?"

"Well, that's a bit trickier. I use my thumb on these two strings and my other fingers on these like this." He pointed out what he was saying, but my hand was not nearly big enough to wrap my thumb around the neck of the guitar, so I flattened out my middle finger and stretched out my pinky to hit the top strings. "Deaden that one on the bottom." I strummed it and sure enough, had an A-minor. I liked the bluesy sound, so I picked my way through a slow, halting version of "Little Red Rooster" that I had heard on a Rolling Stones album, just to get the chords. CD watched me and nodded. I glanced up at Jessie, and her eyes were wide open as if she were surprised at my playing. I launched into the song for real, and I loved how it sounded. Even when I made little mistakes, which I did a lot, they still were on key, so they sounded okay. CD started clapping his hands, and then Jessie did. The door opened, and a couple of the young people from out in the store came in and then a few more. "Slide that note there, Silas LaMontaie. Slide up into the twelfth." I heard what he was saying and tried it the next time through. "Play it through, son." I kept on playing, and CD started singing with my playing. His voice was hoarse and gravelly, and he sang like he meant it. We did the call and response, and then I slid up into the twelfth and CD nodded approval. When we were done with the song, everyone in the room clapped, including Jessie and CD. CD gave me a huge grin as I handed Marie back to him. "You've got talent, young man. You've got real talent."

"You really think so?" My parents had told me for a long time I was good at playing guitar, and my classmates had bragged on me, but I confess I thought the former might be biased towards me and the latter perhaps had too few to compare me to. Having CD say I was good made my head spin a bit.

"Oh, yeah. I know about music. Boy can play a guitar. Yes sir, boy can play."

I turned to leave, my head swollen by praise. "Wait." I stopped at the doorway. "How do you know my Dad?"

CD shot me a grin. "Not only young people want to see Sweet Marie, Silas LaMontaie. Your Daddy has played her too. I know where you got your chops, son. CD knows your chops."

We left with my new clothes and my sense of achievement and my curiosity all loaded into the Buick and drove back towards Marion. All Jessie could talk about was my guitar playing, how much she liked it, but my mind kept going back to CD saying he thought I had talent and that Dad had actually been there before me.

Regarding the time in the loft, Jessie and I did not talk about later. I did catch her giving me a look across the hallway at school sometimes over the following months and years, a look of closeness and femininity that sent a thrill through me, and I was caught looking at her as well, quite often in fact, but we didn't act on it, at least not directly. We did start hanging out together a lot more, but everyone thought that was just because we were best friends from way back, which we were. But she went to the dances with Jeff Clark or Danny Jackson, and I took Susan or Terri Cartwright, a new girl who had moved to the county at the beginning of our senior year from Cadiz. Jessie and I would meet up at the dance sometimes and talk and laugh and even occasionally dance together, but otherwise, we behaved as good friends, best friends. We were best friends. Of course, I thought about our time together in the barn. How could I not? But I also knew what it had been about and why we had shared that intimacy, so I left it alone. In a way, I think I was just biding my time. When your car runs out of gas, you don't push it to the gas station. You bring gasoline back to your car and fuel it up. That was the way I felt I needed to proceed.

Coming back from CD's, we traveled the same road we had taken to get to the city. About the time we went through Corydon, our conversation lagged, and the car grew quiet, and we rolled along lost in our own thoughts, Momma's car taking every bump in the road and making it into a soft swaying. Jessie reached down and grab her purse, more a cloth bag than a purse really, and pulled out a crudely rolled cigarette. Or, I thought it was a cigarette, at first.

"Want to get high, Silas?" She held the joint up to her lips as if it were a cigar and raised her eyebrows twice.

I almost drove off the road, I was so surprised. "Jessie! Are you serious?" She searched in her purse again and found a book of matches from the bank. She put the joint in her mouth and removed a match from the book. "Jessie? What are you doing?" I kept looking back and forth from the road to Jessie.

"Keep your eyes on the road, Sy. I'm going to get stoned." She struck the match and lit the skinny cigarette.

I tried to focus on the road, but it was hard not to notice Jessie smoking pot in my Momma's car. Jessie sucked the smoke into her lungs and held it. Then she coughed and did it again. After her second draw, she held the marijuana out for me. I had no idea what to do. "Here." Jessie croaked out, trying to hold in her last draw while still talking. "Suck it in and hold it there."

I took the joint from her, looked at it a second then imitated what she had done. If Jessie was going to try it, I decided I was too. The smoke choked me, and I started coughing. Jessie laughed. I tried it again and was able to hold it in the second time. We passed it back and forth, and by the time we made Sturgis, I could feel the effects, a light-headed wooziness, and a bit of euphoria. U.S. 60 turns in Sturgis, and I missed the turn, ending up in a residential area, and we started laughing. Once we started laughing, we couldn't stop. We were still giggling when we got to Marion. I stopped in front of Jessie's house to let her off.

"Where did you get that, Jessie?"

"Jeff." She picked up her bag and leaned over and kissed me. It wasn't a long, slow, passionate kiss, but it also wasn't a mere peck. I wasn't sure what to make of it at the time. I rolled down the driver's side window and drove home, trying to air the car out. It smelled like burnt grapefruit. When I got home, no one was there. A note on the kitchen table told me Momma and Dad had gone to the movie house in Marion. Argos whined to go outside, so I opened the back door and let him out. I spied a bag of corn chips on top of the refrigerator and ate the entire bag. I toyed with whether or not I should try some more marijuana. It was, after all, a part of the counterculture we wanted to fit into. The euphoria was nice, but I did find myself looking in the mirror often when I was driving as if everyone in Crittenden County would know I had smoked half a joint and they had notified the sheriff's office. Part of the counterculture too, I supposed. Then I remembered my clothes out in the back of Momma's car. I retrieved them and went up to try them on. I put on my pants and tightened up the web belt and threw on my army fatigue jacket and checked myself out in the mirror. With my scraggly hair and my baggy clothes, I looked like either a hippie or a homeless man, but I knew I was there. Monday would be a new day at school. I decided to see if Jessie could get me another marijuana cigarette. I didn't want to approach Jeff out of the blue. It was illegal, after all.

The next day, Sunday, Jessie called and said we needed to do a protest rally in the school cafeteria the next day.

"What?"

"I think we should start an impromptu anti-war rally tomorrow at lunch."

"Jessie, if we're planning it now . . ."

"And I need you to help me."

"No." I could feel humiliation in my future.

"Sy, we have to."

"Why?" I rolled the idea around in my head.

"Because everyone will be there. It's perfect. Maybe we can have it turn into a sit-in." She was giddy with anticipation.

"What exactly do you want to do?" I imagined her standing on a table yelling anti-war slogans, our classmates stunned into silence rather than chiming in. It would only get her a detention and would not likely change anyone's mind. I could not picture a sit-in occurring in the cafeteria at Crittenden County High School.

"Well, we need to make it seem like it's something other than a protest rally so we can get it started."

"Okay." I had no clue where she was going.

"What if you brought your guitar and we did some protest songs?" She said in a rush. I could tell by the way she said it she had already planned this out.

"What? In front of the whole school?"

"Sure. You play great, Sy." She fairly sighed that last sentence. "That man at the clothing store said you were great, didn't he?"

"Well, he only said . . ."

"You can play anything, Silas.

"If I play, then what are you going to...?"

"I'm going to sing them while you play them. Won't that be amazing?"

My recollection of Jessie's singing was that it was not at all good. I remembered her caterwauling in our living room in Sardis. My picture of this grew from humiliation to absolute ridicule. "Just what is it you want to sing, Jessie?" I was more than dubious.

"Can you play 'Where Have All the Flowers Gone'?"

I knew of the song and had heard it any number of times on WLS late at night. "I'm sure I can figure it out. Seems like it's pretty straight-forward. But. . ."

"Great!" Jesse May could honeyfuggle the wool right off a sheep. I was clearly on the hook to play my guitar while she sang tomorrow in the cafeteria and then be laughed out of school.

"After that, what do you propose we sing?"

"Oh, they'll never let us sing a second song." I decided she was right since I didn't think she would sound at all good. "After that, we sit down and refuse to leave until they end the war. And everyone will join us."

"Jessie, I don't know that we can actually..."

"This is going to be great, Silas. We're going to make a difference. See you tomorrow." Jessie hung up.

That afternoon, I worked out the chords to the song. I did not try to figure out any guitar leads since that wasn't what we were going for. I loaded up my guitar and waited to make a spectacle of myself the next day in the lunchroom with Jessie May.

I wore my new outfit down to breakfast the next day. When I looked at myself in the mirror, I thought I looked downright nobby, if scrawny. But when I walked into the kitchen, Dad's eyes opened wide, and he put down the newspaper he was reading and stared at me. "Well, now that's quite a statement, Sy."

Momma turned around from where she was scrambling some eggs wearing her quilted apron Grandmama had given her, shot me a quick look, then went back to cooking. The kitchen smelled of coffee and eggs.

"Yeah, I've decided to join the counterculture." I sat at the table and drank the orange juice Momma had already poured for me. A fork and a dinner knife were laid out at my place.

"What does that mean, exactly? 'Counterculture'?" Dad took a long drink of black coffee, seasoned with chicory Grandma Boudreaux had sent him.

"Well, it means, not a part of the culture, I guess." Momma put a plate of eggs and toast before me. A pat of butter melted slowly on the toast.

"But if you are joining it, isn't it its own culture?"

"What?" I spread the butter on my toast.

"Well, if it's counter to culture, but it has its own culture, isn't that a contradiction?" Dad put his cup down.

I ate my eggs, mulling over his point. I wasn't sure how to dispute it. After I had eaten all my breakfast, I looked over at Momma who was sitting across from me now. She looked blandly at me, awaiting my response. Her face was inscrutable. "Nobody understands me." I stood in a huff, took my dishes to the sink, washed them off, and put them in the plastic drainer on the counter. "This is why I am now in the counterculture." Then I stomped out of the room to retrieve my backpack full of books and my guitar.

As I left the room, I heard Dad say to Momma, "All I did was ask a question."

I was anxious all morning, but I had told Jessie I would play, so I was determined to do so. I went over the chords in my mind. They weren't hard. I was going to play it in G. I worried that was too low for Jessie and I realized I had not heard her sing since we were little kids. I couldn't concentrate on the classroom lessons either because I felt so scattered. Once, Mr. Whitsell called on me, and I had no idea what the class had been discussing. Classmates tittered just a bit, but Mr. Whitsell moved on, not needing to embarrass me and his point having been already made. I dreaded lunchtime.

When I entered the cafeteria, I puzzled over whether I should eat lunch first, since a sit-in can mean a long period of deprivation, potentially, and I was a little peckish. I saw Jessie sitting at a table in the center of the room, not her normal table, and she motioned for me to come over. So lunch first was out. I walked over and placed my guitar case on the floor next to Jessie.

"Silas, I'm so excited I can barely stand it." She made quick, soundless claps with her hands.

"Jessie, do you think maybe we should . . ."

"Don't do that. Don't chicken out on me, Silas. I need you to play your best, okay?"

"It's just that . . ."

"Silas, we are living through cold, hard times, and here's the thing about cold. It can wake you up, or put you dead asleep. Really depends on how close to the fire you want to stand."

I had no idea what she meant, but I still liked it. And I could not let her down. In fact, I could not tell her no at all. I started reaching for the case to retrieve my guitar, but she stopped me.

"Wait." She looked around the room, surveying. "Let's let everyone get here." I gave a sigh. After a few minutes, she seemed satisfied. "Okay, Silas. It's time we set this school on fire." I took my guitar out of the case. A few students around us took notice and turned to watch. It wasn't unheard of for me to play sometimes, just never before in the lunchroom with pretty much everyone in the school in attendance. I checked my tuning quickly and began playing, just strumming softly. Jessie leaned over towards me. "Louder, Silas, and tell me when to start, okay?" She unfolded a sheet of notebook paper where she had written down the words. I could see the blue ink through the paper. I hit the strings harder and played through once. When I returned to G, I nodded to Jessie, who climbed up on the table and stood tall. Everyone was watching. I lingered over the G until she was ready, then she let loose.

I do believe she sang some notes only dogs could hear. If she was listening to my guitar at all, I could not tell. Midway through the first verse, I switched to the key of A, which required me to rethink things quickly, to try to match her singing. It made no difference. She was off by a good fifth, and I could not wrap my brain around all those chord changes, and I doubt it would have made any difference. She was singing very loud, so I started playing a little softer so her being off would be less noticeable. I glanced around, and absolutely everyone was watching. No one said a word. The teachers who had been sitting at the teachers' table were standing and watching as well. And they were smiling. By the time Jessie had finished the last verse, there was only the rattle of dishes and trays somewhere back in the kitchen. Jessie drew out the last few words dramatically.

"When wi-i-i-ll they e-e-e-e-ve-r-r-r-r-r-r lear-r-r-r-rn!" Then she dropped her head and raised her left fist in the air, and the room erupted into applause and cheers. Even the teachers were clapping. Jessie looked around then looked at me, bewildered.

"Sing another one, Jessie!" Someone yelled.

"Whoooooh!" A girl hooted and raised her fist in solidarity.

Then everyone resumed walking towards their tables and returning their trays. Jessie climbed back down and looked at me, and we both started laughing as hard as we could. About the time we caught our breaths, the bell rang, and I loaded up my guitar and went off to French class and Jessie went off to her English class. The Vietnam War did not end that day.

When graduation came, I told Jessie I wanted to give her a present. I knew she was going to Murray and Momma and Dad and I had decided Western was best for me, so I prepared to be away from Jessie for a long time. Perhaps forever. It was not a happy thought for me. I loved how she saw things in a manner I did not, in a manner no one else ever seemed to, but also how she saw things as they were. I loved her laugh. Listening to her laugh was like looking up at the stars on a moonless night and catching sight of a shooting star, a wonderful treasured surprise that makes you want to keep searching the sky for another. I was going to miss all of that, and her beautiful face. One hot July afternoon, I picked up Jessie in front of her house, and we drove up to the landing to watch the ferry cross back and forth from Cave-In-Rock, and I told her I had her present.

"I don't have a present for you, though, Silas. A present feels too much like forever." I looked at her blue eyes sparkling in the sunlight.

"This is not that kind of present, Jessie. This is a present you can take with you until we see each other again, okay?"

"Okay." She gave me a small smile. I went to the car and took my guitar out of the trunk where I had hidden it so she would not suspect.

"This is called 'Lifeline,' Jessie. I wrote it for you." Then I sang for her again.

"Remember things we said we wanted to be,
Knowing we would make our own path someday.
I saw your heart every minute we shared,
Not understanding the prices we might pay.
Takes balance to cross the high wire.

"If you feel like you're going to fall,
When people are unkind,
You know that you can call:
I will be your lifeline.

"When your dreams are getting battered,
You have no friend to find,
You don't have to sit there shattered:
I will be your lifeline.

"When you are lost on some forgotten road
And sorrow seems to tower from above,
Look around and see me standing with you.
And I will wrap you up in love.
Takes courage to cross the highway.

"If you feel like you're going to fall,
When people are unkind,
You know that you can call:
I will be your lifeline.

"If your dreams are getting battered,
You have no friend to find,
You don't have to sit there shattered:
I will be your lifeline.

"If you feel like you're going to fall,
When people are unkind,
You know that you can call:
I will be your lifeline.
I will be your lifeline."

When I finished, I looked over at my Jessie, and she was a puddle of tears. "Oh my God, Silas. Oh, my God. How can I leave you?" She wrapped her arms around me, and we sat on the grass, holding each other for a long time. Cars came and waited to load onto the ferry, drove on and left. Other cars were unloaded from the other side. If anyone took notice of us, we didn't know, and we didn't care. Then I drove her home, and she got out of the car, and I watched her walking away, again. But then she turned her head around before she got to the porch and mouthed, "I love you."

# The Tetravalence of Jessie May

## Wind

# Chapter 14

The remainder of the summer flew past. We made a quick trip to Louisiana to see family, which I enjoyed, but I missed seeing Jessie one more time before we went off to separate colleges. But I could not complain. I loved seeing Grandpapa and Grandmama. And I got to see Grandma Bailey one last time, although I did not know it would be the last time I saw her, of course. And I met up with Fredrick, too. It was not the last time I would see Fredrick.

Momma let me use her car, and I drove over to Crackletown Road. It was sunny and hot, and the dust rose from the back of the car as I rumbled along the gravel road. I looked like a low-flying crop duster there was so much dust. The sun reflecting off the red dust as it drifted off over the green fields made everything rose-tinged. Fredrick was sitting on the porch with Grandma Bailey, looking in my direction since the dust trail was likely visible from space. I pulled into the drive, and Fredrick stood and walked to the front step, part curious and part protective. When I climbed out, he broke into a smile.

"As I live and breathe, if it isn't Silas LaMontaie?" He came down the step and stuck his hand out. I went to shake his hand, but he turned his hand and gave me a soul-shake, my first ever. It took me a moment to adjust my angle. I liked the feel off the shake but went on in for a quick buddy-hug, a kind of right half of the body event. Fredrick returned the embrace with a couple of quick pats on my back. We stood back from each other.

"Hey, Fredrick." I gave him a once over. He was several inches taller than I now, but most kids were taller than I was. He had let his hair grow out and wore it in an afro, so he looked even taller. He had on a sky-blue dashiki shirt with red and yellow trim. It was gorgeous. "You're looking great, Fredrick. I love that shirt."

"Thanks, Silas." Fredrick glanced down at his clothes as if to remind himself what he had on.

"Is that that boy with the guitbox down there with you?" Grandma Bailey leaned forward in her rocking chair and squinted towards us, but if she was able to focus on us, it sure didn't look like it.

"Yes, it is, Grandmother." Fredrick turned to her. I liked the way he called her "grandmother," using it as a term of respect as well as endearment. "Be careful, Grandmother. He's a musician, you know."

"Ha! You got that right, Fredrick. You got that right. Come here, boy." She waved us towards her with one gnarled hand. "Come here and let me see you." Fredrick stepped aside, and I walked over to Grandma Bailey. "Come closer." She waved again. I stood right next to her, stooped over, and she reached up and felt my face with her coarse hands. "You seen me play some old blues many times with these hands, but they're so crumpled up with arthritis, there ain't no songs left in them. But now, they're my eyes instead. These hands have been good friends to me." She felt my cheeks, my forehead, my hair, ears. Without turning my head, I looked over to where Fredrick stood, just behind Grandma Bailey now. "Oh, yeah, that's our Silas, alright." She put her hand back into her lap. "I've missed you, son. How you been doing?" Fredrick pulled up a cane-bottom chair from farther back on the porch and set it next to Grandma Bailey. He nodded for me to sit, so I did.

"I'm good, Grandma Bailey. I'm good."

"You still playing that guitbox?"

"Yes, ma'am. I still play it."

"You any good?"

"Not bad, I guess. I have a lot to learn still."

"Don't we all, son. Don't we all." Grandma Bailey rocked. "Our Fredrick, here? He's going to college next month. Yes, sir. First Bailey ever. We're very proud of our Fredrick." She gave a big smile. "Very proud."

I turned and looked at Fredrick, who had sat on the other side of his grandmother. "Where are you going, Fredrick?"

"Tougaloo College. It's a private school over in Mississippi." Fredrick waved vaguely directionally.

"Got himself a full ride, did Fredrick." Grandma Bailey nodded while she rocked. "Art scholarship."

"Wow. That's so cool, Fredrick." I had not qualified for scholarships. I did great on my exams in English, but math and science had kept my overall scores middle of the road.

"Yeah. Thanks." Fredrick gave a smile of pride.

"You going to school up there in Kentucky, son?"

"Yes, Ma'am. Western Kentucky."

"What do you plan to study, Mr. Silas?" Grandma Bailey asked.

"Well, English, I think. But I'm not sure."

"Still reading a book a day, Sy?" Fredrick smirked. We once had raced on reading books just for something to do.

"Well, maybe not a book a day. There's lots of other stuff going on."

"Like girls, I'll bet." Grandma Bailey laughed.

"Well, yeah, like girls, and music, and other stuff."

"What is it you dream of, Mr. Silas?" Grandma Bailey leaned her head back. "What are you going to add to this old world?"

I thought about all my plans I had considered, tossed, reconsidered, altered, abandoned over the years. "I don't know, Grandma Bailey. Music, maybe. I want to write songs for people, I think." Until I said it that moment, I don't think I had ever thought explicitly about being a songwriter. A musician, sure, I had fantasized about that often, but not being a songwriter.

"I like that. This old world always needs new songs. Always, whether they're happy or sad."

"Well," I shrugged, although she could not see me shrug. "I don't know for sure, Grandma Bailey. But I think I might want to do that." I don't know why I felt the need to hedge on that goal. It wasn't like Grandma Bailey would ever give me any grief if I did not do that. And, of course, I already was writing songs.

"Let me tell you something, Mr. Silas. Chasing dreams can be like trying to catch a butterfly. The more you chase them and try to hold them down, the more they can change direction and skip just out of your reach. But sometimes, if you just sit still, they will land on your hand and stretch their wings." Grandma Bailey smiled towards me. I considered her words. I liked the idea. She paused to let her thoughts sink in, then added, "You young men go visit some. Grandma Bailey's just going to sit here a spell." Fredrick and I excused ourselves, and he showed me his art he had been doing. I loved it. The colors were brilliant and wild. He had oils on just about anything, from canvas boards that were beginning to warp to plywood that he had sealed to even big squares of material he had stretched on frames and gessoed. He explained the processes he was using, but most of it was beyond what I could follow. I just knew he was fabulous. He had done some drawings of his brother Jackson and his aunts and uncles, but the painting he did of Grandma Bailey playing her guitar on the front porch was unbelievable. I could scarcely stop looking at it. I could tell by looking at it how much love and respect there was. I didn't know artists could show love like that, but Fredrick did. He had a stack of paper in the corner where he had piled assorted drawings and some woodcuts that he had printed off and colored in. One print looked like the drawing he had sent me ten years before of Crackletown Road. I was leafing through the artwork when I stopped at that one. It was beautiful.

Fredrick chuckled. "Yeah, same spot." I shot him a grin and looked back at it. I knew that spot as if I had been there that morning. It was a place between our houses where the road turned along some long-ago abandoned property line, the road rising up a small incline, turning where a giant sycamore tree stood dropping its woody seed balls, its white bark gleaming the sun. Then the road fell back down the small hill, dilapidated fence rows tracing its direction until it angled off towards our old house. We had enjoyed the shade of that tree many a summer day that felt like this day. "That one's yours, Silas."

I looked up in disbelief. "Really? Fredrick, it's amazing." It was printed in brick red ink, and he had colored it in with rows of green crops beyond the fence and green and yellow on the tree. The tree trunk he had mottled with white. I could not believe he was giving it to me, but I didn't ask again if he was serious in case he changed his mind. There were a couple more copies of the print, but none were colored in like this one. "Thank you. I will treasure this, Fredrick."

"You are welcome, my brother." He extended his hand again. He had called me his brother more in the vernacular sound of the day, but I knew he did not use it lightly. We had been like brothers, but we had never used that term. I took his hand, and we shook on it.

Before I left, Grandma Bailey let me borrow her guitar, and I sang a few songs for her. The guitar was badly out of tune when I picked it up, so I knew it had not been played in quite a while. She liked my playing. The last song I ever played for Grandma Bailey was the song I had written for Jessie, "Lifeline." When I finished playing, I looked up, and Grandma Bailey was smiling from ear to ear, but she was also crying. "Oh my goodness, Silas. My goodness, but you have brought some light to an old blind woman's day. Thank you. Thank you."

I turned and looked at Fredrick, and his eyes were open wide. "Shit, man, that's good."

"Fredrick Bailey!" Grandma Bailey barked. "You might talk that way with your friends, but you will not talk that way around your grandmother."

"Yes, Ma'am." Fredrick reached over and stroked his grandmother's shoulder. "I apologize, Grandmother."

"Apology accepted." She nodded with satisfaction. "But that is one damned good song, Silas." She winked one of her blind eyes at me, and all three of us cracked up.

Within a few weeks, I had said goodbye to Argos, which was harder than I expected it to be, and Momma and Dad drove me down to Bowling Green to start college. I had saved up money from working at the Sureway, Momma and Dad were helping me, and Grandpapa had palmed two one hundred dollars bills into a handshake to me as we were leaving Calvin. Still, I would be on a very tight budget. We had been poor before, so I knew what it meant to economize. And I was very eager to start out on my own. Western Kentucky University is on a big hill overlooking a river in the middle of Bowling Green. We had visited before since I wanted to see my options, but I was still a bit intimidated by the sheer size of it all, with different buildings for different classes and miles of sidewalks filled with young people. I was excited, of course, but I was also a little terrified. Momma sniffled into a handkerchief as Dad and I carried my things into my dorm room where I met my roommate Jay, a kid as small and wiry as I was who hailed from Henderson. He was very genial to my parents. It was only later I discovered he could be a lunatic after fraternity parties. Momma liked him, asked about his family, complimented his bedspread even, one that his mother, it turned out, had purchased for his college experience. Dad shook his hand very earnestly, looked hard at him, then at me. If I had not known better, I would have said Dad seemed to know him.

Momma turned to me, her eyes starting to water up again. "Promise me." She reached over and pulled me towards her.

"Promise you what, Momma?"

"Promise me you will finish. You will get your degree."

"Of course." I hugged her too, then she pulled back.

"No, promise me."

It made little sense to me. Wasn't that why we were here, for me to go to college? Why wouldn't I finish? "I promise."

After my parents left, I sat on my skinny bed and looked around me. Jay was rifling through his dresser drawer. "So, you play guitar?" He didn't turn around.

I glanced over at my guitar in my new case Dad had bought me, I think as much to get his back as anything. "Yeah. Yeah. I play some."

"What do you play?" Jay turned around holding a baggy filled with green-brown leaves.

I knew what it was, of course, but it still surprised me. I didn't even know him yet. It took me a second to understand his simple question. "Oh, uh, well, stuff on the radio, you know, and records I listen to. CCR, Joe South, Johnny Taylor, Clifton Chenier, I don't know. Different things. Stuff I write too sometimes."

"Ha. I don't know half those people." Jay dug into his pocket and pulled out a packet of rolling papers, then went over to his bed and started sorting through the pot as if he had lost something. "You any good?" He didn't look up.

"I don't know. Okay, I guess." I shrugged.

"Still learning?" Jay pulled a book from the shelf at his headboard and used it as a base to roll the joint.

"We're all still learning until we die."

He glanced up at me. "Huh. Philosophy major?"

"No, just something someone taught me." I pulled up my guitar case and retrieved my Gibson. "What would you like to hear?"

"Oh, well, I know CCR. Play one of theirs." He stuck the rolled-up joint in his mouth all the way and pulled it out, then lit it with a small plastic lighter. I played "Bad Moon Rising," or at least my version of it. I was heavy hammering on my E and A strings between strums sometimes to create a rhythm, but it's an easy song to play, so it sounded pretty good. By the time I had finished playing and singing the song, Jay was squinting through the smoke from his joint. "Hey, that's pretty good," he said in a voice squeezed by trying to hold in smoke from his draw.

"Well, it's actually pretty easy."

"Hey, maybe you can teach me."

"Yeah, that would work. Got a guitar?"

"Oh, well, no. But you do."

"It's a lot easier to teach you if you have your own guitar, so I can show you while you learn it." In reality, I did not want Jay or anyone else using my guitar, and it suddenly felt very vulnerable.

"Yeah, I guess that's true."

I put my guitar back in its case and slid it far under my bed. If I could have locked it under there, I would have. I needed a second guitar, I realized, one that was not quite so dear to me.

I started classes two days later. It took me a week or so to figure out how to make all of them on time. It was very different than high school. No one seemed to notice or care if I was there, first of all. And there was never any daily homework, at least in the same sense, there had been in Marion. But

Momma had warned me to stay ahead of the class in reading to give myself every advantage, and for the most part, I did so. Some of my instructors were graduate assistants not much older than I was, and a few were professors who had been teaching for years. But I enjoyed it. I was in an advanced English class that focused on southern writers, and I really liked that. The college algebra was still a challenge, made no easier by the fact my instructor was a graduate student with a heavy foreign accent who copied the problems from the chapter onto the chalkboard and never answered questions, although I seriously doubted I would have understood his responses anyway. But I studied pretty consistently and made passable if not extraordinary grades on the algebra exams. I enjoyed writing papers for both my literature class and my history class. I was eager to compare history notes with Grandpapa. I did well in those classes.

Jay, on the other hand, never studied that I could tell. He went to fraternity parties and to local bars using a fake ID, the photo of which looked exactly like someone other than Jay, but it seemed to work. Perhaps the idea was more that he showed an ID rather than it had to be a believable one. I wasn't interested in joining a fraternity, due primarily to figuring I could not afford to, and I had no fake ID, so I did things on campus. I went to athletic events and concerts and movies. The football was tremendous fun, and the team was good. Autumn on a college campus is a treat. I went to a couple of parties with Jay after he told me I didn't actually have to join the fraternity to drink beer. They were okay, but some of the other guys there drank like they had never had a beer before, drinking until they threw up in the bushes outside the fraternity house. I couldn't understand why they did that. We had been given wine with water in it down at Grandma Boudreaux house since we were children. And Dad had been offering me a beer on Saturday afternoons while we watched sporting events for a while now. In fact, I was surprised to discover almost no one else's father did that. In Cajun country, a small drink every now and then just takes some of the sting out of the heat. We didn't drink to get drunk. We drank to quench our thirst and to smooth out the sunlight.

By second semester, I had a new roommate, Jay having been *invited* to stay home in Henderson by the university due to his grades. Bill was a quiet, shy boy from Greenville. He was forever pushing up his black-rimmed glasses while he read, which he did even more than I did, and flipping his bangs out of his face in a twisting shake of his head. But we were a good match. He was unassuming and genuine. It helped that my playing guitar did not seem to bother him, as long as I didn't play too late. And when it did bother him, he asked me to stop. I liked that he told me when he needed me to lay off the music, instead of being grumpy about it. Also, by the end of the second semester, I had a fake ID that Jay had procured for me before he left, and by my second year of college, I had a serious girlfriend.

The fake ID was not really so I could go into bars and drink, although I certainly did that a few times, so much as it was so I could go into bars and play music to make some money and, someday, get another guitar. I started off in a little place called Carla's Hilltop Lounge, which was at the bottom of Kentucky Street. When I walked in with my guitar case that March day, it was early afternoon, and the place was rank from stale cigarette smoke and soured beer. Although it was chilly out, the door was propped open, presumably to let it air out, and a heavy man with a beard and wire-rimmed glasses was behind the bar, gathering glasses, wiping up the bar, and filling a cooler with bottles of Budweiser. I stood there for a moment, watching him work and waiting for him to notice me. He moved fluidly for a big man, almost in a dancing motion, and did not seem at all unhappy to be cleaning up a very stinky bar. Finally, he saw me.

He shot me a big smile. "Hey there. Didn't see you at first. We're not really open yet, except for deliveries and cleaning the place up, but if you want a beer . . ."

"Um, no. Is Carla here?" I approached the bar. The bartender kept smiling at me.

"Carla? No. There's no Carla at Carla's Hilltop Lounge. I own the place now. My name is Jim." He stuck his hand out across the bar.

"Oh, hi." I shook his hand, but not in the soul shake Fredrick had given me.

"What can I do you for?" Jim went back to work, taking glasses and running them up and down on brushes in soapy water in a triple sink, then dunking them in a sink full of water, then again in a sink of blue water, then lining them to drain on a bar towel. He moved like a machine. He had clearly done this often.

"I was hoping I could interest you in hiring me to play in your place here. I'm a college student and need to make some money."

Jim stopped and looked up at me. "What year are you in?"

"Fresh...senior. I'm a senior." I had nearly forgotten I could not play in a bar if I was not 21.

"Uh, huh." Jim looked askance at me. "You have an ID?"

"Yeah." I put my guitar case down and reached for my wallet.

"Hold on. Let's hear what you got before we go to all that. Play something. Not really looking to add music right now but maybe." He went back to work. A big truck pulled up outside, its air brakes hissing in the open doorway.

I put my case on a table. It was still sticky with something from the night before, so I removed it to the red seat of a stiff chair. I pulled out my guitar, slung the strap over my shoulder, and checked the tuning. "What would you like to hear?"

Jim did not look up from his work. "Your gig; your setlist." I looked at him blankly for a moment, trying to decipher exactly what he meant. He did look up now. "What would you play if you were back there in the corner with a dozen drunks up here trying to forget why they came here in the first place?" Jim went back to work. A man with a two-wheeled dolly stacked with beer cases came in through the front door and walked straight past me to a back room.

"Oh." I thought for a moment, then played "Vermillion Girls" for him, singing the French words as Dad and Johnny and Beau had taught them to me. Both Jim and the beer delivery man who was on his way back out now with the empty dolly stopped and watched me. I kept the arrangement pretty simple, so I wouldn't mess up.

When I finished, the beer man nodded approval and walked back outside after handing Jim a piece of paper. Jim kept looking at me. Finally, he nodded. "Okay. Let's see that ID. Play for tips? Fridays and Saturdays, say, nine to eleven." He smiled big again. "I like that song, but learn some country songs too."

I used half of Grandpapa's two hundred dollars that I had been hoarding to buy a small amplifier, two microphones, and two stands. I played at Carla's for quite a while, learning the regular customer's names and, more importantly, their favorite songs. Some of them were generous, others less so. When springtime started warming up Kentucky, I made good tips, making many times over my expense in setting up. My grades suffered a little when I found myself struggling to keep up my reading regimen, but I stayed afloat.

In May, Bill and I decided to get a place of our own. We pooled our money and got a tiny apartment carved out of the attic of an old house. Three flights up narrow, winding stairs, and it was very hot under the eaves during the day. It had two tiny bedrooms, a bathroom, a skinny long living area that was wide enough for a couple of beanbag chairs, and a minuscule kitchen with a two-burner countertop hot plate and a dorm-size refrigerator. I signed up for summer classes and played at Carla's and ate generic boxed macaroni and cheese. I got home to Tolu a few times when I could catch a ride. Argos looked more and more tired, but always glad to see me. While I was home, I washed all my clothes and ate as much as I could hold. Momma's cooking was a feast for me. She didn't know at the time what my diet was, but I'm sure my skinniness told her I was not eating too much of anything.

By autumn, I was also playing at a place called The Red Carpet Inn, a fancy motel with a rowdy restaurant and lounge attached to it. I played during the week there and kept playing at Carla's on the weekend since The Red Carpet Inn had a regular band on the weekends, who were excellent and boisterous. I didn't get tips there, though, just a regular fee for showing up and playing. In fact, I usually made more money in tips, but it all added up to a more or less livable wage. And at the Red Carpet, they sometimes gave me food, so there was that added bonus. It was there one Wednesday night eating some cold French fries and a soggy club sandwich that I think had been sent back to the kitchen that I saw Debbie. She had jet black hair pulled into a ponytail, and dark, brooding eyes. She looked around her as she moved through the room towards a booth where three other girls were seated, and they all burst into conversation when she arrived. I could not stop staring at her, twisting around on my bar stool to watch her progress across the room.

"You finished with this, LaMontaie? Or are you just hypnotized?" I turned back around. The bartender, Henry, was giving me a smirk as he reached for my plate.

"Oh, I'm both, actually." I glanced over my shoulder. "You know her?"

"No. But I'm guessing you're about to."

"Yeah, I'm going to try." I walked over to the table as casually as I could with my knees shaking. I was new to this meeting girls. I tried to think of something I could say to get her attention. "Excuse me. My name is Silas. I'm playing here in a few minutes." I motioned towards the stage with my thumb. "And I wonder if I could have your name so that I might dedicate a song to you." I felt my face flush.

She looked up with those dark eyes and seemed to look right through me, but she smiled, which helped. "You're the music tonight?"

"Yes, Ma'am, I am."

"Well, that's pretty special, isn't it?"

"Oh, I don't know. To a flea, a dog is the whole world. Depends upon your perspective, I guess."

"I guess it does." She looked back down at the glass of water that had been placed before her and took a slow drink from it, then looked at the girl next to her as if she was returning to her conversation. I figured my approach was not well-received, but at least I had tried. I turned, nodded to the girl sitting opposite her who gave me a timid smile and started away. “My name is Debbie.” I looked around and saw her smiling again. There was a meaning to her smile I could not interpret. I would come to find out, though.

# Chapter 15

People like to think the face of death is a horrible skull, all ugly and scary, and it will put you in fear for your life, but I'm here to tell you the face of death can also be a pretty girl with black hair and deep, troubling eyes. Her secret is that she can smile at you so daintily, so sweetly, that it can nearly make your teeth fall right out of your face, all the while taking you down some path you never knew existed that will leave you an empty shell alongside the road somewhere. And can I tell you I know that because I kissed the face of death. But for Jessie May, I would've never made it out alive.

Debbie and I hit it off pretty well. She had been a psychology major, although she was not in school just now. She told me she liked my music and the way I talked since I never quite got rid of the Louisiana drawl I developed in my youth. And she liked the things I said, which more often than not were things I had learned from Grandma Boudreaux, or Grandpapa, or Grandma Bailey, but I never let on; I let her believe I had invented those sayings. She told me I was witty and smart and talented. And that was very intoxicating to me. Why would I disabuse her of that idea? She was a definite beauty, and I actually considered her out of my league, since I had only really dated girls I already knew in high school, and somehow, that just wasn't the same. But when she complimented me, bolstering my feelings and making me feel like I was something extraordinary, that was a new experience for me, to have a woman talk to me that way.

Our relationship progressed very quickly and was very involved. I was reeled in by her beauty and her ingratiating appreciation of me. But she always had that look in her eyes, a look that said, "I have designs on you." We spent many an afternoon and evening at her apartment she shared with three other girls. My roommate Bill was such a homebody, he rarely left, and privacy was nearly impossible at our tiny place. But Debbie's apartment was a newer one in a complex of apartments, and each of the girls had her own space, so we went to her room and poured out our mutual desires upon each other. I was not all that experienced in such things going into this relationship, but she said I was wonderful in bed. I have my doubts. I was a young man with absurd amounts of hormones coursing through my bloodstream, so other than sheer passion, I really don't believe I brought all that much to the bedroom. I suppose enthusiasm does have its appeal. Regardless, we often sat on her bed, spent, satisfied, dizzy with sated hunger, usually with her wearing whatever shirt I had worn over that day. Any man can tell you a woman wearing his own shirt and nothing else is perhaps the sexiest woman alive at that moment.

But there was another side to Debbie Dangerous, as I later came to refer to her. She could be possessive and a bit jealous of my attention, regardless of where that attention might be directed. For example, sometimes when I would study, she would pout and say I was ignoring her and didn't I want to put down that silly book and join her and her friends in the living room watching a program she liked on television. I usually stayed with my studies, but sometimes I took the temptation to skip my studies for the evening because once I left my books, there seemed to be no returning to them that night. And occasionally, when I would be writing a paper, she would come and sit near me and start up a conversation about someplace she would like to go someday or maybe a new club she wanted to go to. It's true, my studies suffered. I did not flunk out, but my grades went down dramatically. It wasn't her fault at all. It was mine because I was so easily distracted by her. Then one day after we had been seeing each other for over a year, she told me she wanted me to stop playing at Carla's because that's when she wanted to go out and do stuff, and I was never around and what was she supposed to do? Again, I was torn. But when I told her, no, I won't quit at Carla's because I needed the gig, and I liked the people, and Jim had given me my first opportunity, she went all Debbie Dangerous on me, which was a side of her I had not counted on. She yelled at me, told me I was selfish and asked me why I didn't care about her. We nearly broke up that night, but instead made up by engaging in satisfaction of furious desire.

It was this anger, simmering just below the surface, that I had seen in her eyes. I had grown quite fond of her, and I thoroughly enjoyed our fun times together, so I did not want to break things off. But I had never seen a woman who could turn around so quickly from happy and fun to angry. I liked her, but I could not fathom her, and I think that made her even more attractive to me.

We took her car to go visit Tolu one rainy summer weekend after my junior year. Bill and I had a phone now, so I called ahead. Momma and Dad were eager to meet Debbie, whom I had been dating for going on two years. It poured rain on us the entire trip. By the time we arrived, I was quite tensed up from the drive, from her questioning my driving and my direction finding (although I was the one driving home), and from my lack of conversation with her while I held the steering wheel in a death grip through the heavy rainstorm. When we drove up in front of the house, I was twisted up as tight as barbed wire. Momma met us at the door. We got drenched just running from the car to the front porch.

"Come on in here. Hurry." Momma held the screen door open for us, and we slipped into the living room, dripping all over the rag rug. "Here. Dry off a bit." Momma handed a dishtowel she had been holding to Debbie, who dabbed her face and clothes softly. It did not seem like she dried very much, but she was evidently okay with it. Momma had on a pretty printed summer dress. I could tell she had made a point of looking nice to meet Debbie.

"Hi, Momma." I gave her a hug. She ignored my dampness.

"Hi, Sy." She returned my embrace. Argos waddled slowly into the room, his tail wagging.

"Argos!" I kneeled down, and he made his way deliberately towards my hands, his head lowered.

"So this is the famous Argos?" Debbie stood behind me.

"Yeah." I stood again. "Debbie, this is my Mom, Abella LaMontaie. Momma, this is Debbie." I spread my arms between them. "And this is Argos." I reached down and scratched behind Argos' ears, just where he liked to be scratched. My father came into the room from the kitchen, the newspaper still in his left hand. "Oh, and this is my father, Ben. Ben, this is Debbie." Dad gave me a funny look then went over and gently shook Debbie's hand. His hair was greying now, and he looked a bit tired.

"Delighted." He gave me another sidelong glance.

"Well, in this family, we hug." Momma stepped forward and wrapped her arms around Debbie's very wet shoulders. Debbie just stood there awkwardly with her hands at her sides while Momma hugged her. Dad gave me another glance.

"Come on in. Have a seat." Dad stepped aside so we could pass. I walked over and sat in the leather chair he usually sat in. Dad blinked once or twice then sat at a chair across the rug from his usual seat and put his folded-up newspaper on the pedestal table next to it. Debbie sat on the couch. Meanwhile, Momma slipped into the kitchen. I knew lemonade was in the offing. "So, Debbie. Where do you hail from?" Dad sat stiffly in the wingback, his hands clasped before him.

"My family lives in Willow Shade. But I live in Bowling Green. I don't go back to Willow Shade any more than I have to."

"Oh. And where's Willow Shade?" My father leaned forward.

Debbie laughed. "Well, you go past Eighty-eight and Summer Shade, and it's before you get to Marrow Bone." She paused, and Dad blinked again. "It's east of Bowling Green," she clarified. "Just a little town where I came from. Again, I live in Bowling Green now."

"I see." Dad leaned back. "Are you at Western like Sy?"

"I was. I'm sitting out a semester or two. Not sure what I want to study yet, so, I'm kind of taking stock, I guess you'd say."

"Ah."

I knew my father was only trying to make conversation, but it was beginning to seem more like an interrogation to me. "How are things at the dam, Ben?" Dad gave me a long, sidelong glance.

"They're good, son. They're good."

Argos meandered over towards Debbie's feet. She pulled her feet closer to the couch. "Silas, um, could you keep your dog off my shoes?"

I looked over at her, then at her shoes, which, if they had once been nice shoes, were quite ruined now by the rain. Now my father gave her the quick sidelong glance. "Argos. Come here." I leaned forward in my father's chair, and Argos stepped to me, his tail wagging gently. I pet his shoulders, and he sat at my feet.

"Sorry." Debbie gave a sheepish smile. "I'm just not a dog person."

Momma came in with a tray of glasses filled with lemonade and a plate of cookies. She offered a glass to Debbie, who took it and held it pertly in two hands in her lap. She did not taste it.

"What did I miss?" Momma brought the tray over, and I retrieved a glass and a cookie. Momma's shortbread cookies were always a favorite of mine.

"Oh, nothing much. Ben here was giving Debbie a quick grilling, is all."

Momma looked quizzically at me. Dad turned his hands up as if to say, "What?" Then he stood, picked up his paper, and walked back into the kitchen.

Debbie stood and put the glass back on the tray. "Excuse me. Where's bathroom?"

Momma stood. "Oh, just past the front door, on your right." She pointed with one long, skinny finger. It was the first time I realized that she was starting to look more and more like Grandmama. When Debbie had left the room, Momma turned back to me. "What was that about? What's gotten into you?"

"What?" I feigned innocence.

"Silas, an old tiger might not growl as much as a young tiger, but it would be a huge mistake to think he couldn't take you apart just the same."

I shrugged, this time feigning indifference.

That night Momma made a roast chicken with lemon and potatoes. I could smell the spices and the lemon all afternoon. When we sat at the table, Dad held the chair out for Momma, the way he had always done at dinner time. He made no big show of it, and Momma simply nodded a *thanks*. I looked over at Debbie, for whom I had not held the chair, and she gave me a quick glance. The chicken was amazing, but Debbie only picked at it, cutting off a few pieces and moving them around on the plate. Dad saw her, and I'm sure Momma did too, but they didn't mention it. We were talking about the Boudreaux's down in near Abbeville and how that's where I first learned music when Debbie took a liberty I was not expecting.

"Well, Silas and I have been talking, and we're going to move down to Nashville so he can become a music star." She lay her fork, which I don't think ever reached her mouth, on the edge of her plate. It was true that she had suggested that we do that, trying to convince me I was wasting my time reading Thackery when I could be making big money in music. What she failed to mention was that I had told her I was going to finish school first. I don't know if she thought my parents would try to help convince me, but if she did, she was wrong.

"What?" My Dad put his utensils down with a clank. He looked hard at me. "What is this?"

I scooted my plate back. I had finished, of course, since Momma's cooking was always just what I craved. "It was only a conversation." I felt cornered between not wanting to throw Debbie over the cliff and wanting my parents not to throw me off.

Momma looked back and forth at Debbie and me. Debbie had that dark look in her eye. Momma leaned over in my direction. I think she was intending to whisper to me, but it came out more like a hiss. "You promised." My foot was in a snare, and I could not free it.

"Silas, son, you are too close to finishing to stop now." Dad shook his head disapprovingly. I pulled on the trap, but I could not break free.

"You promised, Silas. You promised." Momma didn't pretend to whisper. I felt the noose tighten.

"Well, I never said . . ." My head spun.

"There will always be time to pursue your music, son. You need to finish what you've started." The snare clamped harder on my foot.

Finally, I jumped to my feet. "Well, maybe I should burn down a sugar mill and then, that'll be the end of it, Ben." I stomped off, free from the trap I had felt, but I had chewed off my foot in the process.

I spent the evening brooding in my room. Debbie came in just a few minutes later, and we sat on the bed. "Silas, I'm sorry if I . . ."

"I don't want to talk about it." I cut her off.

We didn't talk the rest of the evening, sleeping tenuously on each side of a double bed without touching. The next morning, I grabbed our bags and loaded them in the car first thing. I stood next to the car door, trying to decide how or even if to say I was leaving. Debbie got into the car without speaking. I saw Momma walk out onto the porch and lean against the post, her arms crossed. I walked back up the sidewalk.

Argos was at her side. "Momma, we have to get back."

I leaned over, and Momma hugged me and said quietly in my ear. "Just because you stuck your toe in the ocean, does not mean you know how deep it is."

I pulled back to look at Momma, and I pet Argos on his head. Through the living room window, I saw Dad, sitting in his leather chair, looking back at me, a newspaper folded in his lap. He had that same baleful look I had seen before, that look that gave off nothing. He did not stop looking at me. Finally, I turned to leave.

"You need to apologize, Sy," Momma said to my back. I saw Debbie sitting in the car, watching. I kept walking.

Two weeks later, Momma called me early one Thursday morning. Argos had died. I sat in my tiny room in my tiny apartment and bawled and sobbed over the phone. I could not stand it. I kept seeing Argos, running with me, protecting me, playing with me. I could not stand the thought of not seeing Argos again. In many way ways, he had been what my parents had intended him to be: my best friend. Between sobs, I asked Momma what they were going to do with him.

"Your Daddy is waiting for you to come home so you two can bury him."

I canceled my performances. All the managers and owners were very understanding, telling me they were sorry about Argos and assuring me it would be okay to miss. That afternoon, I drove again to Tolu, this time in my rusty Ford. When I arrived at home, Momma had just come home from teaching summer school. She gave me a quick hug, then pulled back.

"Your father is probably out in the back yard, digging." She turned and walked in the house. She was still upset with me for what I had said. I was upset with myself for what I had said. I had thought about it all the way back to Bowling Green two weeks before, and I could not leave it behind. I had hurt my father deeply. I knew that, but he would not let on. He would act as if it was okay, but it wasn't. I was standing there still on the front porch when a man and a woman in a Karmann Ghia pulled up behind my battered old baby blue Fairlane. The passenger door opened, and Jessie stepped out. I couldn't believe she was there. A thin blond-headed man climbed out the other side. He was tan and wore a blond goatee that was neatly trimmed. Jessie ran up the steps and wrapped her arms around me.

"Silas, I'm so sorry about Argos." Her voice had taken on a whispery sound, airy. She pulled back and looked at me. Her eyes watered, making the blue as lustrous as the July sky that day. "He was such a great dog."

"How did you...?" I shook my head.

"Mom saw your mother at the Sureway. She called me as soon as she got home." Jessie turned as the man who had driven her there walked up the walk. "Dean, this is my oldest and dearest friend, Silas. Silas, this is Dean." I reached my hand out as he took the step, and he gave me a solid grip.

"Sorry, man. It's hard losing pets."

"Thanks for coming. My father's out back." I let go of his hand and motioned with my thumb. We went through the house. Momma and Jessie hugged as we went through, but I kept going. Out back, along the back fence, Dad was in the middle of a shovel full, tossing it aside. A rug lay in front of the hole he had started, and I knew it was Argos. I was torn between running to see him one last time and not wanting to face the pain. By the time I had made the walk out, Dad had stopped digging, watching me make my way. He looked tired. I stooped at the rug and pulled back a corner. There was my Argos. He looked like he was asleep. I just stared at his calm face a few moments, my throat tied in a knot as big as a loaf of bread.

Dean stepped past me up to my father. He stuck his hand out and shook my father's hand, then reached over and grabbed the shovel. "May I help?"

Dad gave him a look, then let go of the shovel. "Sure." Dean started digging. He was wearing nice khaki chinos and fancy boots, but he started digging. Dad came over to me. "I'm sorry, son." He put his hand on my shoulder, and I could almost feel his strength pouring into me.

"Dad?" I didn't know how to start.

"I know. It's okay."

"No, Dad. It's not." I stood and faced my father. "Dad, I'm sorry. I cannot believe I said that to you. I'm sorry." Jessie gave me a quizzical look then she went back to watching Dean dig the hole. He had made decent progress, but his slacks were muddy already.

"Okay." Dad gave me a hug. Then he turned around and looked towards the house. "Where's Debbie?"

"Oh, well, she couldn't make it. She didn't really understand why I was so sad about Argos, I think." Jessie looked at me hard. "Tell you the truth, I'm not sure she's ever had a pet." I shrugged.

"This the same Debbie you've been seeing for a couple of years now?" Jessie's tone was more accusatory than curious. I just looked at her. "Well, it may not only be about the dog, you know?" She looked back towards Dean, but I don't think she was focused on him.

I stepped forward to where Dean was working. "Here. Let me do some." He let go of the shovel, and I finished digging the hole. I dug it deep so nothing could disturb Argos in his repose. Momma came out, and the four of them talked quietly while I worked. I was sweaty and covered with dirt by the time I had finished. There was something cathartic about digging Argos' grave, the physical labor of it being a release. When I was done, Dean and I lifted the rug and lowered Argos down. Momma and Jessie cried. Dad looked so forlorn I wondered if he would cry. I realized then Argos had been their dog as much as mine.

"Want to say anything, Silas?" Daddy reached over and helped me up.

"No. I don't think so. Except to say, he sure was a great dog."

"He was indeed, Sy. He was indeed." Dad watched me shovel the dirt back over Argos. Shoveling the dirt such a final act, I could not bear it, and I felt a deep sob come out of me. Dad stepped forward and continued filling the hole.

I stood back and watched. Momma came over and put her arm around my shoulder. I didn't cry more, but I felt horrible. "Where's Debbie?" Momma asked. Jessie shot a quick glower towards me.

"She had something." I didn't want to go back there. Dean helped dad finish covering up my dog, and I turned back with Momma to return to the house. Jessie walked up beside me and reached her hand into mine.

Momma glanced over to see it, then returned to her focus on the back door. Then she stopped and turned to face me. "Silas, I want you to be happy, is all."

"You need to be sure you have the right one, doesn't he, Momma 'L'?"

Jessie chimed in with her breathy voice.

I stopped walking, and they stopped with me and turned to look at me. "Jessie, you don't even know her. Why are you talking about her?"

"I just think she should have come. That's all. I mean, after two years?" She cocked her head to one side.

"Well." I struggled to find a response. "Who is this Dean guy, anyway?"

"He's a good friend, Silas." She smirked a little.

"What happened to the football player? And then there was the philosophy guy, right? And then, what was it Tim did?" Somewhere within me, I knew trashing Jessie's escapades made no difference, but I felt a bit accused myself.

"Import-export." If I had gotten underneath her skin, she did not show it. "Don't forget Dylan, the Welsh guy." She chortled a little laugh. "Turned out he was from Louisville and had only been faking an accent. His parents were Bob Dylan fans." She shrugged lightly.

"Right. So, why aren't any of those guys here?"

Jessie gave me a thin smile. "Isn't it obvious, Silas? I didn't date any of those guys two years." She let go of my hand, turned, and walked inside.

Momma watched her then looked back at me. "Be careful, Silas. Don't lose sight of what is important to you."

"I know, Momma. You're right. I was being defensive, I guess. I guess it's because I don't know why Debbie wouldn't come." I looked down at the pale blue porch boards. "You know, Momma, I'm not sure Debbie's good for me. But, she's not a bad person."

"No one said she was. Silas, it may not be Debbie's doing. It just may be you are a different person when you're with her. Sometimes it works that way. You decide who you want to be, and it will work out from there. I promise." She said that last part with emphasis as if to remind me I had made a promise.

"Okay, Momma." I went inside. There was a pitcher of lemonade on the kitchen table, rounds of lemons floating around the top, and four tall glasses beside it. Jessie was holding the other glass and taking a long drink of Momma's sweet, sour yellow delight. "Jess, . . ." I started.

Jessie lowered the glass. A drop of condensation dripped along the edge of her finger. "Don't worry, Silas. I'm not mad at you." With the stress on the last word, I wondered if that meant she was mad at someone, just not me. Momma came in a stood next to me.

Dean came through the front door now, knocking as he came. "Hello?" He walked through to the kitchen. "Is Jessie...? Oh, there you are." He wore clean clothes now. I tried to imagine Dean changing clothes out in the street. Tolu was tiny, but not uninhabited. His face was a little flushed from his labors, but otherwise, he looked as if he had just come from a business meeting. "Hey, we need to get going if we're going to make Nashville."

Jessie looked him up and down and shot me a smile. "We've got to run, Silas."

"Is that homemade lemonade?" Dean looked at the table.

"Yes. Please help yourself." Momma waved towards the table.

Dean poured a glassful and drank it down without stopping then put the glass back on the table. "Oh, man. That was delicious. You don't get homemade much anymore."

"Have another." Momma watched him scoot the glass closer to the pitcher. Dad came in, his clothes covered in dirt and sweat. He did a double take of Dean, standing there in a pair of blue slacks with a crease in the legs.

"No. Thank you. We do need to get going." Dean put his arm around Jessie and looked into her face.

Jessie looked up at him for a second, then back at me and Momma and Dad. "We do. Dean has a sailboat down in Apalachicola. He's going to teach me to sail." She almost whispered.

"Ah, well, bon vents et bonne mer." Dad stuck his hand out and shook Dean's hand. "Thanks for your help."

Dean nodded then turned, still holding Jessie's shoulder, and I watched her walk away again.

# Chapter 16

I once heard Grandma Boudreaux tell Beau that just because a pepper was hot didn't mean you could boil water with it. At the time, I just thought it was funny, but now I understood what she was saying. A couple of weeks after we had laid Argos to rest, I decided Debbie was not the one for me. I broke it off as clean as I could, but it was not a pretty sight. In the end, she went her way, and I went mine. I still saw her around town some, since Bowling Green is not so large that you don't end up in some of the same places at the same time, but it was over, and we both were okay with that, eventually. There were a few cases of getting death stares from across the room, and then there was the obvious avoidance and pretending I was not there, but since I was finished with that relationship, it bothered me perhaps less than she would have liked it to. So, we moved on.

I finished my last year of college, fulfilling my promise to Momma in the process, and looked out over my future. I was fully armed with a degree in English, my particular interest being American authors from the south, and ready to, well, I wasn't sure. I did not consider graduate school, since I didn't want to teach, and I wasn't sure what else a graduate degree would prepare me for. My senior advisor suggested law school, but that also didn't capture my attention. As a rule, I avoided confrontation, and being an attorney felt like the opposite of that. I decided to focus, at least in the short term, on my musical career, such as it was. It's true, I had only played local bars and coffee houses, eking out a meager living, and I would need more now that my roommate Bill was finished also and had been offered a position with what I considered a very healthy salary in Atlanta utilizing his electrical engineering degree. So, I either had to find a roommate to stay in the tiny apartment I had been in, which I was not at all excited about doing or find a way to make more money. I decided it was time to step out of my comfort zone. I loaded up my guitars and my list of a two dozen or so original songs and I headed down to

Nashville to find an agent. I had often been told I should go to Nashville; now, I was doing it. How hard could it be? After all, everyone told me I had talent.

I drove down in my old Fairlane, which I had nicknamed Ezra because I just liked the sound of it. I had two guitars now since I felt the need for another one for shows in the rowdier Red Carpet Inn. I packed up a second-hand battered brown suitcase I found at a thrift store with my few articles of clothing, including my show outfit of flared denim jeans, a black tee-shirt, and a denim jacket. I also had my pointed cowboy boots. I thought of it as my signature style, but when I drove down Broadway in Nashville, it seemed every other fellow I saw was wearing a nearly identical outfit strolling along the sidewalk. As I drove along with all the honky-tonks lining the streets, I tried to figure out where to go beg for a gig. It had worked at Carla's and at the Red Carpet, so I figured it would work here. I parked Ezra in a lot, locked my Gibson in the trunk, and walked door to door along the great row of bars, my new backup guitar in hand. It was early yet, but already, many of the places were loud with music and people yelling over the music or sometimes just with people yelling. Each place I went, however, either the manager wasn't there, or they weren't the person who made that decision, or they already had a long list of musicians waiting to play. It was depressing me. I spent hours going from dive to honky-tonk to coffee shop. I got no more nibble than a stale biscuit. Finally, as I was trudging out of one particularly seedy looking and loud bar, albeit with no music at the time, the bartender stopped wiping on the bar long enough to look up and say, "Hey, kid. You any good?" He was older than I, mid-forties maybe, with long brown hair pulled back in a ponytail.

I stopped and turned around. "Yeah. Actually, I am good."

"Who you play?" He went back to wiping up the wooden bar. Names and initials were carved all over it.

"I write my own." I looked at him.

He waved towards a barstool. "Show me." He picked up a different bar rag and started drying beer mugs and putting them in a cooler.

"Okay." I unloaded my guitar from its case, checked the tuning, and played a song I had just written for Argos. It wasn't a sad song, because I didn't want to think of being sad every time I thought of Argos or every time I played that song. Instead, it was a song about a best friend who stuck with me through every kind of adventure. It wasn't until the end that the listener knew it was about my dog. It was a kind of cross between Cajun and slap-strummed blues and the bartender stopped working to listen. At the end, he grinned.

"Hey!" He pointed at me. "Now that's pretty durn good. You didn't lie."

"No. I didn't. Not this time." I smirked.

He shot me a glance. "How long you been in town?" I checked my watch. The bartender smiled a sad smile. "Listen, kid. I've been here for more years than I care to think about. There's a hundred thousand guys out there every bit as good and just as cocky as you. You need to change your approach. Door-to-door ain't going to cut it. Some of these guys trying to make it? Been here for years."

"Oh?"

"Listen, I've stood on the same boards your walking now, and I can tell you, it just isn't easy." I loaded my guitar away. "Here's the problem," he went on while continuing his cleaning. "You have to have an agent to get a booking. Even these honky-tonks don't hire off the street anymore. They let the agents screen everything. The problem is, you can't get an agent until you've played some gigs and someone hears you. You kind of have to be discovered."

"But how do you get a gig if..."

"Open mic nights. Play for free and hope someone hears you. And hope someone doesn't steal your songs."

My eyebrows shot up. "Steal my songs?"

"Yeah," he finished with the mugs and slid the cooler door shut. "Get them copyrighted. Easy to do. Cost you a few bucks but worth it. I can attest. I, myself, wrote a top-forty country hit once and never made a dime from it. If I had copyrighted it, I would've been fine. This town is littered with that sort of story." He spoke so rapidly I could barely follow him. Now while he talked, he wiped down the well on the inside track of the bar. He never stopped moving. "Record companies don't do it so much as other singers. Some other young hopeful hears you play it, likes your song, and pawns it off as his own." He turned and started away, then stopped and grabbed a bar napkin and pulled a pen from his pocket. He jotted down something and handed it to me. It was a telephone number. "That's Pete. He runs open mic night at the bar at the Long Last Inn. It's a motel with a bar, but he gets some scouts in sometimes. Tell Pete, Ted sent you. It's a place to start, anyway." He started walking away, then turned around. "And get your songs copyrighted." Then he waved with his bar rag clamped in his hand and walked towards the end of the bar where a young woman was teetering on a barstool, but asking for another beer nonetheless. I was tired just trying to keep up with the speed of his conversation.

I called the number and got set up to play at the Long Last Inn two weekends later. He said any friend of Ted's was a friend of his. I did not mention I had only just met the fellow. And I went to the library and got information on copyright laws.

I stayed the intervening time back in Bowling Green, filling out copyright forms and practicing and playing at Carla's and The Red Carpet. I had to tell Jim I was leaving, though, which I hated to do, but he only wanted music on Friday and Saturday, and that's when I needed to be in Nashville. I dreaded telling him, but he only smiled that squinty-eyed smile, shook my hand, and said, "Good luck, Silas. Someday, I'll get to say, 'I knew you when.'" I still played at The Red Carpet during the week and stayed in my tiny apartment alone. That went on for another month, but it wasn't something I could keep up. I knew something had to give, so I let my lease go, loaded my meager belongings into a rented moving trailer, and moved to a studio apartment in Nashville. I mentioned before that I knew how to be frugal, and I had saved enough for a deposit and three months' rent and early summer turned out to be a good time to apartment shop since many college students vacated their apartments after classes ended.

I couldn't drive back and forth to Bowling Green to work at the Red Carpet. So I found a job. It wasn't flashy, but it made me some money. I drove the shuttle bus for the airport from the terminal to the parking lots. I drove in a snake-like circle all through the parking lots, helping people with their luggage and taking them to catch their planes. When I landed the job, I was tickled because I needed the income. But days of driving the same circuit turned into months, then years. I worked hard to maintain an upbeat attitude while I helped people so they would tip better, but deep down, I was very tired of it before long. It was quite tedious because it was so repetitive driving around and around, but then I found a way to make my time pass more pleasurably, entertain my passengers, and work on my vocalizing. Yes, then I became the singing shuttlebus driver. Passengers loved it. Nashville is Music City, and folks just relished getting songs on the way to their cars or their flights. I didn't sing my own songs since I was saving those for my gigs, and I did not want someone to steal them, so I learned a whole batch of classic country songs to add to my list of Cajun classics and old southern blues. And my tips went up dramatically. I had not begun singing to boost my tips, but I relied on tips to flesh out the meager pay, and that it worked towards that end was a definite bonus. So I drove a bus, my shaggy hair shoved up under a John Deere cap, singing Hank Snow, Buck Owens, and Johnny Cash. I didn't belt them out. I didn't want to be too brash. But I sang the songs, making sure I included all the lyrics when I could. I also took the liberty of telling folks who complimented me that I was playing at the Long Last Inn and, later, at the Boots Up Bar. But the thought of living a life of being the singing shuttlebus driver crossed my mind in moments of feeling lost and depressed. In those moments, I felt boxed in.

Meanwhile, the years crept by and I played at open mic nights around town and busked on side streets near Broadway when the weather permitted. But I found tourists don't tip much, even if they stop and listen and even have their friend take a picture of them with you. It was fun to play for an audience, but it wasn't very lucrative. Not that I needed a lot. I had my small place, gas, and insurance on Ezra who was on his last leg, and telephone service, which I had to have for that fateful call I knew was coming any day now, my big break. Instead, I got calls from my Momma and Pop, catching up on things and filling me in on family goings-on. I went back to Tolu for holidays when I wasn't driving the shuttle bus. But Nashville was a lonely town for me. I suppose I was skittish after Debbie. I went out with a few ladies, who also were looking to break into the industry, and I had a few tourist girls come on to me, but the women in the first group seemed only slightly less transitory than the last group, who made me feel more like a local attraction than a person, not that I didn't occasionally take them up on it out of sheer loneliness, as much as anything. When I got back home to Crittenden County, I found myself driving by The Dip sometimes to see if any of the old crew was there. Once I happened to see Joey, and we visited some. He told me he was sorry about Argos, which I accepted. It had been a long time since I had had to rescue Argos from him. We buried that hatchet finally. Mostly I saw teenagers at The Dip, which made me feel as if I were aging without taking notice of it.

Another trip home at Christmas, I ran into Jessie at the Sureway. She was picking up a can of jellied cranberries for their meal. I had been sent for marshmallows for the sweet potato casserole. When I saw her, she was reading the back of a can. She had on blue jeans and a faded blue sweatshirt, but she was still the prettiest girl I had ever seen. I walked up beside her.

"Cranberries are good for you, you know." I grinned.

Jessie turned, her face expressionless as if she was bothered by unsolicited advice, but when she saw me, she dropped the can and squealed, throwing her arms around my neck. "Silas! Silas! It must really be Christmas." She pulled back and held me at arm's length, gripping my arms. "Silas. I can't believe it's you." She smiled those sky-blue eyes at me, and I nearly fell over, as I did every time I saw her. She gripped my arms again. "Have you been working out?"

"No. No. I just work hard, in a fashion." In fact, I was pretty skinny, but my arms were sinewy from lifting all those bags. "How long are you in town?"

"Just until Friday. Cliff's taking me to the airport in Nashville. I have to get back to New York."

"New York?"

"Yeah, I have to get back for my job."

"Hey, if you want, I can take you to the airport. I live in Nashville, and I have to get back Friday too. I would love to visit with you on the way down." The truth was I had planned to stay until Sunday, but I would not let the opportunity to talk with Jessie pass me by if I could help it.

"Oh. Okay, wonderful. Yeah, I'd like that. My flight leaves at noon. Pick me up at nine?" She cocked her head to one side as if trying to see somewhere inside my head, although if she could not see what I felt at any moment around her, I would have been amazed.

"Perfect." I reached down and picked up the can of cranberries.

"It will be like having Silas as my very own chauffeur." She took the can from me. She had no idea just how many people I had chauffeured over the years.

Friday came warm, for December, with scattered clouds drifting across the sky. I picked up Jessie, and we drove south. She wore a grey pants suit and looked as if she were going to a business meeting. She had one small suitcase, a roller bag. As many times as I had loaded and unloaded suitcases over the past few years, swinging her little roller bag was automatic. We decided to take the toll road. As we sailed towards the parkway, Jessie settled in. Ezra had a musty, damp smell, but he was reliable, thanks to Pop's help with the mechanics of it all.

"So, New York." I glanced over at her. She had pulled her hair up and fastened it with a giant clip.

"Yeah. New York. I love it there."

"Big change for a girl from Sardis." I kept watching her from the corner of my eye.

"Ha. Sardis. Now there's a name I rarely hear any more." Jessie watched the fence posts pass.

"What do you do in New York, Jess?"

"I work in a bookstore. It's in Brooklyn. Actually, I live in Brooklyn, but explaining the difference to most folks is hard, so I just say 'New York'."

"Oh. I thought maybe you worked in a Manhattan skyscraper, with the suit, maybe an executive at a big bank." I glanced over again.

"Ha." She laughed again, but it wasn't a fun laugh. "This. Mother always told me you get dressed properly before you fly, and I do rather like it. Besides, I have gotten upgrades before, I guess from being dressed up. Most days at work, I wear jeans and a sweatshirt."

I pictured her in jeans and a sweatshirt. I had seen that Jessie many times growing up. "Are you still seeing Dean?"

"Dean?" She turned around to face me. "Oh, Dean. That guy from Florida. No. No. That was a while back."

I took the ramp onto the parkway at Princeton. "Oh. He seemed nice." I remembered his helping bury Argos. He went well beyond what most others would have done.

"Yeah, he was. I meet lots of nice guys." Jessie settled back into her seat. "Nice guys take me someplace new. That's how I ended up in Brooklyn. Met a nice guy, Hank, in Alexandria when I was working at bar in a motel there. He got a job in uptown Manhattan and took me with him. We enjoyed the city. Hank was nice. But then," She trailed off. The car grew quiet for a moment except for the roar of Ezra's tires on the pavement. I didn't press her, but I think the quiet did. "But then I wanted something else, I guess. I moved on." She said the last part blithely, a forced cheerfulness in her tone. "Some girls I met, we decided to get a place together in Fort Greene. I like it." I wasn't sure if that was meant to convince her or me. "Hank calls sometimes, and we go out occasionally, but, no, not much. Lately, I've been seeing a guy from Pittsburgh I met at a flea market. He sells old jewelry and stuff. Nice guy." She paused again. "They're all nice guys," she said softly to the window now. The car wheels rumbled on. Then she turned to me, her mood brighter. "So, you're in Nashville? Where are you playing? Keeping busy?"

I laughed. "Well, I play several sets a day, so, yeah, busy."

"Several sets a day? Oh my gosh. Where?"

"I drive a shuttle bus at the airport, mostly," I confessed. "And I sing old country songs while I'm driving for tips." I hated the sound of that. I felt like a beggar.

"Oh." She looked at the ragged floormat. "Shuttlebus." I could see her turning it over in her head.

"Someone needs to do it." I shrugged. "I play in some bars sometimes too, but it turns out, there are several thousand other fellows down there trying to break in just like me."

"Yeah, but you play great, Sy." Jessie raised her eyebrows.

"They do too, Jessie. Better than me, lots of times. And you know, I never was exactly a great singer."

"You are too."

"No, not really. And I don't dance all that well. Turns out dancing is sometimes a big part of it."

"Well, no, you can't dance a lick." She chuckled. "But what about your songs? No one writes songs like you do."

"Yeah. I do like to write songs."

"Sing me a song, Silas." Her voice was airy now, and I could no more say "No" to her than I could fly. I started singing "Together Again" but Jessie stopped me. "No, sing me one of your songs."

"Okay. Okay. I got it." I tapped a slow beat on the steering wheel and sang her some of my songs as we headed towards Hopkinsville. I finished with "Lifeline" as we pulled onto the interstate near Tennessee. She closed her eyes and listened intently, the most appreciative audience I had encountered for some time. After a while, my voice was tired, so I stopped singing, and we kept heading south with only Ezra's grumbly voice breaking the quiet. Jessie was looking straight out ahead.

"I like clouds," Jessie said softly, breaking the pause.

"Me too."

"You know, no one tells a cloud where to go but the wind." Her voice was wistful, distant. She was gazing up through the windshield when I glanced over. I let that one settle on me for a bit. It seemed to me, Jessie was maybe the unhappiest quaintrelle I ever saw.

I followed the familiar route through the airport roadways and dropped off Jessie. We exchanged addresses and phone numbers to keep in touch, hugged each other next to Ezra, and she gave me that Jessie-look that always liquefied me. I wanted to tell her to stay, that I would take care of her, but I sensed she was maybe not ready for that. A boat adrift on a lake won't stop until it reaches the other side. I needed to wait. Besides, I was barely taking care of myself. I watched her walk away, again, and the curbside security officer came over to tell me to move.

"Need to move on . . . hey, how you doing, Silas?" He grinned. "How's Shuttlebus Twitty today?"

"I'm good, Marty. I'm good." I got back into my car and vowed to make a change. "Shuttlebus Twitty." I drove off to my tiny studio apartment.

Despite bristling at my moniker, I did not stop singing while I drove. The tips were too good, and some business travelers in the area actually were asking to ride my bus so they could hear me sing. It was an odd way to create a following, but I could not be choosey. A week later I wrote a letter to Jessie, wishing her a happy new year, but it was returned, and someone had written on the front "Moved. No forwarding address." I worried about her, where she might have gone off. I wished I had told her to stay. Even if she had said no, she would have known she could.

An icy day in January, the air traffic was slow, so I had fewer passengers, but I sang anyway and told them I was playing that weekend at the Boots Up. My breath frosted in the frozen air as I crooned out, "Walk the Line." I noticed one guy almost the same age as I who eyed me curiously when I sang, almost studying me. He was very tall and quite thin.

He showed up at the Boots Up Bar on the next Saturday afternoon, which was when the open mic was. I saw him come in. The place was full of older people, mainly. It didn't get loud and boisterous until later. But I saw him come in, squinting into the dark after exiting from the daylight. The place was full of cigarette smoke and the sound of people chatting amongst themselves. The last part bothered me at first when I played that people would just ignore that I was playing, acting as if I was the soundtrack in some movie behind their real lives. But after I thought about it, I decided I didn't mind being a part of people's soundtrack. When they got drunk and loud, however, that was harder, but during open mic, it was generally calmer. Of course, many of the folks sitting in the chairs were awaiting their turn on the stage, so they may or may not have even been listening, but they were usually pretty well-behaved. But the tall, skinny fellow came in and stood for a moment, letting his eyes adjust, then sat at a barstool. I was sitting at a table, going over my set of two songs I got to sing. I had planned on singing "Tiger by the Tail," but I remembered I had sung that on the bus when I had serenaded my passengers, so I decided to sing my song about Argos. I had received notice from the copyright office they had received it, and that was enough for me. When Bobbi Lee finished her set, there was a polite smattering of applause. She wasn't bad, but she sounded like an awfully lot of other singers. I took the stage, sat on the stool, introduced myself, and started playing. My first song, I did "Long Black Veil," a classic, but one that is so easy, almost everyone did it. But it was a good one for me to loosen up my voice. Then I sang "My Old Friend." It was something people hadn't heard, of course, so it got a bit quieter. And as people listened, they got even quieter. At the end, I sang the last line, "You were the best dog this boy ever had", and people ooh-ed and clapped loudly. I saw my former passenger cock his head to one side again like he was studying me. He didn't clap.

I took my seat, and he came over. The bartender brought me a beer that one of the regulars at the bar bought for me. That was a first too. The bartender said the patron loved the song. My visitor asked to join me at the same time he sat, which was fine with me, putting down a clear glass with clear liquid in it before him.

"Silas, right?" He stuck his hand out.

I shook his hand. "Yeah. Silas LaMontaie."

"Sam. So, where did you hear that song? The dog one?"

"I wrote it." I took a slow drink from my beer.

"I like it." He smiled. It was the first facial expression I had seen from him.

"Thanks." I had no idea what he was driving at.

"Have you written other songs?"

"I have. I have indeed." I wondered if he was one of those notorious song-stealers I had been warned about. I was tempted to say, "And they are all copyrighted."

"Huh. Okay, then." He reached into his shirt pocket and pulled out a business card. "My name is Sam. Sam Tackerson. I'm a talent agent with R and T Talent. I'm taking it you don't have an agent yet, right?"

My head spun a bit. "No. No, I don't."

"Can I be honest with you?"

"No. I prefer dishonesty." I smirked. He looked at me funny, then I saw him recognize the joke.

"I like your singing fine," he went on. It was as if he was in a hurry. "It's not great, but it will do. You play guitar a little different, so that's good. But in Nashville, that's not the difference maker. Songwriting is. We are always looking for good songs. If you can write, we can use you. Would you be interested in selling your songs? We can sell good songs."

Again, my head felt in a whirl. "I have copyrighted all my songs. Will that make it harder for you to use them?"

"No, not at all. And that's actually a very smart thing to do."

"What about paying gigs?"

"That too, although that takes longer." He scooted back his chair. "If you're game, let's see if we can make this work. What do you think? Come by and play some songs for us, see what sticks?"

It never occurred to me that I might say no. This is what I had been working towards for years. "Okay."

He stood and stuck out his hand. I stood too. He was nearly a foot taller but looked like he weighed no more than I. I took his hand and shook on it. "Come by the office Monday, and I'll introduce you to Connie, my partner.

Bring your guitar and your songs." He grinned at me, turned, and walked out. It all happened in a flash, without ceremony, just business.

That was how I met my agent, Sam, and how I would come to meet Connie, who would become as good a friend as I would ever have in the industry.

# The Tetravalence of Jessie May

## Water

# Chapter 17

You can cut down the oak trees in the forest, but there is something that will grow in that spot afterward. The question is, will it be another oak tree or a bramble patch? I had decided if I was going timber trees in my life, I might as well drop some acorns when I did. I had left behind Tolu and Bowling Green and spent years struggling to make ends meet, all the while writing and working on my songs. I felt like I had been sowing acorns for a long time when Sam came by the Boots Up Bar. Still, I could not believe my good fortune. The first thing I did was call Momma and Pop that evening to tell them. They had always been my biggest supporters.

"Hello?" Momma's voice was almost somber. I immediately worried something was wrong.

"Momma?"

"Oh, hi, Sy!" Her tone brightened.

"Everything okay, Momma?" I pushed my agenda back.

"Yes, Silas. Yes. Just wondering how long a ghost can haunt, is all." She spoke dismissively, but that one had my imagination running wild immediately.

"What?"

"Bennie?" She spoke away from the receiver. "It's Sy." There was a short pause.

"Hey, Silas. Bonsoir, mon fils." When Pop went all Cajun on me, I knew something was up.

"Bonsoir, Papa. What's going on?"

"So, I need to tell you something. Got a minute?" Pop's tone was a forced cheerfulness.

If I had been standing in a burning house, I'm not sure I could have left after that start. "Yeah, sure, Pop. Of course."

"This has been a long time coming, son. How much do you remember about Loreauville, Sy?"

"Well, I remember your shop. I remember starting school there. There was a draw bridge there too." My stomach did a little flip.

"You remember when the mill burned, I know." That part was a little flatter.

"Pop, I'm really sorry I . . ." I hated that this was coming up.

"No. No. You had every right to wonder. I made a decision that changed the rest of our lives. That's okay. You had a right to harbor a little anger too. Tout le monde reçoit un peu de moutarde dans le nez de temps en temps."

"Mustard in my nose?" I was baffled.

"Just something my Daddy used to say. I just meant everyone gets mad sometimes. That's okay."

"What's going on, Pop?" Thoughts spun through my head. Pop rarely spoke French anymore.

"Do you remember Mr. Kohler?"

"Yes, I do. Short, fat, bald guy. Mean. He owned the mill, right?"

"Yeah, I guess you do remember him." Pop chuckled slightly. "Well, I just heard from some folks down there that he passed away last week."

"Oh." I didn't know if I was supposed to be sad or not. I didn't really know the man. He had been hard on our family, but I still could not be happy at his death.

"I wonder where his soul may fly."

"Yeah, I get that."

"Be that as it may, I think that means I can tell you now."

My throat tightened up. "Yeah? Tell me what, Pop?"

"I never lied to you, Silas. Never."

"Okay."

"I didn't set the mill on fire."

"I know, Pop."

"No, I'm not sure you really do. I know you believed me, but you still wondered. Wonder no more. I did not burn the mill, Sy."

I felt a knot in my throat. "Yes, sir."

"But I still made a decision that changed everything in our lives."

"Yes, sir?"

"Silas, I always knew who did. I saw him do it." It came out in a rush, and I heard my Pop catch up his breath as if saying it was a huge release. "But I never told anyone. Except your Momma, of course." A tiny part of me felt irked that she had also kept a deep secret from me, but I quickly dismissed the feeling. Of course, Pop told Momma.

"Yeah?" I kept waiting for the end of the story.

"As long as Kohler were still around, I couldn't tell."

"Why?"

"A good man made a very bad choice. I couldn't let it destroy him and his family. I told him I would not tell, so I didn't."

"Pop." Our conversation paused. "Who was it?"

There was another pause. "Frank Blanchard."

"Charlie's Dad?" My eyes opened wide.

"Yeah. I think the statute of limitations passed some time ago, but until Kohler passed, it didn't feel like we could tell."

"Charlie's Dad burned down the mill?" I was trying to fathom this news.

"Yes, Silas." I heard relief in Pop's voice. I wondered just what the toll of this secret might have been.

I suddenly had a welling up of anger within me I had not expected. "Wait. Charlie's father burned down the sugar mill, and he let everyone think you did it?"

"Well, yeah...but I knew I hadn't done it so they couldn't convict me. And other people's opinions are more about them than anything else."

"But wait." My head raced with thoughts tumbling over each other. "You saw him?"

"I did."

"But you said you were fishing with Beau and Johnny." Had my Pop, in fact, lied to me?

"I did go fishing with my cousins, Silas. On the way out of town, I saw Frank over by the mill, next to the boiler. He saw me, and I saw him. He was setting it up then, I think."

"Did you two talk about this? About your not telling?"

"No. That was my choice. And your Momma's. But I told him later I wouldn't tell."

My thoughts whirled. "All those places, all the talk, Pop. People trashed you. And us."

"I know. But we've been okay, haven't we? We always had each other."

I couldn't argue with that, really. I had called to tell them the great news, after all. "Well, wow. That is huge, Pop." I felt the fever of thoughts calm some. "How are you with this, Pop?"

"I'll tell you, Sy, I feel like a grinding stone has been lifted off my shoulders. I had no idea how heavy it was until it was gone." I heard my Pop's throat tighten. Pop was as strong a man as I ever knew, and a part of that strength was his sensitivity. I wanted to change the subject and share my news before he said goodbye.

"Well, Pop, I have some news to share too."

"Oh?" I could hear him gathering himself.

"Pop, I may have gotten an agent."

"What? An agent?" Then away from the phone, I heard him tell Momma excitedly, "Silas has an agent." Momma squealed an "Oh my goodness" in the background.

"Well, I may have. But I've met him, and he wants me to play some songs for him and his partner day after tomorrow, so that's a foot in the door, anyway."

"He says he has a foot in the door," Pop said away from the receiver again. I had to laugh. It was such an odd part of the conversation to repeat, but he was so excited for me he couldn't help himself. I heard Momma in the background saying she had to call her Mom and Dad.

"Wait. Don't tell anyone else yet until I get signed, okay? I don't want to jinx it."

"Jinx it? Son, you will knock them over, I just know it."

"Thanks, Pop. But wait, okay?"

"Okay, Sy." He paused. "Son, I'm very proud of you."

Now my throat tightened. "Thanks, Pop. You know what? I'm very proud of you too."

I spent Sunday morning gathering up all my songs. I worried that I might freeze up with my big opportunity. I also put the final touches on my latest song about Jessie. I liked it. I thought it was one of my better ones. Sunday afternoon, I went to work, wending my way through the rows and rows of sedans and pickup trucks, singing a mix of country and Cajun songs. My voice was in full force with my excitement, and I made as many tips as I usually made in three or four days.

Monday, I loaded my Gibson into Ezra and drove to R and T Talent just off Music Row. I was a half hour early. I sat in my car parked along the side of the street for what seemed like hours, then looked at my watch and five minutes had elapsed. I couldn't stand the waiting. I got out, retrieved my case, and went in.

The business was small, just a grey front desk where a pretty blonde was answering the phone when I entered, then a short hallway that led to a couple of offices. I waited for the receptionist to finish her conversation. The walls were white and the carpet a light blue. It was fairly sterile, except for the faint flow of music playing on small speakers on the wall. I walked to the other end of the room where photos hung in a tight pattern near a large window. The photos were of musicians, some of them I was well acquainted with. There were also small 45 RPM records framed. I knew these songs. My stomach tightened.

The receptionist assumed her I-have-to-hang-up-now tone. "Yes, Sir. I'll let Ms. Ragsdale know. Yes, sir. Thank you." The "Thank you" was drawn out in a long southern accent. She hung up and looked up at me. "May I help you?" Every time she said "you" it sounded like two syllables. I walked back over to her desk.

"Hi, I'm Silas LaMontaie. I'm expected?" I thought it a poor choice of words when I said it. I sounded like I was pregnant.

"Yes?" She looked up at the plain round clock over the doorway to the hallway.

"Silas." Sam came striding out of the doorway. He was so tall and thin, it seemed that he took three steps to traverse the entire room. He stuck his hand out, and I took it. "Glad you could make it." Again, I tried to imagine a scenario where I would have not made it.

"I'm early." I shook his hand.

"That's fine. If it wasn't important to you, it wouldn't be important to us." He turned to the receptionist. "This is Janine." He waved. "Janine, this is Silas LaMontaie."

Janine stood and reached her hand out as well. "Nice to meet you." Again, two syllables. I shook her hand and followed Sam down the hallway to the first office.

"Connie?" Sam leaned into the doorway. "That songwriter I was telling you about? Silas?" He motioned with his thumb toward me.

"Yeah." Her voice was coarse, crackly. I could tell she smoked. "Take him back and set up. I'll be there in a few."

"Excellent." Sam turned around and motioned for me to follow him. The back room was through a heavy door. It was not a huge room, made smaller by an array of amplifiers and speakers arranged against one wall. The room reeked of stale cigarette smoke. There were several guitars lined up on stands to one side. Microphones and wires snaked around to the middle of the room where a stiff metal chair was positioned. The walls were covered in big rugs hanging from the drop ceiling. Two more stiff chairs sat next to the door we had just entered with a tall white plastic ashtray between them. All of it was glaringly lit with the overhead fluorescent lights. "You need to plug up?" Sam walked towards the amplifiers.

I looked around me. "Uh, no, I can just play acoustic."

"Okay." He flipped on two of the amplifiers. Red lights glowed. He positioned the microphones in front of the chair. He had done this many times, I could tell. The speakers hummed slightly. He stood up and looked at me standing there watching him bustle around. "Get your guitar out?"

"Oh. Oh, yeah." I pulled myself out of the trance I had fallen into. I unloaded my Gibson, sat at the chair, and checked my tuning. Sam shoved the mics again, so they were in front of me. "I'm not sure I need . . ."

"Connie wants to see you use the gear. She likes to know how you sound amplified. Just relax, play like normal."

I had played using mics and such before, it just hardly seemed necessary in this small room, but I was in no place to debate the issue. "Okay."

Sam stood by the door. "You need to warm up?"

I laughed. "Yeah, I've been warming up the whole way over here. I'm ready when you are."

"Great. Hold on." He stepped through the door and came back. Then a woman came in behind him. She was older than either of us, with hair that was colored blonde and looked a bit like straw. She was short and a little frumpy looking. She had on a floral dress that hung unevenly around her shins, and a cigarette dangled from her mouth. She squinted against the smoke as she came in. And ash tumbled from the cigarette to the floor. Sam waved one hand towards her. "Sam, this is Connie Ragsdale." I started to stand to greet her.

"Keep your seat," she growled. "What do you got?" She sat at one of the two chairs, and Sam sat next to her. She snuffed out the cigarette in the ashtray and pulled a half-empty pack of Viceroys from her dress pocket, make a flick of her wrist, then drew a cigarette from the pack with her lips and lit it and gave out a yeasty cough.

"Well, I sing a lot of different stuff . . ."

"Sam says you write," she said hoarsely.

"Yes, ma'am."

"Play something you wrote." Her head was nearly engulfed by an exhale of smoke.

I played a number of my songs. If she was moved, I could not tell, but I was playing about as well as I could play, so if she didn't like me, it was not because I messed up. My voice and my guitar pushed through the speakers sounded awkward to me in the little room, but I had been singing in a shuttle bus, so I was used to just about anything. After I had played seven or eight songs, she just sat there, looking at me. Then she lit another cigarette and grumbled, "What are you working on right now?"

"Well, I wrote a song about a friend of mine. I'm still working on it though."

"Let's hear it." She exhaled another plume of smoke.

"This one is called 'Lonesome Goddess.'" I played my intro and started singing:

"When it comes that fateful day,
"When you would leave and go away,
"Find yourself stranded in some private place,
"I'll be there to touch your face,
"Lonesome Goddess."

"Standing alone on the busy street
"Nothing to follow except your feet,
"Every turn taken but forgotten dreams
"It isn't as bad as it may seem,
"Lonesome Goddess."
"Lonesome Goddess,
"Remember my name.
"Lonesome Goddess,
"I'm still the same.
"Lonesome Goddess."

"When all the worshippers fall away,
"When there are finally dues to pay,
"When all the prayers have all been said,
"No more apostles filling your head,
"Lonesome Goddess."

"Lonesome Goddess,
"Remember my name.
"Lonesome Goddess,
"I'm still the same.
"Lonesome Goddess."

"Tell you all you ever want to hear
"When they don't know what it is you fear.
"They walk away when it gets too close.
"I know what nobody else can know,
"Lonesome Goddess."

"Lonesome Goddess,
"Remember my name.
"Lonesome Goddess,
"I'm still the same.
"Lonesome Goddess."

"You were not meant to be a savior,
"Open up everyone else's door.
"Look back up that abandoned road
"You'll see me standing there in the cold
"Lonesome Goddess."

"Lonesome Goddess,
"Remember my name.
"Lonesome Goddess,
"I'm still the same.
"Lonesome Goddess.

"Gave everyone you saw a song.
"Never stayed in one place very long.
"You should know one thing that's always true;
"I was the one wrote songs for you,
"Lonesome Goddess."

"Lonesome Goddess,
"Remember my name.
"Lonesome Goddess,
"I'm still the same.
"Lonesome Goddess.

"When it came that fateful day,
"When you would leave and go away,

"Find yourself stranded in some private place,
"I'll be there to touch your face,
"Lonesome Goddess.

"Lonesome Goddess,
"Remember my name.
"Lonesome Goddess,
"I'm still the same.
"Lonesome Goddess."

I played a fade-away chord progression and stopped. Connie stood up and walked towards me. "For a friend, huh?" She smirked. "I like it. I like it a lot." Her voice was a bit less growly now. "I can sell some of your songs. A few need tweaks, but you're good." She stuck her hand out towards me. "If you want to make some money off your songs, we can do it. What do you say?"

I stood to shake her hand and bumped against the guitar microphone, and it gave a shrill feedback through the speakers. I stumbled trying to grab the mic and my guitar and shake her hand all at the same time. Sam took two steps and was at the amplifier flipping off the whining feedback. He was beaming. I shook Connie's hand, and we became partners.

We signed a lot of documents to make it all legal out in the front office. I was still flabbergasted. Sam kept patting my shoulder and saying to Connie, "See? I told you he was good."

My hand was shaking as I signed the agent agreement. "Sorry." I tried to gather myself. "I just can't believe my luck."

"Luck?" Connie rumbled as she let out a cloud of blue smoke. "Roman philosopher once said, 'Luck is where preparation meets opportunity,' Mr. LaMontaie. You make your own luck."

I looked up from my signing. I liked that take on it. "Call me Silas."

"You got it, Silas." She turned and walked back to her office.

It would be a mistake to think success came holus bolus after that. It did not. I still worked as the singing shuttlebus driver, and I still lived in my tiny apartment. I did spend more time writing since that was what Connie thought was my first step into the industry. Connie had a rough exterior, but her knowledge of the music world and her connections were something of a legend, it turned out. She had once been part of a bigger agency and had retired, but she had grown bored with retirement and went back into business at Sam's behest. He was her nephew. After several weeks, she got me a paying gig at The Silver Bird Saloon, one of the clubs on Broadway. It was one I had visited that first day so many years before without getting a nibble. I opened, and the crowd was tamer than it would be later, but it was still hard for me to be heard over the din, so Sam found me a couple of studio musicians to back me up on stage, a bassist and a drummer. Walt and Tony. They were amazingly talented, and I was stunned they were still looking for work. We practiced in the basement of Tony's parents' house out in Franklin and honed our sound. They appreciated the Cajun background my music had, so we ended up playing a kind of Zydeco-country-blues blend. I liked the sound. I did have to buy a new electric guitar, but there is no shortage of guitars at pawn shops in Nashville, unfortunately. We called ourselves The Bayou Glad Band, after a place I used to fish with my cousins and my Pop. A month in at Silver Bird, we had a few followers, and people actually became quieter during some of the songs - never completely quiet, but quieter. One day, that bartender who first told me about open mic night at The Long Last Inn came in. He looked rather beaten down, but I recognized him by the long grey ponytail and his gaunt face. He looked at me oddly, probably trying to figure why I seemed familiar. I decided to play the same song I had played for him that first day I was in Nashville. We hadn't really practiced it much, but Tony and Walt picked it up as we went. I saw the old bartender take notice. He watched me playing the song with rapt attention, and when I finished, he raised his brown beer bottle in a salute.

# Chapter 18

We were halfway through recording my first and only album when Momma called. I was beat from playing in the studio all day for the tenth straight day. It was exhilarating and exciting, but also enervating, no doubt in part because my emotions were running so high. I had just returned home to my tiny apartment that I was looking to vacate now that several of my songs had been sold and I had a decent boost to my income. I grabbed a beer from the small refrigerator and sat down to gather my wits about me. The jangle of the phone startled me from my reverie on the loveseat that served as my couch since it was all I had room for. I put my beer down on the metal side table I had found in a second-hand store and grabbed the phone.

"Hello?"

"Hi, Silas. It's Momma." She always started her telephone calls to me that way, as if I might not recognize her voice. It was really more rote now than anything else.

"Hi, Momma. What's up?" I leaned back onto the loveseat and reached for my beer.

"Honey, I have sad news for you." Her voice was soft, filled with tenderness. My mind immediately raced. I had several relatives who were getting older now.

"Oh. Okay. What's happened?" I sat up straighter and put the beer back down without taking a drink.

"Grandma Bailey has passed, Sy."

"Oh, no." I relaxed some. It wasn't that I was okay with Grandma Bailey dying, but that with her diabetes and age, it was not totally unexpected. But then I felt guilty for feeling relieved. "When?"

"Monday."

"Oh." I don't know why it meant anything what day she might have passed away, but it seemed like a reasonable question at the moment. "How did you find out? Grandmama?" Then my throat tightened.

"No, Fredrick. He got our number from Daddy and called just now. He asked for your number, but he was pretty upset, so I told him I would call you."

"Yeah. I'll bet. Damn." I pictured Grandma Bailey, sitting in her rocking chair, staring blindly at the peanut fields across Crackletown Road, slowly keeping the rhythm of some long-forgotten song running through her head. I wanted to ask her what song she was hearing and ask her to sing it for me. I saw Fredrick, kneeling beside her chair, shucking corn with me. We used to race to see how fast we could finish our ears of corn so Grandma Bailey could can it up. We would spend all morning yanking open the green husks, the golden corn gleaming in the summer sunlight. There was a sweet, green scent everywhere. By midmorning, it would be warm and thick with humidity, and we would be sweating, but Fredrick never slowed down. He always won those contests. Grandma Bailey would laugh to watch us competing, admonishing us to not leave any silks between the rows of kernels. The basket would be full of shucked ears of corn, and the porch would be festooned with husks and stalks everywhere. Grandma Bailey would heft the basket inside, and we would clean the porch. Grandma Bailey always kept some of the silks for making tea to treat people along Crackletown Road with kidney stones.

"He wants you to speak if you would." Momma's soft voice brought me back.

"What? Speak where?" I blinked back tears.

"At her service in Winnfield."

"Oh. Okay. When is the service?"

"Tomorrow. You remember the church she took you boys to? Over off Coldwater Road." Momma's voice was heavy with sympathy.

"I will be there." I stood now, as much to gather myself as anything.

"I'm so sorry, Silas. I know she was very important to you."

"Thanks, Momma. I did love her." I paused. "Did you know she raised Fredrick and Jackson from the time they were babies. Actually, right after Jackson was born. Their mother died when he was born. She always told us the lord took her baby girl but gave her two baby boys in exchange."

I called Sam and told him I needed to go down for the funeral. He understood and even loaned me his Oldsmobile to drive down since Ezra was no longer road worthy. I found my copy of *We Were There at Pearl Harbor* Grandma Bailey had given me when we moved and took it with me. I hadn't looked at it in years, of course, but I knew Grandma Bailey was with me. All the way to Calvin, I saw images of Grandma Bailey in my head: her hanging out the laundry in the back while we three boys climbed around on the tree out front; her hugging people who came to her porch, regardless of who they were or why they were there. I wondered what might become of Crackletown Road without her. I crossed over the river at Vicksburg, and suddenly had a feeling of home. It had been many years since we lived in Louisiana, although we did visit, somewhat surreptitiously, as often as we dared. Maybe it was the news that Pop no longer had anything to fear about the mill. Maybe it was going back to Crackletown. Maybe it was Grandma Bailey's passing. Whatever it was, I had a strong sense of going home. I stayed with Grandmama and Grandpapa, who loaned me a suit coat to wear since mine had evidently been purchased when I was four inches shorter than I now was. Grandpapa's was long on me, but long looked better than mid-forearm.

I drove over to the church well ahead of time. I had jotted down my comments on a piece paper I found in Grandpapa's library, aware that there were a number of speakers. It was folded in half lengthwise and in the inside pocket of Grandpapa's suit coat. I was not prepared for what I encountered, however. The place was packed. I guess two hundred mourners were in attendance, the women wearing beautiful dresses and hats and the men with polished shoes and three-piece suits. I had on a coat and tie, but I definitely felt underdressed. By the time I had found a parking place and made my way in, it was nearly time for the service. I did have the opportunity to speak briefly with Fredrick beforehand. He had grown even taller than the last time we had spoken, but his body was stooped by sorrow. Faint organ music softened the many conversations into a steady hum of voices. We agreed to talk later, after the service, so I took my seat. The gathered included people from all aspects of Winn Parish. The wealthy, the poor, local businesspeople, workers, black, white, brown: Grandma Bailey brought them all in. As I settled in near the front of the section where those speaking were seated, I saw that there were many of us scheduled to talk. The organ music grew louder, and everyone took their seats, shuffling a bit. I looked at the program and saw that I was the seventh listed. I had been to funerals before, of course, elderly family members on both sides, and Edward May's too, but this was not like those services. This was very much more a celebration. Grandma Bailey's niece Louella rose first and welcomed everyone, then she and her sister, whom I had not met before, sang "Crossing Chilly Jordan" in harmony. It was breathtaking. Then a woman who taught school down in Alexandria rose and talked about growing up along Crackletown Road and how Imogene Bailey had told her she was the smartest and prettiest every day and had encouraged her to go on to college. I could hear people murmuring, saying things like, "That's the way she was, all right. Mmhmm." The banker in town came up and talked about her legacy, what she had built in her years in the community, richer than it would have ever been without her. She was known for taking food to families who had come upon hard times, whether that be losing a loved one or losing a job. She had been a moving force in her church also. And local politicians always courted her approval, since her opinion carried so much sway amongst people in the area. If she liked you, she would let you know. If she didn't, she'd also let you know. Fellow mourners nodded their heads in affirmation. "That's true. Yes, sir, that's true." The organ then played a somber version of "Bye and Bye", and everyone retreated into memories of Imogene Bailey, who seemed to be everyone's grandmother. Then Fredrick's Uncle James, a very hefty man, stood and talked jokingly about Grandma Bailey's wonderful cooking making him the man he was today as he patted his large torso, making everyone laugh a little. He talked about how generous she had been, although she never had much. Somehow, she always found enough to share. Again, people spoke softly while he spoke: "She made the best cornbread dressing I ever had." "Never met someone she didn't want to feed them." "Food is love, she said. Food is love." I did recall Grandma Bailey saying that. Another musical interlude, this time with guitars and banjos, filled the room with "Just a Closer Walk with Thee" that had everyone clapping and then several of the women singing with it. I wasn't familiar with the song before then, but I vowed to learn it. I loved it. Then it was my turn. Although I had stood before audiences hundreds and hundreds of times, this was different. I walked up to the microphone that was next to Grandma Bailey's casket. She lay there unperturbed by all this fuss. I glanced over, then looked out at the rows of people gathered before me. I didn't take out my notes from my jacket pocket.

"Imogene Bailey," my voice cracked. "Imogene Bailey was my Grandma. She gave me love, and she gave me music and, yes, she gave me food." Several people chuckled. "She was my Grandma not because she was born to it, but because she wanted to love me, just like she wanted to love everyone."

"Amen." A voice came from the pews.

"She gave me so many gifts that I can never repay, except by paying it on to someone else." My eyes watered.

"Yes sir. That's right."

"Grandma Bailey shared her home with me and my family, shared her music, shared her heart. If we were hungry, she fed us."

"Uh huh."

"If we were sad, she hugged us."

"That's true."

"If we were sick, she treated us." The brightly colored dresses and suits before me blurred.

"Yes, she did."

"She once told me, we are all but a dapple of sunlight coming between the leaves of a cottonwood tree, here and gone in a brief warm moment."

"Mmm hmm."

"Our job, she told me, is to spread that light. To let others know that the light is within them too."

"That's right."

I looked over towards the casket. "Grandma Bailey, I promise you. I will spread the light you shared so generously with me." My voice was shaky, my knees quaky as I made my way back to my seat. I had intended to speak longer, but I couldn't. Besides, I had said what I wanted to say.

Another musical interlude followed, then more speakers, and finally her minister, a small, dark man who held his Bible close to his side. He started out talking about God's love and ended up getting filled with the spirit, calling out a sharp, "Hah!" after each line he spoke. Many in the crowd were calling out also, urging him on. When he had finished, and two of Grandma Bailey's nephews-in-law had helped him back to his seat, there was another song on the organ. I thought it was an amazing and wonderful service, one I thought Grandma Bailey would have loved.

We went outside to the gravesite that had been dug in the churchyard next to an array of markers inside a wrought iron fence. That service was much shorter, and then the crowd meandered back inside to eat since everyone had brought casserole dishes and platters of chicken and rolls. I stood, looking down at the casket, which six men had lowered down into the grave. Fredrick and I were the only ones left now, except for a man who stood off to the side leaning on a shovel, waiting for us to say our final goodbye to Grandma Bailey.

I walked over to Fredrick. "Fredrick, I'm so sorry."

Fredrick turned and leaned onto my shoulder. "What a wonderful woman. I can't believe she's gone." He wrapped his long arms around me and began to cry.

"I know, Fredrick. I know." I hugged him back.

He pulled back, stood up straighter with obvious intent. "But she's resting now." He set his lips tightly, then added, "It's selfish of me to want her here. She was sick and hurting. Now she's not." Another tear welled up, dropped to his cheek, and ran down his face. The air was full of earthiness. A small breeze wagged the willow leaves next to the graveyard. Across the fence, hidden in a shrub near the church somewhere, a white-throated sparrow gave out a trill of "Old Dan Peabody Peabody Peabody," as Grandma Bailey always described it. Fredrick wiped away his tear, found a smile. "Grandma always said she would love to come back someday as a sparrow so she could sing all day long. 'And one of them shall not fall on the ground without your Father.' Guess maybe she did." The bird sang again, and Fredrick leaned over onto me again and sobbed deeply.

I wanted to bring him up some, but I didn't have any words that would change a thing. I needed to do something, not say something. "Hey, Fredrick?"

He pulled back and stood. He was at least eight inches taller than I. "Yes, my brother?"

"I'm working on a record."

"That's good, Silas. That's good." He sounded like he wondered why that was apropos in the current situation.

"We've been talking about an album name. The producer wants to just use my name, but I wanted something more, something about my music, my life. I know what to name it now."

"Yeah?" He wiped away another tear that had trickled down his cheek.

"Yeah. 'Crackletown Road.'"

Fredrick found another smile. "I like it, Silas. I really do."

"Can I use your woodcut for the cover?"

He leaned over and hugged me again. "I would be honored, brother. I would be honored."

I pulled back from him. "Let's go eat, Fredrick. 'Food is love.'"

"Yes. Yes, it is." He threw his arm across my shoulders, and we walked back into the church. I would have thrown my arm over his shoulders too, but I couldn't reach them.

Once the album was finished, I did get more gigs in and around Nashville, and the album sold enough copies that I knew people were hearing my songs, and I loved that part, but it wasn't a huge seller, not that that was what I was necessarily after. I felt humbled that people wanted to listen to my songs, to my singing of my songs. A number of my songs had been done by others by now, including several that were pretty big hits. But these folks were listening to me singing them. I hoped I lived up to expectations.

We went on a kind of mini-tour the following year, opening for a number of big names. In places like Oklahoma City and Little Rock no one knew who we were, but it felt good to get out in front of new people. We traveled in a bus that someone else had outgrown, but it was just right for me and my new band members, Dave on bass and our drummer Jimmie, whom everyone called "Crash." It was exciting for us because it was new, but three weeks into our tour, we began to understand why so many artists talk about life on the road being so hard. We weren't exactly suffering. It was the monotony of the road, the drudgery of loading and unloading, the boredom of sitting all day looking out the window. And we were only a few weeks in. By the time we got to Bakersfield, the whole touring scene was beginning to jade us. Crash was ready to go nuts, sitting for so long on the bus. He drummed his leg, tapped his drumsticks on the back of the seat in front of him, fidgeted in his seat, and smoked one Marlboro after another until everyone in the bus reeked of cigarette smoke. Dave was naturally more laid back, but he too, was showing signs of stress, strumming the same chords on an acoustic guitar over and over. I spent the hours jotting down lyrics for songs, or for what might become songs. I wanted to be doing something productive, but I was getting stir crazy as well. But Bakersfield proved to be different.

The first thing that was different was that we opened for a very big name. In some places, we opened for a regional bigtime band, and a few places we opened for a band that had seen its glory days a few years before, although they were still well-known. But here, we opened for a band that had a current top forty song and had had a top ten song just recently. I felt a little intimidated, in fact. The venue was sold out ahead of time. This would be our largest audience.

We set up early, knowing we needed to keep our set simple since we had to take down between acts and the headliner had elaborate sets and lights. We tuned up backstage and waited. It was around ten after the hour when the promoter, who wore a buckskin jacket with fringed sleeves, walked out onto the stage and introduced us.

"Ladies and Gentlemen! The Silver Palace proudly presents, Silas LaMontaie and the Bayou Glad Band!" The applause was solid, but nothing like the headliner would receive. People were still finding their seats, and there were lots of conversations going on, but that was not unusual. We walked out, waved, and went to our spots. Crash climbed behind his Ludwigs and gave them a rat-a-tat. Dave plugged in his Hoffner, and I sat on the stool I always sat on and hooked up my Fender. I had a quiver in my belly, but I had done this enough, I knew I could push through. Besides, I always had a case of nerves before a show. That was normal. Then I looked up to take in just how big the audience was. The house lights were still up since people were still milling in. In the front row sat Jessie May, smiling at me. I nearly fell out of my chair. She looked a little different, her hair was longer, but her eyes were still that same deep-water blue, and her smile was still like a book from my past I had never stopped reading.

I turned around to Dave and Crash. "Fellas, remember that song we practiced before, 'Say Goodbye'?"

"Yeah," Dave nodded. Crash gave me a thumb's up.

I turned around and nodded towards the crowd. "This was the first song I ever wrote," I said into the microphone. My voice carried across the sea of heads and still settling bodies. We played "Say goodbye" and Jessie covered her mouth as if stifling a scream, but she did not cover her eyes. The audience liked it and clapped loudly. I gave Jessie a grin, and she waved at me. We played our usual set after that, all of the cuts from the album, and everyone seemed to like it, but at the end, I added "Lifeline." Jessie sat in the front row, crying now, but still smiling. My queasiness had gone away as soon as I saw Jessie. I couldn't believe she was there. I had heard through the family and friends she had ended up in California, but I did not expect to see her. I really wanted to play "Lonesome Goddess" too, but we had reached our time limit. We took our bows and walked off to very nice applause. I decided I rather liked Bakersfield. As we walked to the curtain, I turned to a stagehand.

"See the beautiful woman in blue there? Looking at us?"

"Yeah, she's really..."

"She is welcome backstage." I cut him off before he said something to make me mad.

"Oh, okay." He looked a bit dumbfounded.

As the opening act, we did not have a huge dressing area but instead shared an area cordoned off with speakers and equipment, but we never needed more than that. It wasn't our act to dress in a certain way or put on a big visual effect. I liked those shows fine, it just wasn't what we did. We played our music, or, rather, my music, since I wrote all the songs. When Jessie came peering around the corner looking for us, Crash and Dave made themselves scarce. I had mentioned she might be coming back. Just before he left, Crash gave me a glance with both eyebrows up, as if to say, "Way to go, LaMontaie." I ignored him. The lead act was still setting up, and we could hear the guitars tuning, some horns playing random tunes somewhere else backstage, and equipment being pushed around the stage. Jessie stood there looking at me for a moment from the other end of the backstage area.

"Hi, Jessie." I walked towards her, and she came towards me. We met in the middle with a hug.

"Oh, Silas. I just can't believe it's you." She pulled back to look at me. Her voice was smooth, languid, calm. "I saw the advertisement and saw your name, and I could not even think of missing the show." She leaned in towards my chest and rested her face against me. It felt to me like she fit right there next to my chest.

"So, you live in Bakersfield now?" I held her close. I was a little afraid if I let go, she might be gone.

"No, I live in L.A., Silas. I only came up for the show." She looked up at me. The noise level increased so I led her to our dressing area, farther back behind the stage where it was quieter, although we could still hear some of the sounds of preparation.

We sat facing each other on the tired sofa in the dressing area. "L.A., huh? How did you get all the way out here, Jessie?"

Jessie gave a short laugh and looked down at her hands. "Oh, who knows? Some path of least resistance, I suppose."

"Are you working?"

"Yeah, another bookstore. This is more about rare books than anything. I like it."

"You like L.A.?"

"Yeah, usually. Sometimes L.A. is like cheap bourbon: it only tastes bad the first ten drinks. After that, it still tastes bad, but you can't tell anyone about it."

"Ha, I get that."

"I've missed you, Silas." Her voice was more serious now.

"I've missed you too, Jessie."

"You know what people ask me out here?" She looked at the floor as if she were hoping to gather herself.

"What?"

"What my last name is. They think Jessie May are my first and middle names." She smiled thinly.

"You look wonderful." She really did. She looked calmer, more relaxed than I had seen her in years.

"You are very sweet to say so, Silas." She ducked her face slightly, then looked back up at me. "But what about you? I would ask how you got out here too, but I guess I know. You're a star now."

I laughed loudly. "Oh, no. I am not. Not at all."

"Well, you're on tour with these guys. That's big."

"Well, we aren't really on tour with them. We have some shows together, but mostly we're just traveling around opening for a number of bands. Connie set it all up."

"Connie?"

"She's my agent. Been in the business for something like forty years. She's amazing." I thought I saw just a tinge of jealousy run across Jessie's face when I mentioned Connie, so I decided to make sure she knew Connie was not a romantic interest. The nod Jessie gave told me she understood that.

"Are you touring a lot?" Her question seemed perfunctory as if she were not sure what to ask.

"No, just this tour. I'm not that well known. And I don't love touring that much."

"I love your album."

"Ha. So that was you who bought it!" I pointed at her.

"You're funny, Silas. I'll bet lots of people bought it."

"Well, no, really, not a lot. But I'm not worried about it. I wanted to make an album. I wanted to do that, you know? To have that experience. But honestly, I think I like writing songs better. Let other folks tour, and I can just sit back and write some more songs and take it easy."

"But they make the big money then, don't they?"

"Yeah, but it turns out, I do okay, and I don't have the same pressure. No one notices much, but I've gotten something of a reputation as a songwriter, so Connie sells them just about as fast as I can write them. One of mine is actually top twenty right now. I like that arrangement."

"But you're touring now." She looked around the space. The headline band was almost ready to play somewhere in front of us, the speakers facing away from us, giving a subtle thumping of a bass beat.

"Well, again, something I wanted to do, just to have the experience." I shrugged. I had not told this to Dave and Crash yet, but the truth was, my heart was not into touring. My bandmates would be perhaps disappointed to find that out. "I won't do another, I don't think."

"I'm very glad you did this one." She shot me that smile that always disarmed me utterly. "I can't believe you played my songs, Silas. You are so surprising. I think I'm beginning to learn a few things I maybe always knew, Sy." She was sitting sideways on the couch, facing me. She looked as comfortable as if she had sat there a hundred times, leaning her arm against the back of the couch. There was a brief pause as I let her comment sink in.

"You're still my best friend, Silas, aren't you?"

"Yes, I am. Now may I carry your books for you?" I pictured that walk home from The Yale School once again.

Jessie laughed. "Yes, you may."

"I have another song I wrote for you, Jessie. We didn't have time to play it. Can I play it for you now?"

Jessie looked quietly at me for a long moment, her eyes the color of the ocean. "I would be honored, Silas," she finally said. She took a deep breath.

I took my Gibson out of its case and played "Lonesome Goddess" for Jessie. At the end, my voice cracked just a little as it always did when I played it, even though I really tried to keep it from breaking. But when I sang the line, "I was the one wrote songs for you," I knew how deeply I meant that and my voice quaked through the knot in my throat. I repeated the chord progression and faded out as best I could acoustically. When I looked up, Jessie was staring at me, a tear running down her cheek.

We sat there in silence for a moment, just looking at each other. Jessie let the tear run its course, down to her jaw, while she stared at me. I reached over and wiped it away with my palm. She kept looking intently at me. "Silas?" She said finally. "Silas?"

"Yes, Jessie May."

"I know...deep down...I have always...how could I not...?" She reached her arms out, and I put the Gibson aside, and we kissed. It was the kiss I had waited for since I saw Jessie May throwing dirt clods in Sardis. My heart raced. I was holding and kissing my Jessie May. My head swam. My head was dizzy and hot. I pulled back for just a moment to look at her face. She looked up at me, her eyes wide now. That's when I knew Momma was right. Love conquers all.

# Chapter 19

I drove to the airport to pick up Jessie. It brought back memories of being the singing shuttlebus driver. It was funny, really, that essentially busking on the shuttle bus to increase my tips had led me just where I wanted to be, fulfilling my dream I had told Grandma Bailey about. But I no longer drove the bus, and even Ezra had been laid to rest. I was now driving a late model Pontiac. It was perhaps an unusual choice for an up-and-coming songwriter, but Pop said it was solid and would need little maintenance, and that suited me fine, and the price was good. I stopped at the curb and saw Jessie, walking towards me now. We had spent the last few months getting our separate lives in order so we could be together. We talked on the phone every night, remembering things from long ago and planning for our future. I could not have been more ecstatic. Each morning I awoke to a feeling of disbelief. Had I perhaps dreamed that I had finally gained her love? If so, I did not care to awaken. I jumped out of the car and ran over to her.

"Silas!" She dropped her suitcases, and we kissed. I vowed to never take those kisses for granted.

"How was your flight?" I reached down and grabbed her two suitcases.

"Long, but wonderfully uneventful. You are such a welcome sight, Silas. I am so glad to see you. But I am bushed." She did look a bit fatigued.

I looked behind her. "Where are your other suitcases?"

"This is it, Sy. I got rid of everything else." She waved her arms into the air. "I didn't need it and, I realized, I didn't even want it. I gave it all away. I want to start all over again, you and me. What else could we possibly need? They were things." She let her arms drop onto my shoulders again. "And you are the man of my dreams, Silas LaMontaie." We kissed again. I had a nagging worry about being parked too long along the curb.

"We need to move the car, Jess."

"Okay." I led the way back to the car. She fairly sashayed across the sidewalk, as if she had let go of a heavy weight. She let her hands float up in a kind of happy dance as she walked, but she also looked exhausted. I put down the heavy cases and opened the trunk. "Did they throw you a going away party at the shop?"

"They did. It was really quite nice. I will miss some of those friends. They were good people. You'll never guess what they gave me as going away presents." She flitted over to the passenger door.

"Books?" I opened the door for her.

"Ha. Yes, they gave me books."

"That explains that one suitcase."

"It was heavy, wasn't it?"

"Well, at least they didn't have to go far to buy your presents."

"Yeah, and they knew I love books. Did you do that to me? You've always had a book in progress, haven't you?" Jessie swung her legs in, and I closed the door. I went around and got into the driver's seat.

"I got that from Momma and from her Daddy both. I never met folks who love to read any more than they do."

"Where are we going now, Silas?" She yawned.

"Home."

"Are you going to sing to me while we take the bus, Shuttlebus Twitty?" She teased.

"Ha. No, maybe you should just rest some."

"Good." She leaned her head back, and I thought she would fall asleep before we got to my now larger apartment in the Gulch area. When we arrived, I led her up to our place, and I loved being able to describe it as "our place." She lay across the bed. Just before she fell asleep, she opened one eye, smiled at me, and said, "I'm so glad to be here with you, Silas. I just realized: I'm home."

"I'm very glad you are here too, Jessie." I caressed her arm.

"I love you, Silas LaMontaie." Then she fell asleep. My throat was tight. I watched her sleeping for a long time and then went and got her suitcases.

I slept sideways on the bed next to Jessie. When we awoke the next morning, she said she couldn't believe I let her sleep with all her clothes on. I told her undressing unconscious women was not something I hoped to be good at for a whole variety of reasons. I made coffee while Jessie looked around the apartment. I had emptied out the drawers in Grandma Boudreaux's dresser that Momma and Pop had given me and she unpacked. She brought a stack of old books into the kitchen.

"Look at this." She placed the books on the counter. "This is what my friends at the shop gave me. These are really nice books." She picked up a battered book with a marbled cover. "This is a second edition of Jane Eyre. A little rough, but still rare." She placed it aside. "And look at this one. This is so interesting." She opened a blue box that I would have thought had 33 1/3 albums in it. "It's a picture book with beautiful paintings for children and the pages all have moving parts. 'My Whirligig Fair.' It's so cute! Carly said it's for when we have kids." She cut her eyes at me, smirking.

I shot her a grin. "Well, first things first." I put a cup of coffee with a dollop of cream in it on the counter for Jessie, just the way she liked it. "How about coffee first?"

She gave me a furtive smile and picked up the cup and smelled it. Then she smiled bigger. "Chicory?"

"Well, yeah, you're with a Louisiana man now." I grabbed my coffee, and we headed for the living room area. It still wasn't a huge place. Lots bigger than the last one, but when I had rented it, it was only me, so I had not figured on getting a big place to keep up. Now all those ideas seemed like dandelion seeds drifting away on a hot summer breeze.

"I really like your place, Silas." Jessie looked around.

I looked over at her. "Our place." I corrected her.

She nodded and sat on the sofa. "Yes. It is our place now, isn't it?" She took a long drink from the cup. "Wow, we've taken a twisted road to get here, haven't we?"

"All the way from Yale to Nashville."

Jessie laughed loudly. "I love telling folks I went to Yale. Wow. It really has been a lifetime." She drank again from the cup. I realized I was watching her every move, and I didn't want her to feel odd so I made a point of taking a long drink of my black coffee. "Silas?" She looked up at me, and I sat down next to her. She twisted around and put her feet under her as she faced me.

"Yes, Jess?"

"Do you remember the first time we did something together?"

"I remember everything, Jess." My mind went through all the times we were together. I wasn't exactly sure what she meant by "did something together."

"We went fishing."

"Oh, yes. I do remember. We brought the fish home in a coal bucket."

"It's a wonder we weren't poisoned or something." Jessie laughed.

"I know." I took another long drink of coffee. I made strong coffee, the way the Boudreaux's and LaMontaie's liked it.

"Do you remember what I asked you to do for me that day?" She looked at me with those incredibly blue eyes.

"I do for a fact."

"No, you don't."

"I assure you I do."

"What? What did I ask you?" She cradled the coffee cup in both hands. The sun streamed through the sheers at the window, filling up the room with light.

"You asked me to show you 'Bayou.'"

She dropped her jaw. "Oh my God, you really do remember everything, don't you, Silas LaMontaie?"

"Well, everything about you, Jess."

We didn't come out of the apartment for days.

We drove up to Tolu and Marion the next week to see family. Mr. May looked as old and tired as if he had been ninety. It was as if losing Edward had taken thirty years off his life, and he just kept aging from there. Cliff was running the farm now, and, in fact, was doing it very well. He had even bought up several of the surrounding farms. He had married a woman named Judy he had met in college, and they were expecting twins. It was great to see Cliff again. Mrs. May was chatty and bubbly, telling us about people at her church and who had been in town and the latest goings-on around the county. It didn't matter that we knew hardly any of the people she talked about. We listened, sitting on the Mays' divan, our arms interlaced like a honeysuckle vine, holding onto each other as if one of us might somehow slip off from the other. Jessie asked questions about who had ended up where, although I knew she really didn't care. But her mom wanted to share it, so Jessie showed her interest. Jessie said she did that every time she came home and even when she called from California. Jessie said it made her mother happy to catch Jessie up to speed, so she let her.

When we got to Momma and Pop's place, they greeted us on the front porch. Momma had a look in her eyes. Pop could be inscrutable when he wanted to be, but not Momma. She had news of some sort. But Pop being on the front porch was also different. He usually waited inside, reading at his chair.

"Come in. Come in." Pop patted me on the shoulder while Momma hugged Jessie.

I led the way in. There were boxes everywhere. I spun around. "What's going on here?"

"Hold on. Hold on." Momma walked past us and into the kitchen. I looked around at all the boxes, some of them already taped up. Momma came back with a tray of glasses and lemonade. She held the tray out, and Jessie took a glass. She turned to me. "Sy, you want some lemonade?"

"Give the man a beer, Bele." Pop grinned and went into the kitchen himself. He came back with three cans of beer. "Jessie?"

"I'm good, Papa L." Jessie raised her glass of lemonade and drank.

Pop handed me a beer. I could see him turning over the moniker in his head. I could tell he liked it. "Have a seat." Pop waved towards the couch with one beer. I took one of the beers from him. Jessie and I sat on the couch as close as we could get to each other. Three more people could have sat on the couch, no more room were we taking up. I held Jessie around the shoulder. Her warmth was fuel to me. Momma put the tray on the coffee table and took a glass for herself. She sat in her usual wingback. Pop ensconced himself in his leather chair.

"So, what's going on? Are you guys moving?" My voice echoed in the room. I smelled Momma's scented candles from somewhere, perhaps the box behind me. I took a drink of my beer, the hops bringing a pleasant bitter taste forward.

"Yes, we are, son. We're moving home." Pop looked more serious now, but he also looked like he found a ten-dollar bill in his overcoat he had forgotten about. He was as happy as I had seen him in a long time.

"Home? I thought this was home, Pop." I took another drink. The beer was cool, light.

"No, we're moving to Abbeville, Silas." Momma chimed in.

"Abbeville?" I looked at Momma and then Pop. Jessie was watching the conversation like she might watch a tennis match, her head turning back and forth.

"Where's Abbeville?" Jessie took a sip of lemonade and put the glass down on a coaster on the coffee table.

I shot her a smile. "That would be bayou country, cher." Jessie smiled back at me. I looked back at Pop. "So, are you not worried about...?"

"I worry too much." Pop drank from his beer. "Listen." He leaned forward, holding his beer can in both hands between his knees. "I owe you an apology. Both of you." He looked back and forth between Momma and me.

"An apology? For what?" I shrugged.

"I took on something as a kind of personal mission in life, something I didn't even have to do, and I made a decision that affected you both without even giving you an explanation."

"Bennie, I never needed an explanation to be with you." Momma sat calmly, familiarly in her chair.

"Thank you, Bele. But I made you leave everything, leave family and friends and everything else."

"But Pop..."

"I had no right, though."

"But Pop..."

"No. A man made a huge mistake and then I made it my mistake."

"Wait. Pop."

"I'm sorry." Pop looked at the floor before him. Momma stood and went to his side, rubbing his shoulder.

"Thank you, Pop." I put the beer on a coaster in front of me. Pop looked up at me sadly. "Thank you for moving us from Loreauville and Calvin." Pop's expression changed, his eyebrows furrowing up, confused.

"What?"

"Pop." I glanced over at Jessie. I know she saw where I was going because she began to smile at me. "Thank you."

"Yes, Papa L, thank you." Jessie looked at my parents, who were huddled together by Pop's chair. Pop had turned grey for the most part. Momma's hair was paler too, although still auburn. They both suddenly seemed very vulnerable to me. Momma patted Pop's shoulder. She knew. Pop was still looking sorrowful.

"Pop, if you hadn't brought us where we ended up, I never would have met Jessie. Don't you see? It happened this way because it was the only way it could happen. Heck, I should be calling up Charlie's dad and thanking him for burning down the mill."

"No, he shouldn't have . . ." Pop shook his head.

"I'm kidding, Pop. But it all came together for me to find Jessie, you know? You don't owe me an apology, Pop. You never did. If I had never found Jessie May, my life would be empty, vacant." Jessie looked at me with those blue eyes, and I stopped just to look at them. "See?" I finally regained my focus and looked at my parents. "Can you imagine not seeing those eyes?"

"You're sweet, Silas. But that's enough." Jessie leaned forward and picked up her glass. She gave me a coy glance then looked at my parents. "Abbeville, huh? And that's home?' She turned her head and looked at me. "Is that where you had all those crazy experiences with your cousins, Silas?"

"Grandma Boudreaux lives there. She's getting older and needs some help." Momma walked back to her chair and sat. "We're going to go and help take care of her."

"Tolu has been fine, and between the rivers was okay, but I am eager to be going home." Pop looked towards the door, focusing on something far away. "I won't lie; I have missed my home."

"And it's closer to my Daddy and Momma so we can see them also. It's a good move." Momma nodded.

"You know, down there, no one thinks it's odd when I say something in French." Pop had a wistful look.

"Well, I think that's great, guys. I am tickled to hear this. You need to be home, 'Frenchy.'" Dad shot me a quick smile. I stood up and raised my nearly empty beer. "To home!"

"To home," Momma, Pop, and Jessie all said. I looked at Jessie, and now she was looking a little contemplative also.

We left after dinner, heading back to Nashville. I started telling Jessie more about Vermillion Bay and Abbeville. I told her about Johnny and Beau and how they used to tease us when we were children. Now, Johnny was a fairly prominent lawyer in Abbeville and Beau ran a hospital in Lake Charles. I recounted stories to her about fishing in the bayous and about the wonderful celebrations we had with étouffée and gumbo and fish and even alligator sometimes. Even though I had told her some of these stories before, I was having fun retelling them. She let me talk. I told her how we all had wine and beer, the kids with a healthy dose of water in their wine glasses, but we were part of the celebration. And then there was the music: Cajun ballads and rousing zydeco songs played by the family while all the kids hopped around in the yard, dancing. I told her about how hot and wet it could be in the summer, but how it never kept us from being outside, swimming in creeks while we watched for alligators, climbing up in the live oaks, making our way through pine forests, the scent of the trees intoxicating, collecting pine cones to toss into the bonfire later throwing sparks into the heavy night sky, so humid we could feel the moisture. I even told her about Sophie, to whom I had played my first music with an inspired if childhood version of "Low Down Blues." Then I told her about all the festivals. Every little town in south Louisiana had a festival in the fall, each one celebrating something unique to that town. There were food festivals to honor boudin, pecans, oysters, shrimp, and crawfish all across the region. There was a music festival just about any time of the year, from jazz to blues to country to Cajun. I told Jessie how Pop and Momma loved going someplace nearly every weekend, and they always took me. I talked about Christmas in southern Louisiana being an entirely different scene, with big bonfires and oyster dressing and the singing of French carols. Once I got started, I couldn't stop. I was very glad Pop and Momma were going back. I told her, don't even start talking about New Orleans around me. New Orleans is a great place, I told her, complicated, sometimes, and not simply a tourist destination, but the mix of cultures and the almost European feel to the city was what I liked. Jessie listened quietly the whole time I went on and on about Cajun country.

Finally, as we passed Clarksville, she looked over at me during a rare pause in my stream-of-consciousness recounting of southern Louisiana, and said, "Sy, where do you write your music?"

I looked over at her. A part of me was still wanting to tell her about Momma and Pop going back home. "In the other bedroom?" She knew where I kept the keyboard and my guitars, where I spent my time writing. I didn't understand the question.

"No, that's not where you write it. That's where you play it, but you write it in your head." She watched the highway now.

"Well, yeah I suppose that's true."

"Sy, I've never heard you talk about any place the way you talk about Louisiana."

I laughed. "There aren't any other places like Louisiana."

"You don't talk about Nashville like that." She looked back at me.

"I love Nashville." I shrugged.

"I know you like it there. I do too. But I've never heard anyone talk about a place like you just did unless it was home."

"What?"

"Honeybunch?" Jessie took on a mock southern accent, but her midwestern twang still shone through. She leaned towards me, taking hold of my arm.

"Yes, cher?" I tried my best to say it like Pop did.

"You reckon maybe we ought to move back home too?" She leaned her head against my shoulder now.

"Home is a box you fill with memories." I still tried to sound like my father.

"But, Darling, you have a head full of memories already. So wouldn't 'home' be where the memories need to be put?"

I didn't answer right away. The little game of southern drawls took a break while I thought about Jessie's point. I'll admit, I had never considered moving back to Louisiana after the fire at the mill. But then I remembered how much it felt like going home crossing the bridge at Vicksburg when I went to Calvin for Grandma Bailey's funeral. I even waxed nostalgic over the peanut fields and the muggy, hot summers. I realized then how much I did miss my time in Cajun country. I turned it over in my head for a few minutes. It made all the sense in the world. "You're really amazing, Jessie May. You know that?" She was still leaning against my shoulder, and I raised my arm to put it around her and held her against my side.

I talked it over with Connie and Sam, and they said I had no reason not to live anywhere I wanted to. In fact, they noted that my songs were in high demand so that they were sold nearly as quickly as I wrote them. They also told me if we ever wanted to make another album, I could always come in for that. Lots of people make records and don't live in Nashville. With that assurance, Jessie and I traveled south several times to scout where we would live. While I had tremendous memories of small-town life, I found myself drawn to New Orleans. We decided we could go out and see Momma and Pop and enjoy the old Boudreaux place and still live in the city, thereby having perhaps the best of both worlds. It was on a visit to check out places to live that we rode the St. Charles Street trolley just to take a break from the house hunting. It was a balmy spring morning, and we were enjoying the "clack-clack" of the trolley and the rhythm of the movement, huddled together through The Garden District. Once we got to the park, we wandered around for a bit then decided to go back. We were on the number 11 bus coming back up Magazine Street when Jessie saw it. Suddenly, she focused on a building along the street. She sat up straight and stared out the window. She stood and pulled the bell for the next stop. I had no idea what was going on. She hustled me off the bus and kept saying, "Wait. Wait. You'll see." She was in a hurry too. I could barely keep up with her. Then she stopped before a shop. The rustic hand-painted black and white sign said it was White Cat Bookshop and another sign in the window said it was for sale. We went in and spoke to the owner, an older woman who was ready to retire and move in with her daughter in Metairie. For now, the woman lived in an apartment in the back on the second floor of the shop.

The bookstore needed updating, but Jessie had been working in a variety of bookstores, and if we could live in the back of this one while she rejuvenated the shop, my income was plenty to make a go of it. I loved the location; the accounting was good also. I asked Connie to look over the profit and loss statement, and she said it was making money, just not a lot of it. Jessie was confident she could bring it up. Within a few months, we were moving into the apartment we had painted and fixed up some, living and working in New Orleans. Jessie worked on the store, especially on setting up events and signings to bring people in. She filled in the holdings and set up some cozy areas for people to come in and read. I helped out when I wasn't writing songs, my longstanding love of reading making me a decent resource for customers looking for a good read. Then I suggested we set up an open mic night. It would be a great way to bring people in, plus I wanted to give someone else the chance I had. We had poetry and short stories as well as music. I sometimes took a turn, playing whatever song I was working on, which gave me the opportunity to try them out and slaked my desire to play my music for folks. Since some people knew my songs, that increased the audience, and the bookstore started making a bigger profit. I doubted it would ever be a huge enterprise, but neither of us wanted a big store to take care of. We liked it the way it was. Jessie even went to the shelter and rescued a white cat to wander the premises since the original stray the previous owner had named the store after had long since passed away. And the open mic nights didn't bother her a bit since she was as deaf as the queen of spades. We named her Bastet.

It was after several months of turning the bookstore around that I sat on a plain wooden chair and played a song I had been working on for a long time. I waited until Jessie was sitting behind the checkout counter, sipping a cup of tea.

"Good evening. We are pleased you are here." I tested the microphone distance and pushed it back enough so that my "P's" didn't sound like firecrackers going off. The twenty seats were full, as they usually were for open mic night. As a rule, customers in bookstores are not a rowdy bunch, and this audience was also respectful. "I'd like to play one I've been working on for some time now. Even my Jessie May hasn't heard this one yet." I saw her look up and several people twisted in their seats to ascertain her whereabouts. It's called 'I hope you always heard what I never said'." I played a simple fingering opening, then went into my song:

"Climb on the beaver dam, wait for the moon,
"Walk down gravel roads, hide in poplar trees,
"Hold your hand as we walk on home from school,
"Steal some berries, scratches all on our knees,
"Trying to show what I couldn't seem to say,
"Just what I was feeling every day."

"The way that you look right through to my soul,

"Knowing without you I'd never be whole,
"The thoughts turn me round in my head,
"I hope you always heard what I never said."

"Came high school and you were always the queen,
"Daring and crazy and free as the wind,
"Hoping you'd find me someplace in between,
"Writing love notes that I could never send,
"Trying to show what I couldn't seem to say,
"Just what I was feeling every day."

"The way that you look right through to my soul,
"Knowing without you I'd never be whole,
"The thoughts turning me round in my head,
"I hope you always heard what I never said."

"Dance in the kitchen to our favorite song,
"Watch the children playing out on the lawn,
"Any time away is always too long,
"I need to hold you right here in my arms,
"Trying to show what I couldn't seem to say,
"Just what I was feeling every day."

"The way that you look right through to my soul,
"Knowing without you I'll never be whole,
"The thoughts turning me round in my head,
"I hope you always heard what I never said."

I played a fadeout and looked up. The audience applauded, but it was Jessie's huge smile that made me happiest. I made way for the next performer, a teenaged girl whose poetry was heartfelt anguish, if a bit coarser than I cared for, with one poem being little more than one curse word repeated seventeen times. But that's open mic night. Anything goes. By the time I made it to the glass cases that served as the checkout counter, Jessie was ringing up a sale to two thin, jabbering, long-haired fellows. I touched Jessie on her shoulder, and she turned around to give me a hug. Then she whispered in my ear as she hugged me. "I heard you every day. Sometimes, hearing isn't enough. Sometimes I have to be sure to listen too." I pulled back to look at her. Her eyes had a royal blue tint. Jessie said. "Thank you for the song, Silas. But it isn't quite accurate."

"I know."

"We don't have children."

"I know. Think we should do something about that, cher?"

"Yes, I do." She leaned her head against my chest, then pulled back to look at me again. "Let's go out front and listen for the stars to come out."

"Okay, cher. Let's do that."

# Chapter 20

*Jessie May*

I met Silas LaMontaie when I was a little girl at home between the rivers in western Kentucky. When I met Silas, he was a scrawny kid with a big heart and a love of books who had recently moved near Sardis Church. I, on the other hand, was born in Carmack, Kentucky, in a ramshackle farmhouse near the Kuttawa Ferry that crossed the Cumberland River. I knew everyone in our community. Many of them were related to us, and even those who were not kinfolks were much like relatives, even to the point where we sometimes didn't really like them very much, but we would do anything in the world for them if they needed us. Daddy farmed, growing hay and a small tobacco plot that supplied most of our cash income for the year. Mom gardened and canned and sang in the little choir at Sardis on Sunday when the preacher came through, which was every fourth weekend. I discovered later that we were what most people would call "poor." The funny thing is, I never knew that as a child. It was just childhood. I had everything I could ask for. I had ponds to swim in, lakes to fish in, trees to climb, woods to explore, deer and fox and raccoons to spy upon, birds to sing to me. I had a bed to sleep in, and I never went hungry a day in my life. I had all I could dream of asking for. And I had a very best friend, once I met Silas. He was different from anyone I had met before. He was both fearless and inquisitive, which could have been a dangerous combination, but he was also smart. He was smart enough not to get himself or me in any real danger. He had these green-blue eyes that seemed to be always studying me like maybe I had a secret to tell at any moment that he wanted to hear. And maybe I did.

One day, the government decided they needed to build a big dam across the Cumberland River to make electricity for the TVA and to help control flooding, which was pretty much an annual problem. When the government built the dam, the waters rose and flooded my little hometown community.

They washed away my roots. I was left adrift. It was something I felt deep within me, a kind of losing my ground, I guess. In Carmack, I had answers to every question. It's perhaps true I was young enough that my questions were built on naïveté, but of course, I didn't know that then. But I knew where to hike to find mulberries, and I knew how to run a tractor. I could out pitch just about any boy in the area. I knew what trees were good for making chewing gum, spruce being my personal favorite. I really had no idea all the things I didn't know. What I found out was that when we were forced to leave, and, even more, when they tore down our old house and flooded our family's land, I was untethered, set free like a toy boat on a creek, sailing downstream and unable to find a mooring. Downstream proved to be exciting, but often unfulfilling, in the end. Yes, I saw the world, and I am glad for those experiences, but ultimately, they did not fill that longing within me to be home. I mistakenly thought if I looked enough places, I could eventually find home. I discovered I couldn't find home; I could only make home.

Silas and his family were new and different from anyone else between the rivers. Silas' Daddy was even colored different, like olive oil, almost. And he and Silas both had that hair as black as the new moon. Silas' Momma, though, was fair, with the prettiest auburn hair I ever saw, and she was where Silas got those blue-green eyes. The color of her eyes always reminded me of the slag rocks we used to find around Mammoth Furnace back before my Daddy's leg got twisted up in the bailer and we would hike all over the area. Silas' Momma loved books, and she gave that too to Silas. It was one of the things we shared. I read a lot too, although I maybe didn't devour books the way Silas did. But we didn't have extra money for a lot of books, so I learned to treasure them when I got them. My brother Ed always gave me a book for Christmas. He was big enough to help with cutting and stripping tobacco and wiry enough to climb into the top of the barn to hang it, so he always made some money in the fall, and he would spend a lot of that money on our family at Christmas. But then they took Ed away from my family and me during the Vietnam War. That was the worst thing. They took our home, our land, our roots, and then, just for good measure, they took our Ed. That's a pit that can't be filled.

A part of me always knew Silas loved me. He had a crush on me when we were children, and later, when we found each other again in high school, he would watch me with those eyes that had no bottom, and I knew he loved me. I just didn't appreciate what that meant. There were lots of boys who wanted my attention, and I saw no reason to be selfish with something I could so freely make, but Silas was different even then. He watched me. He didn't just look at me. He watched me. To tell you the truth, it was a little unnerving sometimes, knowing he was watching, waiting, as it turns out, for me to wake up and know what he always seemed to know.

When we were children playing outside in the hot, sticky Kentucky summer, we often ran all day without shoes. They were too much trouble. But the blacktop road that coursed through Carmack would get heated up with the sun and burn our feet, so we learned to walk on the painted stripe in the road because it was cooler. Of course, the stripe was in the middle of the road, so we kept a watch out for traffic, which thankfully was never heavy, but we listened and kept our eyes open, and then one of us would yell, "Car!" and we would scamper off the road until the cars passed, the drivers waving to us since we surely knew them. Then we would gingerly make our way back to the stripe for the next leg of our adventure, whatever that might be. When I look back, that seems like what Silas always did for me. He was looking out for us both while we went about learning who we were.

Silas is a wonderful songwriter. He writes songs for me and sings them for me while he plays his guitar when I'm feeling anxious or worried. His voice is like a song from the summers of my childhood that I remember hearing played on wind chimes, rustling leaves, and katydids. It's always a beautiful song, even if there are no words, and it always lulls me to sleep with a smile on my face and calm in my soul. It's as if when he sings, he has just protected me again from a passing farm truck, and I can go back out on the cool white stripe.

Silas and I married out at Grandma Boudreaux's house near Abbeville. It was the most amazing celebration I ever saw. It was in April, and everything was full of life and color. The magnolia trees were ready to burst with blooms, their leaves a deep green. Grandma Boudreaux's hollyhocks and azaleas were in full bloom. The entire lawn was framed by patches of blue-eyed grass. Cliff and Judy brought Mom and Daddy, of course, and they had a wonderful time. It was the best I had seen Daddy in a long time. Mom made a lot of new friends, and I think they were nearly ready to move down after the wedding as much as they enjoyed it. We had made long rows of tables out of sawhorses and boards and old doors and the like covered it all by rolling out bolts of bleached muslin. We had bouquets of blue hydrangeas in glass jars along the center of the tables. I met all his family, including Beau and Johnny, who were still wild, even though they had real careers and real responsibilities. I sometimes wondered if going back to Grandma Boudreaux's just let them revert back to their younger days. But in any case, they were crazy. Momma L's parents were there too, of course, and Silas's Grandpapa sat on a rocking chair on the porch, his cane across his lap, and held forth with a number of the youngsters in attendance who sat all over the porch around him. Cliff and Judy's twins were there too. Grandpapa told tales of woodland spirits and a story about how the opossum got her pouch. The children were enthralled, and Grandpapa was having the time of his life.

I also got to meet Fredrick Bailey, Silas's old friend from Calvin, who came down for the wedding. He's a fascinating man to talk with since he's terrible with small talk. As a result, he says things that are almost startling.

For example, I asked him, "So, Fredrick, what do you he do?" It seemed pretty innocuous a question to me.

"I'm a revolutionary." He looked down at me, his hair braided and draped down his back. He said it very matter-of-factly.

"A revolutionary. Well, I guess someone needs to do it." I didn't know exactly what to say. I took a sip of my muscadine wine one of Papa L's cousins had made. It was fruity and tart.

He nodded and looked across the lawn to where Silas was standing. "I am what many call an 'artist.' What I believe is that all true artists work in the same medium regardless of what vehicle they used to express it. That one medium is truth. True art," he said, "reveals truth, and speaking the truth, especially to power, is subversive, revolutionary. Consequently, all artists are revolutionaries. That is what I consider my profession." He saw Silas turn his head and focus on him and Fredrick excused himself to go speak with him. I watched him go hug Silas, and I mulled over that surprising forty-five-second conversation. Silas told me later that besides being a revolutionary, Fredrick was an art professor over in Lafayette. I told Silas we needed to see him more often; I liked his revolutionary friend.

After Papa L's priest had pronounced us married and we had jumped over a broomstick, we served up étouffée and jambalaya and every kind of local delicacy we could come up with. The boudin balls were a huge hit. We all feasted, then the music started, and since no one could dance until Silas and I did, we danced the first song. It was Jole Blon. We let the violin and accordion swing us around the yard in a circle, and soon everyone was dancing with us. We danced until early the next day, the Cajun music keeping us energized. Beau and Johnny got pretty loaded on the muscadine wine and took over the dance floor at times, leaving their wives at the edge. They started dancing a two-step with each other but ended up in a jitterbug. Everyone hooted and laughed and urged them on. Silas thought there might have been some brandy involved as well. Even Mom got a bit tipsy, and I had never seen her drink any alcohol whatsoever. We all had the best time.

We love the bookstore. It's not at all hectic, so we can make plans on what to do next and where we want it to go. Silas is still writing songs and has played a few gigs around the Garden District, but he says he's doing it to keep in touch with his music and how people respond to it more than for the money. Some of his songs have been pretty big hits, so that's always interesting, to turn on the radio and hear a song he wrote being played over the airwaves. We have built a life that just works. When I was running everywhere looking for answers the questions I could not formulate, I never dreamed I would end up here at The White Cat Bookstore with Silas and Bastet. But like Silas's Grandmama says, "If you throw your dreams to the wind, you shouldn't be surprised if you find yourself someday flying a kite all alone." I didn't want to fly a kite alone.

Silas and I are expecting. It's a boy. We want to name him Silas also since Momma L was mostly right about the book Silas Marner. Love does indeed conquer all, but even more, love redeems us all and makes us whole.

# Afterword

These days, we are increasingly disengaged from our world. We move around in a bubble of our immediate concerns, unaware of anything beyond a few feet from us. We so rarely are actually involved with our world in a way that fulfills us that disengagement becomes the norm. For the most of us, we don't plant or harvest. We don't create or build. We don't sit under a tree and feel the cool earth below us, hear the rustling of leaves in the wind, lean against the trunk, and trace the patterns of bark against our backs. As a result, we have holes. We have holes in our souls, holes in our spirit, that make us feel empty, wanting, enigmatically alone amidst the crowds we walk within. We feel those holes as a kind of longing as if we have forgotten something and recognize that we have forgotten it, yet we cannot bring it to mind. We try to fill the holes, too often, as we are told: buy something, eat something, be distracted by something. But it is the nature of this alienation that such superficial fillings are by their very structure incapable of holding in our holes, so the holes return, made larger by the transient effort, in the same way, a hole in the quilt is made larger by the little girl's worrying it with her finger. The issue is that we cannot fill the holes. We must stitch them back together, sewing with threads of engagement, needles of awareness. A basting stitch won't do. It calls for a back stitch, strong, solid. Sometimes, we have to listen to the silence to hear the answers we are looking for. We might start by sitting quietly under a hickory tree.

# Note from the Author

Word-of-mouth is crucial for any author to succeed. If you enjoyed the book, please leave a review online—anywhere you are able. Even if it's just a sentence or two. It would make all the difference and would be very much appreciated.

Thanks!
Lawrence

# About the Author

Lawrence Weill is a Kentucky author and artist whose previous books include *The Path of Rainwater, Out in Front, Incarnate,* and *I'm in the Room.* His fiction, poetry and nonfiction have appeared in a wide range of local, regional, and national journals. He also is a visual artist and an avid outdoorsman. Lawrence and his wife live in the woods overlooking a beaver pond next to a wildlife preserve.

www.ingramcontent.com/pod-product-compliance
Lightning Source LLC
Chambersburg PA
CBHW030412310726
48979CB00002B/384

* 9 7 8 1 6 8 4 3 3 3 8 0 6 *